THE APOLLYON GAME

A Horror Short Story by CLIVE REZNOR

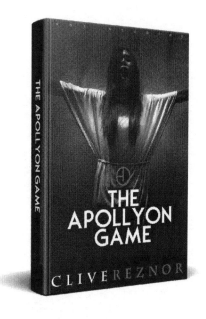

From new horror author **Clive Reznor** comes a twisted horror short story where you inner demons can cost you your life.

Portia is a strange girl who has spent most of her life isolated and ridiculed for being different. On this night however, she gathers five friends to take part in **The Apollyon Game**, a macabre mix of truth or dare where if you get the answers wrong, or are not truthful, the consequences will tear your soul apart.

The demons are watching.

For fans of stories like **The Hellbound Heart** or **Night Shift**, this short story injects the reader into the middle of a terrifying nightmare that will have you questioning what you believe about personal truths and the justifications for revenge.

www.aoestudios.com

THE IMMANENT WORLD
VOL. 2
CLUICHI

CLIVE REZNOR

AOE STUDIOS

Published by AOE Studios

THE IMMANENT WORLD: VOL. 2: CLUICHI
Copyright © 2017 by Clive Reznor. All rights reserved.
Printed in the United States of America. For more information contact AOE
Studios: contact@aoestudios.com.

Cover Design KC Hunter

AOE Studios publication: First Edition October 2017

ISBN: 978-0-9829533-4-1

CONTENTS

INTRODUCTION

♣

When I was asked to take over for the horror anthology series *The Immanent World* it took me a little bit by surprise. The previous installment was an anthology of various authors, poets, and illustrators contributing to a unique style of weird fiction. At first, I thought I was going to be a contributing author but later found out that I was being given the entire series, the task of rewriting a previous entry into the series, and creating a concept that was entirely my own.

It couldn't have come at a more opportune moment as my desire to move from being an anonymous writer on the internet to an actual writer of a book fell in line with what was asked of me. There are several stories that have been burning in my head for months now and I had no idea how to get them out. Some were tales of terror while others were dark comedies poking fun at many things in society over the last decade or so that I find absolutely absurd and prime for ridicule.

The first night I sat down to write the wrap-around story (as they call it) proved to be the start of something new for me as a writer. Without the constraints of what usually passes for internet articles and blogging I can explore all manner of wonder, horror, joy, fear, perversity, pleasure, and pontification. For fifteen years I have written short fiction for my own personal use and the enjoyment of the occasional friend or lover. To have those ideas manifested in words for the world to see, if it so chooses to, is both terrifying and exhilarating.

My private life is going to remain just that: private. *The Apollyon Game* rewrite brought attention to my name in rather quick fashion with thousands of people purchasing and reading that short story in a matter of weeks. Like many authors I am very much an introvert (and quite proud of it) so you will not likely see pictures of me holding this book up on social media for a selfie or going into details about what my home life is and how I got into writing.

This falls right in line with the title of this series.

Immanence is the divine within that manifests itself in the most mundane and unassuming parts of daily life. It is a notion that the human mind in particular holds the keys to God's door as opposed to the metaphysical being one removed from humanity. All is united through a continuum that only the sharpest sighted or the keenest of minds will witness if they know which curtain to pull, which window to look into, which gatekeeper to coerce.

It is very much my philosophy of storytelling and even life beyond that. The stories found here—while containing some personal truths and observations—are not intended to be mantras to live life by. They are experiments in thought, eruptions of emotion, and at times confessions of fears that we all find inherent within ourselves, poured out into the darker corners of imagination.

-   *Clive Reznor*
    October 2017

GAMES ARE A TEST OF OUR WITS,
INGENUITY, AND IN SOME EXTREME CASES,
OUR WILLINGNESS TO LIVE.

THE IMMANENT WORLD

VOLUME TWO

CLUICHI

The Death of Omar Snellings

We are all one unforeseen breath away from death.

That last breath, the final inhalation and exhalation, has its own mind and its own unique chemistry that is unlike any other drawn before it. Whether it's a short gasp, a long sigh, muffled by a groan, or pierced by a shriek, that last ritual of consumption and expulsion summarizes for its master what his life was and, in a sense, how he had used it.

It has its own rules. But, as with any rule, they can be broken.

Omar Snellings drew in a deep breath just before his graceless tumble down the stairwell. His head bounced into the stained plaster of the walls, blurring his vision and muting his hearing. He feared that these bumbling moments would be his last; a fear that crept into his bowels, causing them to spill their contents just a little.

His mind rapidly scanned through his memories, trying to relive the most meaningful before the end. All that he wanted to see, all that he wanted to be, the people he would miss and—he hoped—would miss him came rushing into his brain with as much insistence as the throbbing pain he felt with each tumble.

This shouldn't be how it ends. Focus on how not *to die.*

The base of his skull struck the metal steps once, twice, and then a third time. Fortunately, that was the end. His body slid to a halt at the bottom step.

No blood. No bumps. I'm fine, Omar thought as he pulled himself up from the filthy floor. He took this time to adjust his leather jacket, run his hands over his thinning head of hair and, most importantly, find his glasses. Thankfully, they had not been broken during the fall. He did his best to wipe them clean, sliding the lenses back and forth between a portion of his shirt that he held between finger and thumb.

Good enough. Time was wasting.

♣

The twenty-second block of Hanover Street was halfway between abandoned city blight and gentrified urban renewal. While many of the row houses remained in a state of disrepair, every third or fourth one stood refreshed. A new coat of paint, modern interior design, and a charming red and blue sign displaying the name of its seller flapping against the refurbished front doors. They seemed to mock the other homes, proudly boasting their value and newness while the others depressingly sagged into their concrete moldings, occupied by owners, renters, and sometimes vagrants who cared little for their well-being.

Omar could relate. He often identified more with the dilapidated than the decorated. It was not as if the new homes didn't possess character, but they were a symbol of this neighborhood—where he had spent his childhood—changing away from what was and into something that, quite frankly, didn't belong.

Stammering out of one of the older homes, he immediately became dizzy as he entered the afternoon's chilly air. It was late fall, and winter was already whispering her chill a month early. He stopped moving and took a moment to steady himself, his breaths short at first, creating translucent white clouds as they exited his lips.

The street was unnaturally busy today. The neighborhood children were gathered on the stoops near the end of the street, some chattering outrageously while others busied themselves on their smartphones. The older kids, who knew Omar by reputation, kept an eye on him as he composed himself. And there, across the street, was one of those new houses.

What an obnoxious sight. The damn thing might have very well been mocking *him* now. Omar's clothes were not new, his face that of a man who lived a rough and challenged life. The first few patches of gray had shown up in this last year, hurting his vanity and forcing him to shave his beard. He had seen the owners of the new house and knew they were younger, more accomplished, and better looking.

They were probably there now, the couple with their designer clothes and fashionable hairstyles, looking out the window at him as if he were part of the entertainment: a living display of urban life. Perhaps the older of them, a man in his forties, would be more respectful, but his partner, a much younger man in his early twenties with an undeniable love for hair dye and orange shoes, was certainly watching. He had caught the skinny twerp doing it before, the look on his face that of inquisitive busybody.

I'm not here for your entertainment.

Omar stumbled again as he tried to find his car. Where had he parked it? The throbbing in his head was keeping him from focusing. Too many thoughts were racing through his head, back and forth from the room he had just left to the fall to the street, the houses, and the neighbors, but where was his car?

Another spasm in his skull forced him to double over, grabbing at the side of his head. He'd have to go to the hospital first. Something was wrong. He thought that the fall hadn't harmed him, but that was turning out not to be true.

"Mr. Omar!" he heard a young voice call out. What did these kids want? He wasn't working now.

"Mr. Omar!" the voice called again. The pain was shooting on the other side of his head now.

"Mr. Omar! Mr. Omar!" now came several voices. Why in the world are they yelling at him?

He forced his hand from his temple, knowing that as soon as he did, the headache would intensify, but he needed to know what was so damn urgent. Angrily, he lifted his chin up and stared in the direction of the voices. Before he could yell at them in response, the breath he was taking to do so was knocked out of him.

The impact of the truck was sudden and violent. How Omar had not heard the horn or the screeching tires no one quite knew. Neither did Omar. The truck's metal grill seemed to appear out of nowhere as he turned to see it just before its pattern was embedded in his face.

A crowd quickly gathered around the scene of the accident. The driver of the truck was in utter shock; the amount of blood and tissue that splattered across the front of his vehicle made him sick.

"Didn't you see him?" a voice cried out.

"Is that Omar?" another said.

"Yeah, that was Omar."

"Someone call an ambulance!"

"What for? Someone get a shovel!"

The children who had been content to play games at the end of the street before all of this had happened were now consumed with using their smartphones as recording devices. Every single one of them was taking pictures, recording videos, and some even were streaming live on social media to show this tragedy to the world in real time.

"Stop that," one of the older females of the neighborhood said as she tried to usher the younger children from the scene. "You don't need to be seein' this. Certainly, the rest of the damn world don't neither! Go on, get outta here!"

Ms. Page had some respect for the body but the other adults in the neighborhood had as little compassion as the children. Many of them were recording the event in the same way. The chatter continued in the crowd, people asking questions, throwing accusations, speculating on whether or not Omar had heard the truck or whether the driver could have stopped. A few even vomited at the smell of Omar's remains.

While many knew it was wrong on one level to be gawking at this scene—the gruesome dismemberment of a fellow neighbor—they also couldn't help but indulge in their voyeurism. Who was to say they were wrong? They were all guilty of it, even Ms. Page who told the children to leave was now just as consumed by the scene as they had been. How many times do you get to see a mangled corpse?

"Tell me I'm dreaming. I have to be. This has to be a dream. Tell me I'm dreaming!" Omar said to himself as his panic grew.

No, it was true; he had taken his last breath. He was dead. He knew it. He saw it. And now he roamed outside of his body as a spirit, he could only guess, viewing his initial wake and the reactions of those in attendance.

Their visible lust for seeing a mauled body—*his* mauled body—made him ill. Mrs. Sherman had known him his entire life, and here she was taking pictures while Dre, Tony, Wayne, and Russell were too busy recounting what happened in colorful and exaggerated ways to mourn his passing. In fact, it seemed like no one was mourning what had happened to him. It was a show for them and nothing more.

"Fuck you all," he said.

The sight of his disfigured body disgusted him. His nerves were still firing, making his limbs (or what was left of them) twitch in a heap of broken, exposed bone and meaty flesh. It was too much to witness. He turned his back and walked away back towards the house. There must be something he could do. This couldn't be how his life ended.

"Not that way," a voice called from behind.

Omar turned in its direction but saw no one. His neighbors were gawking at his body, and now the police were arriving along with the paramedics. Perhaps he was confusing their chatter for someone talking to him. Back upstairs is where he had to go.

"I said not that way," the voice came again.

This time, Omar whipped around and looked in all directions for a face to go with this disembodied voice. It was talking to him, no mistaking that now. But who would be speaking to him here? God? The Devil? Another ghost?

"You have no need to go back up those steps. None at all. You've done what you've done, and the only thing up there for you is more grief."

The words were spoken by a small man in a pastel yellow

suit. It was blindingly bright, unnaturally so. Both the jacket and slacks were such a vibrant yellow that Omar wouldn't have been surprised if the man told him it was made of pure sunlight. But how immaculate this little man was, from his expensive cufflinks to his perfectly folded handkerchief to his freshly polished shoes. Either an insurance salesman or a lawyer, Omar suspected. Certainly not someone of the afterlife. But how could he see Omar?

"You're talking to me, right?" Omar questioned, testing whether or not this was real.

"Of course, I am talking to you," yellow suit responded, his accent suggesting he was British but had spent a considerable amount of time in America as well. "Who else just had his entrails sprawled across the asphalt?"

Omar's panic started to return. "So, this is real? I'm dead? I'm fucking dead!"

"Calm down," said yellow suit as he pulled a cigarette from his blazer. "You're not the first one, and you won't be the last. Why don't we go for a walk and get away from this, yeah? No need for you to watch any of this. It can be ... troublesome."

Walking proved harder than Omar had anticipated. There was a sense of vertigo that overtook him as he got farther away from his body. The sidewalks and streets seemed to shift while the air felt stiff against his skin. It was like trying to walk underwater. Above, the sun was pulsating, and the clouds were twisting in on themselves. This was not at all what he imagined the afterlife would be like.

As they continued to walk and Omar strained to adjust to his new existence, the little man in the yellow suit took account of Omar's life history. He couldn't tell whether trusting all this information to yellow suit was wise or not, but at this point, what could happen to him? He was already dead.

"... and when was the last time you saw your father?" yellow suit asked.

"It must have been at least ten years ago. We had a five-minute conversation on the phone that went the way they usually went ... With him insulting my mother and me hanging up the phone. That was the last I ever heard from him. Is he still alive?"

"Him? Yes. Very much so."

"Wow. I died before my father. And he'll likely not know for days or weeks. I wonder if he'll miss me when he finds out."

"He won't."

"How do you—"

"Trust me about these things. The more I know about you, the more I can read the people in your life. I've been doing this for some time," yellow suit said with a dismissive confidence that bothered Omar.

"How long is 'for some time'?" Omar asked.

"The answer would make you uncomfortable."

"So what are you? Some kind of angel or something? Are you here to have me confess my sins?"

"Would you?"

"I have none to confess," Omar said defensively. "Look, I never believed in any of that nonsense my mother and grandmother had me listen to all those years at church. Endless Sundays of old women and castrated men mindlessly repeating 'amen' and 'Lord Jesus' like they were out of some bad Blaxploitation movie. I never bought into any of it."

Yellow suit tapped his lower lip at Omar's outburst. "You are a brave one, aren't you? Defying the name of God only minutes into the afterlife. How do you know that everything they said wasn't true?"

"Because I'm not an idiot. As you said, I've been dead for some time now, and there are no pearly gates or winged angels or horned demons coming to whisk me away to some eternal land of righteousness or damnation. No, it's just the world the way it was, and I'm walking the streets with you."

Streets noticeably devoid of pedestrians or vehicles.

"Is that right?" yellow suit said flatly.

"Hey, don't get it twisted. I loved and respected my mother. She just fell for that whole church thing—a giant scam to take money from old ladies. Her mother did it, and her mother before her did it. If there is one thing I can say for my father, he didn't buy into any of it either."

"He is an atheist, correct?" asked yellow suit.

"And Mexican, so you know he got it double on all sides from his family and my mother. It's probably why he bolted when he did. Enough about me though, you still haven't answered any of my questions."

"You are so right, sir. Ask away," yellow suit grinned.

Omar was growing weary of the attitude.

"First off, who are you? What's your name?"

"Those are unimportant questions for you. Anything else?"

"Don't play games with me," Omar said, his anger returning.

"Or what?" yellow suit asked, stopping dead in the middle of the empty street and turning to face Omar. "Are you about to make some threat? Come now, I figured you to be much smarter than that. Sure, you have the class and social skills of a gorilla ..."

"What did you say to me?"

"But I figured you to be street smart at the very least. Isn't that how you survived past your thirtieth birthday in your old line of work? Most who traveled the path you did don't live that long."

"What are you trying to say?"

Yellow suit's tone dropped, and his face tightened around the corners of his eyes and mouth. "I'm saying, you should know it isn't smart to threaten someone who clearly knows more about your situation than you do. I know your soul is still in shock, but you are, in fact, sir, dead. You are a spirit wandering around in this seemingly empty space between life and whatever comes next. You are here for a reason, and I am here with a proposition."

"Proposition for what? You said it yourself, this is an empty space. There's nothing here. No people, no cars, no animals, even the fucking air has stopped. What the hell is this?"

Yellow suit turned on a sly grin and started walking again. Omar watched him briefly, waiting for an answer, and then followed when none came.

The disorientation increased with every step. It felt as if the pair had been walking for hours, but in truth, Omar had no sense of time whatsoever. For all he knew, they had been walking for days or weeks. Occasionally, yellow suit would make a comment about his life or an observation of their surroundings: the empty cars, the silence, the stillness of the grass and leaves, just about any random thing he could think of about this purgatory they traversed.

"We're almost there," yellow suit said as they turned down Telegraph Street.

"What is this place?" Omar asked.

"Our destination. Or should I say your destination."

They were now in the warehouse district. Omar knew it well; he worked for two factories in this same area some years back when he was attempting to correct his lifestyle and live like a normal citizen. As with everything else, it was abandoned by living souls and just as quiet as a morgue.

"I guess I should tell you now the reason I brought you here," yellow suit said, straightening his pastel tie, which Omar had just noticed was, in fact, orange. "You see, your life, sir, was indeterminate. Not by my judgment, but by something or someone way beyond me. The only reason I know this is because you're here, and I was sent here to show you the way."

"The way to what?"

Once again, yellow suit withheld his answer. He cleared his throat and took several steps towards the street, his hands extended towards it like he was unveiling some grand prize.

"That is for you to determine," he finally said.

This stunk of treachery.

"I don't believe you," Omar said. "Who sent you for me anyway? What do you get out of this?"

"Oh, come now," yellow suit sighed. "You hurt my feelings. I was sent here by those who employ me. They don't tell me why. I don't even see them. It isn't my concern. What is my concern is that I get the job done. And now I have done so."

Yellow suit walked back towards Omar, patted the lost soul on his shoulder, and then continued past him. Omar stared down Telegraph Street blankly, trying to see what possible destination could be here among the cold brick buildings and cracked sidewalks.

"What am I supposed to do here?" Omar asked.

Again, no answer. Yellow suit's games had grown tiresome at this point. With a great swell of anger, Omar asked again, this time turning to face his guide.

There was no one there.

Omar looked in all directions. He even searched the skies. There was no sign of the man in the yellow suit. Just as strangely as he had appeared, he vanished without any useful instructions. All that remained was the street and the warehouses. With no other options, Omar turned his attention back to the empty path ahead and began walking.

♣

Telegraph Street didn't stretch very far. Omar didn't know if that was intentionally meant to be a sour joke or if there was some other oddness that would occur once he reached his destination. This wasn't a major thoroughfare; it ended just eight blocks ahead with a cautionary sign that warned against the power grid just beyond an eight-foot tall cyclone fence.

This makes no sense, he told himself. If this was the afterlife, he wanted back into the land of the living. It was empty here—lonely. He couldn't imagine an eternity in this still painting of the world, stiff and stagnant. Whatever lay at the end of this street, he hoped it would, at the very least, change his surroundings.

As he continued his walk, he felt a sudden pull inside his gut, forcing his attention to his right. There wasn't much there, just a warehouse in an advanced state of disuse, the windows without glass and the doors textured in patches of brownish-orange rust.

Despite its state, he pressed on towards the opening. It was one of the taller structures on the street that had the same personality he loved from the older homes in his neighborhood. It wasn't newly fashioned or renovated. It was weathered and used, carrying with it the histories of whoever had passed through it in the land of the living, now cemented in time in the land of the dead.

His hand pressed gently against the double doors of the entrance. Omar didn't know if this was the right move. He was supposed to walk down the street. Briefly, he turned to look back at his prior destination; the old chain-link fence, the metal warning sign, the grid of generators and conductors just beyond. But this was more interesting. This door, this building, and whatever pulled him towards it. He didn't know why, and he didn't care. Time didn't matter anymore, and he'd have all of eternity to walk another five blocks down this street. He just wanted to satisfy his curiosity.

His mind went back to his body, sprawled out in so many pieces in the street. Omar knew that he'd be the topic of conversation for weeks on end following his death. Maybe he'd be the center of a cautionary tale for children to not dash out into the middle of the street. That was it. He could do some good for children in the end, even if it had cost him his life.

As he continued to replay the events of his demise in his mind's eye, his right hand—as if under some other control than his own—pressed against the rough surface of the outer doors. With little effort, he forced them open, and immediately, he was blasted with a cool breeze. Yes, there was *movement* here. The air was not still but alive, swirling around him as if it had waited for someone to break the seal and free it from this prison.

The chamber beyond was nothing more than an empty room. The ceiling stretched high above, the walls striped with the stains of rot and decay. Rust had overtaken the geometric system of pipes and air ducts that weaved throughout the warehouse, drawing Omar's eyes down to the floor that was littered with filth, trash, broken machinery, and the occasional rodent.

What a disappointment, he thought. He had no idea what force had called upon his curiosity, but it had failed him. Or had it? Just as he was about to turn and head back out into the day, a distortion caught his vision.

On a platform just a few yards away from him, he could see wisps of light and dark, each streaking in arcs above the floor, crisscrossing one another in a dance that was so subtle that it was no wonder he had not seen it before. It required patience to stand and stare, to strain his sight so it could catch the distortion making another stroke of color in the air.

"What is that?" he asked as he approached the platform.

He expected to hear a sound of some kind, a whizzing as the colors streaked around an invisible bubble and then disappeared, but heard nothing. The distortion was larger than he had thought. As he got closer, he could see that it was taking up the entire platform, and at its center was a dirty old table, the only one of its kind in the entire warehouse.

This must have been the source that called upon his curiosity. He had to see it through. What harm could come of it now? As he neared the outside edge of this invisible sphere, the streaks of black and white became a blur, and just as he reached the table, something deep inside him sent up an alarm. He felt as if his insides were being rearranged, a chill welling from his stomach and up through his throat. Until now, he hadn't felt such sensations since his death. They were alarming but, at the same time, welcoming. To feel anything was intoxicating. He wanted more.

Against his better judgment, Omar pushed his hand into the invisible sphere. Nothing happened. Perhaps this was just an illusion.

He pressed on, now with his elbow. Nothing. Next, his shoulder. Still nothing. Now, completely confident, he took a step forward, immersing his body into whatever this anomaly was. It was then that he realized the great error he had just committed.

What had been hidden behind the distortion was something equally absurd as it was disarming. The streaks of black and white he had seen were the movements of the two creatures that sat on opposite sides of the table. Now that he had entered this sphere, their true nature was revealed to him.

To his left was what he could only assume was an angel, given the ivory wings that sprouted from its back. That was the only traditional clue he had because the entity, female but with a figure that could have easily belonged to a teenage boy, had a lit cigar in one hand while the other gripped at a stack of cards.

Her hair was white with a dash of blue, her dress clean except for around the ankles where the dirt of the warehouse had stained the fabric. Her face was dotted with sparkling makeup, vivid colors around her eyes, on her lips, and accenting her cheeks over skin that was as powdery as fresh snow.

Opposite the angelic figure was her polar opposite. It was male and proudly so. He wore no shirt to cover his rock hard muscles, nor did he wear pants to obstruct his enormous phallus that dangled between his legs and nearly touched the floor. His skin was a deep red with streaks of black like the markings of a tiger, curling over the muscles of his shoulders, abdomen, and thighs. The demon's face was chiseled and hard, the bones of his cheeks pressing against the flesh of his face. His long hook nose hung over cracked lips, and a long beard tapered to a point, almost mirroring his dong in the way it hung beneath his pointed chin. Two large horns jutted out from the top of his skull and curled forward while another set, shorter and more pointed, sprouted from beneath a set of ears the shape of bat wings.

Omar couldn't move. As much as his soul screamed to run, the sight was so unexpected, so fascinating, so iconic that he didn't want to leave. He had to take this in. Here before him were an actual demon and angel sitting at a table and, of all things, engaged in a card game.

Slowly, both entities turned their gaze from their game towards him. Their eyes—the demon's white with black pinpricks and the angel's bright blue—sent a chill through him.

"We have a spectator," the angel said, tapping away at the stack of cards to her left.

"It does not matter," the demon replied, his voice deep and proper. "The game is still the game. We won't stop because of this stray."

"A stray," the angel repeated the word, letting it hang for a moment. "Look at him. Confused, I assume. Are you new, stray?"

Omar understood the question but didn't have the compunction to answer.

"Do answer the question," the demon followed.

His voice struck Omar more than the angel's. Every syllable was pronounced with a measured precision, his tone heavy and deep. It unnerved him to hear the creature speak.

"I think I am," Omar answered.

"He thinks he is. You hear that? He thinks he is," the angel said, smiling falsely as she looked at the cards in her hand, seemingly bored with Omar's presence.

"Clearly, you haven't the manners not to intrude. But you've drawn yourself here and interrupted us." The demon seemed to be getting angrier with each word. "Now, you must feed me as I shall feed you."

The words were not lost on Omar. He didn't like the sound of them either. Whatever the demon meant by feeding each other, he wanted no part of it.

"Wait, wait," Omar pleaded. "This is a mistake or something. I was told to walk down to the end of this street."

The angel continued to look through her cards. The demon began salivating at its potential meal.

"There was a man. A man in a yellow suit who told me to walk down this road."

The demon darted a look at the angel who in turn put down her cards. Yes, Omar thought, they knew the man in the yellow suit. There may be a way out of whatever damnation he had unwittingly called upon himself.

"They are always meddling," the angel said.

"I don't care!" bellowed the demon. "So what of it? How does that change my appetite?"

"Now, calm down. You know the rules. You know the laws. Besides, we have a game to finish as you said yourself. There's no harm in waiting."

"And what is he to do then? Just stand there?"

"Let him watch. Let him learn. Let him know a little something of how it all works."

The demon grunted, his bat ears twitching as he gently scratched at his temple. Omar could now see the open sores that decorated the demon's skull—several infected rashes breaking out on his skin from beneath his temple and down the slope of his shoulders.

"So be it," the demon conceded. "You! Come and sit. Come and watch."

Omar reluctantly stepped towards the table, pulled out one of the other chairs, and sat down. His eyes were wide, still in shock, and the look on his face amused the angel. The demon kept his eyes on him for a few more moments before taking a sip from a filthy goblet. The creature was sloppy, the thick green fluid flowing down his chin before he wiped it away.

"What am I to watch? A game?" Omar asked.

"The only game that matters," answered the angel. "The living think they have absolute control over their lives and souls."

"And how wrong they are," the demon said.

"And how wrong they are," the angel echoed.

Omar caught on to what was happening here. These creatures were playing a game for human lives. As hard as it was for him to accept, he had no other choice.

Feeling less threatened now, Omar looked at the playing cards on the table to get a better understanding of what he was watching. These cards were old and worn but had an ancient elegance to their craftsmanship. Each was designed with spirals and symbols, none of which Omar understood, but he appreciated their beauty just the same. There was a deck in the middle of the two players while both angel and demon had their own stack beside them, presumably of hands won, and a fan of eight to six cards in their hands. The demon picked another card from the center pile and added it to his hand. Omar could have sworn he saw the images on the card shift, but the demon was keeping the face of his cards hidden.

"Are you ready to continue?" asked the angel.

"Yes, let's continue this game. We have many hands to play, and when we are done, I will have my meal."

The Shadows at 2:22 a.m.

Shimi spent most of Friday afternoon on the internet, something his parents repeatedly warned him not to do. It's a sinner's toolkit. It would corrupt his young 12-year-old soul. These and other shaming claims were drilled into him by his mother and father after he was caught a few months ago reading secular news on his iPhone. It wasn't how a good Hasidic Jew, in their opinion, spent his time.

But the boy was innovative and had managed to get an outdated smartphone to access the online world. He was good with electronics, even though such things were frowned upon by his family. His friends often called him *nebbish*, sometimes in a playful manner, but also when they grew annoyed with his constant info-dumps about the outside world. Shimi didn't care and was so quick-witted that whatever insults were thrown at him were immediately deflected by a careful turn of a phrase or an observation of others' shortcomings.

Today was different. He had a mission. It was research into old customs that neither his family nor their Rabbi had passed down to his generation, if they had known about them at all.

"Shimi!" he heard his mother calling from the kitchen. "Shimi, come out of that room! You've been in there all day."

"Yes, mamala. Coming!"

Carefully, he slipped the device into the emptied-out bottom of a toy truck which he cunningly hid underneath his bed among a menagerie of other toys. He took a look in the mirror, straightened his clothes, and then ran out of his room before his mother called for him again.

Shimi's three sisters were already at the kitchen table and glared at him, as they often did, with mocking faces. The relationship between the siblings was forced at best. The sisters had no use for their middle brother nor did he have much of a use for them. They usually behaved respectfully, with the occasional disagreement, but Shimi had figured out early on that it was best to spend as little time around them as possible.

"Were you studying?" his mother asked him as she made the final preparations for lunch.

"Yes, mamala. We have a test on Monday," Shimi answered.

"And what subject is it?"

"Science. Biology to be exact."

His mother's face tightened with displeasure. Shimi had expected as much. His father had allowed him to attend a different school that leaned more towards a modern education than a strict religious one. It was a choice that she did not agree with but she accepted. She still oversaw most of Shimi's textbooks and homework assignments to make sure there was

nothing offensive in them. There were only a few
where she had to censor the misinformation, as
being sent home from the school.

"I want to see what you've been working on tomorrow. I
have to take your sisters to Temple tonight so I won't be able
to help you. I trust your father can help if you need any."

"It's pretty easy," Shimi said, wanting to avert any reason
for his mother or father to go into his room. "I can handle it."

"Still, I want him to look it over. I haven't had the time."

Two of his sisters started laughing. There was a split second
where Shimi feared that they knew his secret, but that wasn't
possible. The only other people who knew he had a
smartphone were his closest friends Yakov, Joseph, and Omri
who lived next door.

"Can I go over to Omri's after lunch?" he asked.

"Eat your food first Shimi and I'll let you know. You still
haven't done your chores today and that must be finished
before you can leave this house."

"You haven't talked to Omri in weeks," his oldest sister,
Sara, said.

"No one goes over there," his middle sister, Eliana, added
with a dismissiveness that Shimi picked up on. "They are not
polite people. I wish they'd move away."

"Enough of that," their mother admonished. "Here, eat your
lunch, and afterwards I want all of you to finish your chores.
Only Lila has done what she was supposed to today and she's
the youngest of you all. You should be setting a good example
for her, not the other way around."

Lila had nothing to say and instead just grinned as she
started eating. Even though the girl was only ten years old, she
had clearly mastered the art of gaining favoritism.

Of the three, Shimi was least threatened by her. They were
close until a few months ago when her older sisters, who were
now teenagers, had convinced her that his being a boy made

nim the enemy. While she had a close attachment to Sara and Eliana now, Lila did not treat her brother as poorly as they did.

Given that Shimi's father had not returned home, his mother had little choice but to let him go over to the neighbor's house while she chauffeured the girls to Temple. This wasn't the first time he had spent an afternoon or an overnight stay with Omri's family, but it had been months since it had happened.

Shimi's mother and father, and the rest of the community, had stopped visiting the Rabin family around early winter. Hanukkah was the last time Shimi could remember seeing anyone visit the house, and rarely did he see Omri's parents anymore.

Unlike Shimi, Omri had no sisters, but he did have an older brother who was in and out of the home. Joel was rumored to have been a troubled boy and had spiraled down the road of drugs and alcohol, shaming the family and self-excommunicating from the community altogether. Every so often Shimi would see him return to the house for a few days, only to disappear again for weeks on end. Omri had been a spirited and happy kid for as long as Shimi could remember. They were only six weeks apart in age, but now Omri carried himself like an old man, taking little interest in anything.

And it all started around early winter.

"Hello Shimi," Omri's mother welcomed him into their home. "Omri is in his room. He'll be out in a minute. Would you like anything to eat?"

"No, I just had lunch, thank you," Shimi said.

"Okay, well I have some things to do. You can sit in the living room until Omri comes out. I'll make sure you don't have to wait too long."

Mrs. Rabin was excessively nice. She had never been an unpleasant woman but there was something a bit rehearsed about how she talked. Shimi didn't think much of it and sat on the sofa where he waited patiently for his friend.

On the coffee table was a family portrait. They looked like a perfect Hasidic family, the father and mother standing proudly with their two sons surrounding them. Their smiles, especially those of the boys, could fool someone at a casual glance. However, looking at the portrait longer than just a casual glance revealed the superficial nature of the photograph.

"Nice of you to come over. How long are you staying?" Omri said as he strolled into the living room.

He had lost a lot of weight since the last time Shimi had seen him.

"Just until my mom gets back. I get to stay away from my sisters for a few hours so that's a good thing."

"You shouldn't talk like that, Shimi. They're your family."

"They're also annoying."

"Shimi ... always the smart mouth with you, Shimi," Omri said.

"Are you feeling better? I haven't seen you in school for a while."

"I'm fine now," Omri said, turning towards the picture Shimi was looking at and taking it up in his hands. "Things are better this week."

"Was it the flu or something?"

"Something like that."

An awkward silence followed. Whatever had been going on at this house was not going to be revealed here. Shimi knew Omri was in no position to talk now. It might have been because they were in the house or that he just wasn't ready to speak, but soon he'd talk.

"Let's go out to the park. Yakov and Joseph are there with the others playing a game. We might not be able to join but at least we can watch."

"Sounds good," Omri said. "Mamala, I'm going to the park with Shimi."

"Make sure you're back before dinner, Omri. Your father will be home late tonight so it'll be just us for dinner."

"Yes mamala."

The neighborhood was a typical street in any town with the addition of a park built at the end of the road. Since the weather was warm today, the kids had taken over the park to work off winter's unrest.

Yakov and Joseph were brothers from a much larger family that had ten children in total. They were the youngest with many of their brothers and sisters already out in the world to start their own families.

"You two finally made it out of the house," Joseph said, his hands wiping a bit of dirt against his fat little belly that pushed his white shirt over his trousers.

"I've been busy and Omri's been sick," explained Shimi.

"Yeah, yeah, we know what you do Shimi," Yakov said dismissively. "You two want in on the next game?"

"You're playing basketball?"

Shimi looked at the court where there were older boys well into a game. Basketball had taken on popularity in the neighborhood recently due to one of the neighborhood kids actually making it to college on a scholarship for his high school play. Since then, every kid from the area decided they'd try their hand at the game.

"Yeah, are you scared Shimi? They're not going to hurt you," Joseph said.

Shimi looked Joseph up and down. The boy was clearly delusional if he thought that his short, stubby, fat body would be able to do anything on the basketball court against the much taller and more athletic teenagers. More bravado than brains, but that was Joseph. His brother wasn't any better.

"He just wants to play with his computer stuff," Yakov added. "I'm surprised your mom hasn't found it yet and punished you."

"I don't think we even want to know what you're doing with that thing or what kind of websites you're looking at," said Joseph.

Before this got out of hand, Shimi sought to put a stop to it.

"I was looking for an answer to Omri's problem," he said.

The two brothers stopped grinning, their faces turning serious. Omri immediately put his hand on Shimi's shoulder and shook his head in disagreement. He didn't want this brought up, not here of all places.

"You know we can't talk about that," said Yakov.

"I know you don't want to talk about it, but we all know what's going on. We know Omri's got problems. And there has to be something we can do about it."

"Leave it alone, Shimi," said Omri.

"You hear him! He doesn't want to do anything. Don't force it Shimi. Leave it alone. If the rabbis can't help him, what can we do?" Joseph said, now turning his attention back to the basketball court.

Omri and Yakov joined him, stepping away from Shimi who looked at the back of their yarmulke-covered heads in dismay. They were running from this, like the whole community was running from it. No one wanted to talk about what was going on in Omri's house but given how emaciated his friend looked, how awkward his mother had been, and how distant the whole family was from everyone else, it was only a matter of time before something tragic happened.

"I don't want anything else to happen to you, Omri. Your dad can't—"

"Stop it, Shimi!" Omri yelled.

Not waiting for his friend to protest, Omri stormed off from the boys and the basketball court. Shimi had pushed it too far and the brothers were just as angry with him as Omri was.

"*Nebbish*," Joseph called him.

Yakov had more to say, "That's right. *Nebbish Shimi*, always going where he shouldn't. It's not Jewish at all what you're doing. We don't do any of that weird stuff you read on that phone of yours. You can look up all the articles you want. It's not going to solve the problem."

"Then what will?" questioned Shimi.

He got no answer, just faces turned away.

"Look, for your information I did find something online. I think it might help Omri."

Yakov looked up at Shimi now, his disdain for even having this conversation as clear as the sky.

"This can't be some psychologist or anything like that. We don't want this getting to outsiders," Yakov said. "My parents talk all the time about how they want to find any little thing to make us look bad."

"Actually, it's a Jewish remedy. It's old and the website I found it on said that it has helped kids like Omri before," Shimi said.

Yakov and Joseph wanted to help their friend. That was never in question. What they did not want was to draw any attention to themselves or be involved in any way. They had seen how those who went against the orthodoxy had come under fire.

"Okay, what exactly is this?" Joseph asked.

"Meet us later at Omri's place. We'll talk about it there."

"Are you sure he's going to want to talk about it?" Yakov asked. "Look at him. He looks like he's about to cry or something."

Shimi turned to see Omri just staring off at the trees on the border of the playground. There were smaller kids there playing in the grass, not a care in the world except for their own imaginations.

There was a simple sadness about the image of him standing there. The amount of weight he had lost made his clothes fit loosely. His black suit coat looked like it was for a larger boy while his pants were bunched up at the bottom around his ankles. Even the payot (or side curls) on either side of his face had a grayness to them, still dark brown but with just a hint of discoloration, like a faded photograph. No matter what he said, or what the other boys wanted to accept, he had the look of a soul that was withering quietly away while the world could care less that it was.

It was this image that swayed Yakov and Joseph.

"We'll be there," Joseph said.

Late afternoon had come and the sun was already setting, casting a golden light across the neighborhood. Joseph and Yakov had managed to convince their parents to let them spend the night over Omri's house.

Shimi managed to get back into his house before his mother and sisters came home and snagged his secret phone from under his bed. Omri was waiting for him outside in the backyard, trying to look as coy as he possibly could.

"What are you doing, Omri?" asked Shimi as he exited the backdoor.

"I don't know. I just thought you wouldn't want anyone to see us," he answered.

"It's my house, Omri. No one is going to think it's weird for me to go into my own house."

"You have a point. Did you get what you needed?"

"Yeah, no one in the house knows I have this. But I have to ask you, are you okay with this? You looked really upset at the park."

Omri sucked in a deep breath and then looked over at his house. For some reason, it was strange seeing his house from the other side of a fence like this. These were old, large houses that were three stories high and had storm doors in the back that lead to the basement. Farm-style houses in the suburbs, a holdover from decades forgotten which suited the families of this neighborhood just fine. Right now, it creeped him out.

"I don't know, Shimi. I do think ..." he paused as he lost his words. "Maybe, just talking about it will help. Maybe. I don't know, let's just do this and we'll see."

"Anytime you want to stop we can. We'll just hang out and play games if you really don't want to get into this. Let's get inside before it gets dark."

The two hopped over the cyclone fence that separated the two properties and walked to the front door. Joseph and Yakov arrived at the same time and the four stopped to talk before entering.

"My mother really doesn't like this," Yakov said.

"Yeah, she asked us like fifteen questions before letting us leave. We're all spending the night, right?" asked Joseph.

"That's the plan," answered Shimi, his secret phone clutched against his chest.

"You might want to hide that if we go inside," Joseph suggested. "If your parents don't like it, I'm sure Omri's mom won't."

"We should really go inside before my dad gets home if we're going to do this," Omri interrupted.

The other three boys stared at him for a minute, noticing a certain amount of fear in his face. They knew why he said that and immediately regretted their poor choice of doing this in such a rush. They hadn't considered Omri's father when they made this plan, but it was too late for that now.

Although they didn't want to look suspicious, the four boys

marched through the house and up the stairs to Omri's room as if they had something to hide. Omri's mother noticed but brushed it off as boys just being boys. She gave them a quick glance as they passed by her while she folded laundry, paused for a moment as if to say something, but thought better of it. If anything, she was simply happy that her son had friends visiting.

This was the first time Joseph or Yakov had been in Omri's room and they were a bit taken aback by how empty it was. An old wood frame bed, a nightstand, a polished dresser, and a handful of pictures made up the decor of the bedroom. To the left of the bed was a closet. One of the sliding doors was off track so it wouldn't close all the way. The walls were plain white plaster with a few pictures of relatives hung on the opposite wall near the door.

"Nice room," Joseph said unconvincingly.

As sparsely as it was decorated, it was not the most noticeable aspect of Omri's room. That came from the unusually high number of lamps and flashlights that surrounded Omri's bed. They were haphazardly strung up with tape and string, hanging around his bed from all sides like a theatrical lighting kit assembled by a mind afield. A few were turned at odd angles towards the windows, around the edges of the headboard, and even towards the dresser and closet, but most were aimed so every inch of the bed could be bathed in electric light.

"Are you filming a TV show in here or something?" Yakov quipped as he carefully observed the mess of wires and that lead from the lighting rig to an overused power strip. "That could start a fire, you know."

"Yeah, what is all this Omri?" Shimi asked.

"A project," Omri answered flatly.

Stranger and stranger, thought Yakov as he turned to the window, shaking his head dismissively. He could see most of the backyard from here but the light was pouring in so strongly from outside he could barely stand it. He went to pull the curtains closed but noticed there were no curtains.

"So, what did you find that was so important Shimi?" Joseph asked, trying to change the subject.

Shimi sensed an unconvinced tone from Joseph. It was times like this that the fat boy's arrogance graded on his nerves. Joseph always acted as if he was the leader of the group, but to the rest of them, except for his brother Yakov, this was only in Joseph's head.

"I think we should let Omri talk if he wants to," Shimi said.

"No, you said you had something to help him with his problem. I think we should get to that," Joseph bit back.

"Are we fighting already?" Yakov asked, annoyed.

"I think we need to finally talk about what Omri's going through. We can't even call it what it is," Shimi protested.

Joseph was beginning to rethink his decision to come here, "And what good is that going to do?"

"Look, how are we going to help him if we can't say what it is? That's the whole problem to begin with."

"There's probably a reason our parents won't talk about this. Did you ever think what it might do to the community?"

Shimi scoffed at the argument. "Did you ever think what it's doing to Omri?"

"Okay, okay, stop it you two," Omri said in the loudest voice they had heard from him in months.

His hands were down at his sides, fingers stretched out like sunbeams and trembling as he unnervingly stared at his friends. If anything could make this worse, it was being talked about as if he wasn't there.

"Sit down and I'll talk about it. But I don't want you arguing about me as if I'm some pet you need to figure out what to do with."

The other boys nodded in awkward agreement and took a

seat on the floor. Omri waited for them all to be settled before going to his bed and pulling a small box from under his pillow. He carefully placed it in the middle of their circle, sat back on his haunches, and sighed as if he was relieved to finally have this unveiled to someone else.

It was a plain box made of wood that was splintering on the sides and could have used a good cleaning. Flecks of dust rose up from it in the shafts of sunlight. Joseph, who had always been the most inquisitive of the bunch, immediately went to open the box before Omri slapped his hand away.

"What did you do that for?" Joseph shouted as he tried to wave off the pain in his hand.

"Don't touch it. You don't want to touch it," said Omri.

It was a concerned tone rather than an admonishing one. Omri's eyes gave away how much he actually feared whatever was contained within the box. Why he had brought it out and placed it in the middle of the floor was another mystery. Shimi's impatience for games however would not let this go on.

"Is this what's been causing you problems, Omri? This box?" asked Shimi.

No answer.

"What's in the box?"

No answer.

"Omri, did you hear me? I asked you what was in the box."

Still no answer.

"He looks strange," Yakov commented as he started to get back to his feet. "I'm not liking this at all. I think we should go."

"Sit down, Yakov," his brother barked. "You get scared at everything. He's just unsettled."

"It's not how he's acting that scares me. It's *why* he's acting that way that scares me."

"Shush!" Joseph said.

"It's old. It's very, very old," Omri spoke all of a sudden, as if unaware of anyone else in the room. He was speaking more to himself than his friends. "He told me not to take it. He told me not to touch it. But I did, and now this is what has happened. It's my fault and I deserve it."

"What are you talking about, Omri? You're not making any sense," said Shimi.

Omri didn't answer. His eyes were darting back and forth between his three friends, boys he had known since as long as he could remember. For an instant, he questioned what he was doing. Was this right, he thought? Could he live with himself? What would their parents say?

"Enough of this," Joseph broke the silence, pushing past Omri and heading toward the bed. "Take all of this garbage down. It's not right. It's not what we do!"

Omri took a quick look at his watch and then turned to the window. The sun was starting to dip below the tree line outside his house.

In a panic, he grabbed Joseph's hand before the fat boy could reach one of the lights. Joseph shook his hand free and pulled away from Omri in a huff. This was becoming all too much for him.

"Knock it off, Joseph," Shimi said.

"Yeah, this is getting too weird. Let's just go," Yakov suggested.

Joseph and Omri were locked in a battle of stares. Both boys had their hands balled into fists. Being the larger of the two, Joseph wouldn't shy away from a fist fight if it came down to it. He knew Omri was a gentle soul and even if he had the gusto to take a shot, the only one of them who would regret it would be Omri.

"Don't touch them!" Omri growled. "You don't touch anything. Any of you!"

"We're leaving," proclaimed Joseph.

He backed away from Omri, keeping his eyes locked on the troubled boy in case he got any ideas. Yakov grabbed his brother's arm and both headed out of the room.

Shimi wasn't giving up so easily, "Wait! Come on, we're supposed to be here to help him."

"Shimi, he doesn't want our help!" Joseph said. "He's in some weird world of his own and if you want to stay here and be a part of that then fine. We're leaving."

"You can't leave!" Omri shouted, his face morphing from anger to worry in an instant.

"What is going on, Omri? You have to tell us," Shimi pleaded.

"I can't. I can't."

"It's the only way anything will start to get better."

Joseph had reached the limit of his patience, "We all know what your dad does to you. He touches you, am I right? He does things no right-minded Jew would ever do. Right?"

Omri glared at Joseph again. Another shift in attitude, this time more venomous than before. Joseph stopped walking towards the door and instead went back into the middle of the room.

"Is that it?" Shimi asked Omri, ignoring their friend's blatant lack of tact. "I mean, that's what we've all suspected but we didn't know."

"It's nothing for you to be ashamed of," Yakov added. "I've heard the adults talk about some of the other parents who do things like this. The Rabbis do nothing. It's disgraceful."

"You're not the only one though," Shimi continued. "I've read of others online. Some in Brooklyn. In communities all over."

"So, that's what you've been looking up on that computer phone of yours," Joseph concluded.

Shimi nodded in agreement. There was no use in dancing around this subject anymore. Not speaking of it did little to help the situation and, in fact, made it worse. In all the research Shimi had done online, he had come across dozens upon dozens of news stories the outside world had done on children in the Hasidic community who had been abused by older men. Some were momentary, others went on for years. Children grew up distorted and disillusioned with the faith; a faith that would willingly turn a blind eye to such horrors either out of willful ignorance or flat-out shame.

Omri pushed Shimi away even though he felt a slight bit of comfort in having this secret revealed. He wanted to tell others, his soul had been scratching at his mouth to release some whispers, some hint, some sign to anyone who would listen. If not his best friends, then who?

"Look, I'm sorry for getting angry at you," Joseph said solemnly.

"We're all sorry," Yakov added. "We should have been your friends and instead we turned away from you just like the adults did."

The sun was nipping at the tops of the trees outside now. The darkness of night was coming rapidly.

"Is that why you have all these lights around your bed? Do you think it protects you?" Shimi asked.

"Cast a light on sin," Joseph said, as if the line came from scripture.

"More like keeping sin away with light," Yakov's voice came from behind them all.

Joseph and Shimi turned to see Yakov knelt down above the box. He had opened it while they were talking. Inside were a few pieces of parchment that were worn and weathered. The handwriting on them was old, dried, and written in increasingly chaotic hand with each page revealed. Yakov had been reading them during the last few moments, his curiosity (and general nosiness) driving his hand.

"What is that?" Joseph asked his brother.

Yakov now stood, holding a few pieces of the frail paper in his hands as his eyes scanned back and forth to absorb what was written. The young boy's face turned to that of an old man, wrinkles forming in his brow and his eyes squinting as it worked out each stroke of ink.

"Is this real?" he asked Omri, pushing the papers towards his friend.

"That's what I was going to talk to you about," Omri responded.

"Is this real?" Yakov asked again, in a more threatening tone.

"Alright, alright, what is going on?" Shimi asked.

Yakov waited for Omri to talk. Seemingly struggling for words, Yakov didn't wait and instead turned the pages over to his older brother while he explained what they had all walked into.

"Joseph, do you remember Uncle Abraham?" he asked.

"Yes, *abba* used to say he was right out of his mind. He spent way too much time in Germany doing things he shouldn't have."

"Remember the stories he used to tell us kids? Stories he swore were true about demons from the old world."

Shimi's ears perked up, "Demons?"

This was ludicrous territory. Demons were a construct of another culture, one that the Hasidic community gave no validity to. While it was true that there were demons in their faith—their scripture and other accounts hinting time and again at stories about malevolent creatures from a darker dimension—most of that had died with the older generations. If anything, demons were seen as a manifestation of man's own mind, not physical entities that needed to be exorcised. That was the stuff of the Christians and Hollywood, not any proper Jew.

Joseph had started reading the papers, "Mom and dad told

us that Golems and demons don't exist. It's all stories and folklore."

"*Se'irim*, he used to call them," Yakov continued. "Uncle Abraham knew the Kabbalah like the back of his hand. These aren't really Jewish things though. They are usually from the outside world, if they exist at all."

"What are you reading there?" asked Shimi.

He took the papers from Joseph, scanned a few paragraphs as much as he could, and then joined the brothers as they all were now focused on Omri.

"This is just a story, right Omri? You got this from some weird *Goyish* bookstore in town, right?"

Shimi was trying his best to rationalize what was going on here. This was making even him uncomfortable, which took him by surprise as he colored outside the lines of orthodoxy in his thoughts often. What Omri may have done here—even just the hint of it—was way over the line and far beyond what Shimi had imagined.

"I ... I ... I needed to stop him. He wasn't going to stop," started Omri, his eyes getting wet with tears. "Papa wouldn't stop touching me. He just wouldn't! Every night he would come into my room when it was darkest and mama was asleep. He always said 'It's not proper to speak of this to others' or 'You don't want mama to know how dirty you are'."

Shimi felt a sudden sadness for his friend, "I'm so, so sorry."

Omri continued as if he hadn't heard him, "And when Joel left, it got worse. I could talk to my brother and he'd tell me we would stop it. We would stop him from doing this to us. Then he just left one day. He was gone. His room was empty and mama and papa wouldn't tell me where he went. That's when I found that under his bed."

He pointed to the papers, his finger trembling now. Omri's face had gone ashen. While he continued to talk, Shimi noticed

Omri looking back at the open windows again and again, then checking his watch, and then back to the windows.

"He told me Bubbe gave this to him. Where she got it from, he didn't know. But he was going to use this to keep him away. We talked about it for so long. Then I used it last year ... followed the words as best I could. And all it did was make things worse," Omri said.

"It's a way to call Se'irim," Yakov said, still unsympathetic. "Things like this were thrown away a long time ago."

"What does all of this mean?" Joseph asked.

He wasn't picking up on what was going on, being the least intelligent of the four. Yakov sighed and turned to his brother to give a quick explanation in the most condescending of tones a boy his age could muster.

"What he's done is call Se'irim to his room in the middle of the night. Like he said, his father would visit him when it was darkest, so to keep him away he called the Se'irim with this," Yakov shook the papers in Shimi's hands.

"Let me see that," Joseph snatched the papers back from Shimi.

It was Yiddish, which he could read, but the handwriting was so faded and poorly scribed that he was having trouble with the words. He began to repeat them out loud to sound out what they were.

"Don't do that!" Yakov warned, knocking the papers out of his brother's hand.

Joseph howled, "What did you do that for? Why does everyone keep hitting me?"

"Mashugina! That's how he called the Se'irim! Don't read it out loud!" Yakov said.

While the brothers argued, Shimi was feverishly typing away on his smartphone. He was quite proficient at doing searches online and had already found quite a bit of information on Se'irim, demons, Yiddish spells, and all manner of forgotten Jewish folklore that he had never heard of before and, quite frankly, made him uneasy.

"They come from the shadows, don't they?" Shimi asked Omri.

His friend nodded.

Shimi continued to tap away at his phone, "But they can't come into the light. They can only stand in the shadows. So, that's why you have the lights around your bed. They form a ring around the bed. The demons can't harm you but your papa can't get in either, right?"

Again, Omri nodded in agreement.

"This is silly," Joseph cried out. "There are no such things as demons. You all have lost it, especially you *Nebbish*, feeding into this sick story Omri's telling us. He's trying to find a way to deal with his abuse ..."

Joseph could go on for minutes when he got into one of his tirades. He had lost control of the group, as he saw it, as they clearly knew more than he did on this subject. Beyond his suppressed fear of what Omri and his family were involved with, his ego was taking over. He barked at his brother for listening to their wacko uncle, Shimi for spending too much time looking up secular websites on that ridiculous phone of his, and Omri for causing all of this.

As he continued to chastise his friends, Omri's eyes went to the window and saw the sun taking its final dip behind the trees. The shadows were beginning to creep along the wooden floor, reaching from the window towards the center of the room where they all stood.

He whimpered and suddenly rushed to his bed, turning on all the lights before taking a spot in the middle. Shimi and Yakov were shocked at the seriousness with which he did this while Joseph continued his rant, now annoyed that they had turned their attention away from him.

"I'm getting out of here," he proclaimed, giving up on his

tirade.

It all happened so quickly it was hard for any of them to comprehend what was going on at first. Omri's eyes and mouth went wide as he watched Joseph reach for the door. A shadow was already striping the top half of it right above the doorknob. Before he could warn his friend, several slivers of darkness reached out from the striped shadows snatched Joseph by the arm.

The boy squealed like a pig. He tried to shake off the shadow but its grip was vice-like. He pulled and pulled but couldn't break free. He'd break his wrist before the shadow would let him go. A sick voice started to float around his head, a whispering of something looming and malevolent, speaking in many tongues but all calling his name: *Joseph, Joseph.*

"Hold on! Hold on!" Yakov screamed as he and Shimi grabbed Joseph by the waist.

They all tugged at the boy's rotund midsection. When that didn't work, Yakov pulled at his suspenders while Shimi kicked at the door. Without warning, the shadow let go of Joseph, sending all three boys tumbling to the floor. A wheezing cackle echoed throughout the room just before the door opened slightly, and then slammed shut with a violent thud.

All three of the boys sat on the floor in stunned silence before looking around and realizing that the shadows were growing along the floor. That was enough for them to believe Omri's story. In a mad dash, they all rushed for Omri's bed, being mindful of the wires and lights around it, and dove into the flood of electronic light next to their friend.

"What in the world ..." was all Joseph could get out, his entire body now shaking from the top of his head down to his black leather shoes.

Yakov started praying frantically. Of all of them, he was the most devout and his faith would have to help them all right now. What sickness Omri had brought into this world was now surrounding them at dusk, effectively trapping them in this bedroom.

◆

Over the next few hours the shadows took over the room. They were in control now, gradually pulling the room itself into their realm. The far wall opposite the bed had fallen so deeply into the shadows that it resembled an abyss more than a construct of wood and plaster. It was solid black, deeper even, with its many appendages of various shapes and sizes stretching towards the bed. It would swallow them whole if it could.

Around 9 pm, the guests started to arrive.

Omri had seen this before but his friends had not. The first Se'irim passed through the veil of darkness, as if it had pushed through a membrane of thin spider webs, the traces of its black dimension falling off of its body as it entered the bedroom.

The beast drew closer towards the bed with steady, measured steps, its cloven hooves clicking against the hardwood. It had the look of a middle-aged man who had a taste for young children, a pair of ears that were wide and pointed with many rings piercing the cartridge. It had the yellow eyes of a lizard and the curled horns of a goat. A thick layer of hair, stiff and prickly, covered its naked body from neck to groin, leaving its muscular legs and its deeply wrinkled skull exposed. It stumbled towards the bed and stopped just short of it, the light rig above Omri's bed providing a barrier. It didn't dare push its unholy flesh into the light.

The boys observed the beast carefully as it neared the

bottom of the bed. The reflection of the lights allowed them to see just enough of the creature, its eyes seeming to glow in the darkness, wide and wild. White teeth shined inside a broad, gaping smile as it breathed through its nose and growled with each exhale.

Over the next hour, others emerged from the darkness. Each new Se'irim came with its own unique (and terrifying) visage. The menagerie was something out of an 18th-century painting of religious monsters. Filthy creatures, each of them, some covered in oily hair while others were adorned with greasy scales. A slender, skeletal creature with large alien eyes lingered in the corner next to a shorter, portly beast with fangs hanging from beneath its puffy red lips. Both arrived at the same time and found their place near the back of the group. Next came a small imp of a creature with strands of straw gripped between stained teeth, long slopes for eye sockets, and a mohawk of horns stretching from its forehead to the base of its neck. Another entered the room with a bulbous head, three times the size of any of the boys, that pressed against the ceiling as it bobbed up and down, held up by a neck split into three strands of pale flesh. Just beneath the window they could see a pair of chicken legs scratching the wood floor, the body they supported twisted above the waist like a towel wrung out to dry. An awkwardly constructed monstrosity it was, its top half falling forward under the weight of enormous bare breasts dotted with sores and rashes, the nipples leaking a thick fluid onto the floor.

Oh, the smell! With each new visitor, another wave of rot filled the room. The stench was like raw meat left in the sun mixed with the sick perfume of vomit. It clung to every inch of the bedroom. It hung over the bed, seeped into the sheets, and wrapped around the bedposts.

By 10 o'clock the number of Se'irim had grown to two dozen, each one gathered around the bed. In the dark, the boys could see their demented faces and giant eyes all just out of reach of the bed, like hell-spawn parents watching fresh newborns through the glass of a nursery; close enough to be observed but unable to touch.

"I don't know how much more of this I can take," Yakov muttered under his breath, quivering next to his brother.

"This is insane!" Joseph said. "We have to get out of here. We can't just sit on this bed."

"What else do you think we should do, Joseph? You want to fight them or try to run past them?" Shimi countered.

"I see this every night," Omri said flatly. "Every single night. They can't come close. They can't touch us as long as the light is on."

"So, they just stand around your bed and stare at you?" Joseph asked.

Omri nodded. The poor boy, Shimi thought, spending every night of his life locked in this room with these monsters staring down at him for hours. No wonder he looked as if he hadn't slept in months, he likely hadn't. To see the night coming through your windows and know what terrors awaited—to cower under your covers and pray that not a single light bulb went out or a thunderstorm would knock out the power—all just to keep a darker human monster at bay.

"I have to pee," Joseph said. "We have to get out of here."

"We can't leave," Shimi answered. "I'm sorry, but you'll have to hold it."

"Are you insane? I can't hold this until morning, Shimi! I have to pee!"

"Well, wet your pants then," Yakov said, becoming annoyed with Joseph's complaining. "We have much bigger problems than you having a full bladder right now."

"It's going to be everyone's problem if I pee in this bed!"

"Here, take this," Omri ended the debate by handing Joseph a bucket that was on the nightstand.

"Are you serious? I'm not peeing in a bucket," Joseph protested.

"Fine. Then pee on yourself, I don't care."

"You use this?"

"It's clean."

Now Shimi had become frustrated, "Just pee in the bucket! No one cares."

But Joseph cared. The thought of taking a piss in front of a crowded room of monsters who were watching every move they made was disturbing but his friends being around was probably worse for him. Beneath the modesty factor was the truth of the size of his boyhood: nothing to be impressed. His current state of terror didn't help matters.

While Joseph did his business, trying his best to hide as much as he could, Shimi and Yakov continued to look around the room for a way out. Why hadn't Omri's mother come to check on them? Where was his father? How could this have gone on for months?

"We'll just have to wait," said Omri.

Color was coming back to the boy's face and a normalcy returned to his voice. He was more confident in this nightmare than he was in the park with other kids. It was his new reality in a sense, to the point where he had given names to some of the Se'irim.

While there were different ones every night, he had some regulars. Tubehead, The Gash, Skinny Frankenstein, Neb-Nub, and on and on he pointed out the ones he knew. To him, it diminished the fear he felt. He was no fool, it didn't make him comfortable and he knew that the second he stepped foot outside of the light or the lamps failed him, they would rip the boy limb from limb and lick the blood from his ravaged bones. But he had to deal with this someway.

One eluded him though, staying to the back of the pack every night, hiding so Omri never could see much of it. He knew it was there, he could see the shift in the darkness behind the mob. It always paced back and forth in waiting– what for, Omri couldn't guess. Tonight was no exception as the midnight hour approached.

"I don't know what it wants," Omri said. "It won't ever come close to the bed. It's different though, I know that."

"There has to be a way out of here," Yakov said, ignoring Omri's story. "What if we grabbed the lights and kept them away from us."

"Not a good idea," Omri answered. "You'd make a shadow somewhere, and once you do ..."

"By yourself maybe, but with all of us, we could each hold a few flashlights and make enough light to get to the door," Yakov argued.

"It took me weeks to figure out how to get these lights just right so I wouldn't be attacked. Believe me, you don't want to move them.

"Well what did you do before you put up the lights?"

"The first few nights they just tormented me. They were working up to something worse, I knew it, so I put up the lights. The more lights I put up, the angrier they got when they couldn't figure out how to turn them off. The last time they got close enough to grab me, it wasn't good. Not at all. That's when I left school. Mamala didn't know what to do, but she knew why it happened."

Shimi turned his attention from the glaring demons back to his friend, incapable of believing Omri's parents knew about this.

"How can your parents know and not have done anything?" he asked. "What do the Rabbi's say?"

"The Rabbi's won't talk to us because of ..." Omri stopped just short of repeating the atrocities of his father.

"Got it," Shimi said. "So, they let you stay here in this room all night. What are they doing out there?"

"No idea," Omri said, and until this moment, he had never thought about it. "But if it keeps him out of my room."

"Yeah, this is much better," Joseph said, the sarcasm still there beneath the fear and embarrassment.

The fat boy had finished urinating and put the bucket on the nightstand. As he did, he saw the shadows against the wall shift towards him violently. They wanted him badly, he could tell. Just a taste before, but now they wanted the whole meal.

"When does this end? Sunrise?" Yakov asked.

"We've got seven hours until the sun comes up," Shimi answered, using his smartphone to get the information.

Wait a minute, he thought, *my phone still works.*

"Well, you finally found a use for that thing after all," Joseph remarked while Shimi feverishly pressed buttons on the screen. "What were you going to tell us anyway?"

Yakov added, "Yeah, you were supposed to have something you wanted to show us. Something to help Omri."

"There were stories about Jewish counselors up north who could have helped him. They were from Israel and had dealt with this in their own communities over there. The internet was the only way he could reach them."

Shimi explained this in a rather detached way. He was busy searching the web, and not for counselors for his abused friend.

While he wasn't the most spiritual of souls, Shimi did have a respect for the old traditions and had researched them from time to time. Se'irim were something he rarely read about; he didn't even believe they existed, and even if someone had told him twelve hours ago they did, he'd have laughed at them along with his friends. But he had this device—something that had caused him such ridicule from family and friends for so long—and it might be their only chance of surviving the night.

"*He promised us,*" a strained voice came from the darkness.

Which of the demons had uttered the words wasn't

apparent, but a grumbling started among the clan. In various languages, some human and others guttural, the small army that surrounded the boys began vocalizing. Bass-heavy growls, nasally snarls, breathy moans, and psychotic threats were bubbling from the mass of Se'irim.

Joseph was beginning to panic again, "What are they saying? I wish they'd stop!"

"Promise what, Omri? What did you promise them?" Yakov asked.

How to answer this question? Did Omri dare tell his friends that he had suggested a sacrifice in exchange for them leaving him alone? They'd take it the wrong way, thinking that they were the sacrifice, which wasn't the case at all. He had someone else in mind for the Se'irim to quench their bloodlust upon. The boys had invited themselves over and even though the thought had crossed his mind, there was no way he'd give up his friends.

"Not you, if that's what you're thinking. But I wanted your help. I didn't want you to leave because I wanted someone else to see this. I was trying to tell you about this before it got too late and you started messing around with the lights," he reminded them.

"Then what?" asked Yakov, now highly suspicious of Omri's motives.

"Stop arguing," Shimi interrupted. "I think I know how we can get out of here."

The stench in the room was growing stronger. A few of the Se'irim were shifting back and forth, each one rambling nonsensical phrases to themselves and becoming increasingly agitated. The beasts were no longer content to stare and frighten children in bed. That was an old, tired game now. Whatever language they were speaking meant one thing to the boys; the Se'irim wanted flesh to tear, bones to break, hearts to roast, entrails to suck between their lips.

"That smell!" Joseph commented. "It's getting worse."

"I've never seen them like this before," Omri admitted, his face now lacking the familiarity it showed before. "I'm sorry. Shimi, Joseph, Yakov ... I'm really sorry I did this."

"Stop it, Omri," Shimi said. "Pull yourself together, because you're the one who has to end this."

"What are you talking about?" said Omri.

"I've read some of the writings about Se'irim here. It's old text but these people seem to repeat the same thing over and over again, so it has to work."

Joseph remained skeptical, "Who are these people, Shimi? Some people on the internet? You're trusting that?"

"What else do we have?"

"We can just wait it out. Isn't that right, Omri?" Yakov didn't want to risk anything if this would all just go away come the morning.

Omri didn't appear to be convinced. "That worked for me," he said as the Se'irim continued to grow even more restless, "but this is different. I don't know if they're going to stop."

"Listen!" Shimi broke in again. "We have to use the lights. Joseph was right in a sense. If we use the light we can get out of the room."

"Now he listens to me," Joseph grunted.

"We have to turn them to the door and make a path."

Omri saw holes in the plan, "I said it before, if you mess with the lights you'll make shadows you don't even know you're making. That's all they need, just a sliver of a shadow. You saw what happened to Joseph earlier."

Yakov's attention was drawn to the floor where he could see one of the smaller Se'irim creeping along the border of light. It was an impish creature with elongated limbs, pointed ears, and a hook of a nose. Yakov could see what it was trying to do.

"They're trying to take out the lights," he warned Omri.

The other boys turned to look at the outlet on the wall.

Indeed, this little monster was doing its best to withstand what it could of the light to rip the network of plugs from the wall socket. No use. Omri's placement of the lights cast enough brightness around the outlet that the creature could only stand a few seconds in it before retracting its spindly arm in pain. It cursed and spat at the boys, knowing it had been caught in the act.

"They're going to figure it out," Joseph cried. "Once they do, that's it."

By 1:30 am the boys had still not worked up the courage to try to leave the room. Yakov had made use of the pee bucket twice, Joseph's body started to cramp up from being curled up next to the headboard in an attempt to stay as far away from the Se'irim as possible, while Omri and Shimi tried to find other means of escape that wouldn't put them in so much danger.

The smartphone, although full of information and folklore about the Se'irim, hardly provided anything credible about what to do with them. For Shimi, using the lights to carve a path to the door made the most sense. That theory was offset however by how bold the Se'irim were becoming with trying to cross that barrier around the bed.

Within the last hour, the demons who were content to tower over the much smaller boys before, were now doing their best to touch the bed. A few actually made contact with the bedposts, jerking the entire bed a few inches across the floor. Yes, it was done to scare the boys and keep that fear fresh in their little hearts, but at the same time, Shimi and Omri knew what the demons were up to. They were moving the bed inch by inch towards the shadows and out of the protection of the lamps.

The wall outlet was also tried and tested. The imp from

earlier had enlisted the services of its apparent relatives to take turns at reaching for the wires. Just one good tug, that's all it'd take.

"I want to go to sleep," Yakov said, his mouth opening for a big yawn. "My body wants to. But at the same time, I can't. I'm too scared to close my eyes."

"Why don't they just go away?" Joseph shouted. His outburst had grown louder and louder each time. "You hear me! Just go away! Leave us alone!"

Omri and Shimi started to whisper to one another which didn't help Joseph's anxiety at all. They're going to keep secrets from him now? It was their fault that he was here in the first place.

"Do you want to tell me and my brother what you two are chattering about over there?"

Shimi raised his finger to his lips to quiet Joseph's complaining. It wasn't going to do any good. Joseph had been on the verge of cracking for hours. He couldn't take another whisper, another threat, another repugnant scent filling his nostrils.

Yakov tried to calm his brother's nerves but that wasn't going to last long. They needed to get out of the room before he totally lost it and did something that would get them all killed. It was now or never. Shimi and Omri pointed to a number of lamps and flashlights they could disconnect from the rig around the bed. Carefully, they began pulling a few down, making sure the light they emitted didn't allow any shadows near them. Yakov saw what they had done and followed suit, grabbing two flashlights and an old desk lamp which he handed to his brother.

"We're getting out of here," he said to Joseph.

Still shaking with fear, Joseph took the lamp in his hand and held it up towards the monsters. The cord was long enough for them to get to the door but it was a risk, the lamp was old.

"When I count to three, we get off the bed on the left near the door. Keep your lights aimed at them and stay back-to-back. Don't let any shadows get near you," instructed Shimi.

"And what happens when we get to the door?" Yakov asked.

"We'll get to that when we do."

Shimi counted using his fingers. One. Two. Three!

The boys slid off the bed, flashlights and lamps pointed in all directions. The Se'irim were keen to their plan and all swarmed near them, hoping for just a slither of darkness where they could reach the boys. The light was more powerful and painful than they realized. Shimi lifted the two flashlights he carried and aimed them at any demon that got too close. They squealed in pain, then cursed him in six languages as they shielded themselves with their deformed hands.

Formed like a four-leaf clover, the boys were just a few feet from the door. Omri was the one facing it, taking cautious steps forward while he kept his light focused on the entire door frame. The closer he got however, the smaller the light became, and the more the Se'irim encroached around the entrance. They'd have to be quick once they got to the door. A second maybe was all they would have to get out of the room.

"I can't do this," Joseph began to whimper. "They're getting too close."

Shimi peered over his shoulder and saw the hooked-nosed Se'irim towering over Joseph. It was in pain but absorbed it, growing in anger as it bore down on the child. A stream of saliva slid between its sharpened teeth onto Joseph, its white bloodshot eyes wide, its pupils pinpricks.

"Keep it together, Joseph," Yakov whispered.

A few more steps and they'd be there. Omri began to wave the light around, trying to make up for its shrinking coverage on the door by wiggling the flashlight in all directions around it. A long, drawn-out groan came from his right as he reached out for the doorknob on his left. He looked through the corner of his eye and saw a towering figure behind all of the other Se'irim—the one who had been there all along—and even though most of the creature remained hidden in the shadows, its face was not.

Its head was a white oval with a red spiral spinning from the outside edge to a pinpoint at its middle. Long strands of black hair draped over its face, but didn't diminish the hypnotic effect of the spiral. Omri knew what this was and he turned away before he felt its effects.

Yakov was not so fortunate. He was facing the creature and, unaware of what the spiral was doing to him, slowly started to drop his flashlights. His face stiffened in shock, his mouth opened in awe, and just as Omri's fingers touched the doorknob, Yakov's hands opened and the flashlights fell from his grasp, clattering on the wood floor.

"Yakov!" Joseph cried out.

"I've got it!" Omri shouted.

"*Yessssss*," the spiral Se'irim hissed.

Omri twisted and pulled at the doorknob, opening it to the hallway beyond. He and Shimi flung themselves through the doorway, relieved at their escape, but their companions were not as quick.

Yakov was still mesmerized by the spiral-faced Se'irim, his hands stiff at his sides while he stood like a statue. The flashlights he dropped were keeping some of the demons away but not for long. They were quickly finding their way around the light source and closing in. Shimi took a hold of the boy's suspenders and dragged him out of the room, through the door, but pulled too hard and collapsed on the floor. It was enough. Yakov woke from whatever trance he was in, shaking his head to clear out the hypnosis the monster had drowned him in.

Joseph was another problem entirely. The boy had spent

more time flinging his lamps at the smaller Se'irim to even realize the door had opened. Omri called out to him several times, no good. Consumed with his own fear and panic, Joseph didn't notice the larger, more formidable Se'irim, glowering over him from the side.

"For crying out loud Joseph, get out of there!" yelled Yakov.

This, Joseph did hear. Turning to look behind him and seeing the open door, he dropped his lamps and hustled as quickly as he could. His girth was working against him.

With one last push Joseph forced his way out into the hallway. Halfway through, he felt a painful clamping around his ankle, so tight he thought his leg would snap in two. With a scream he turned and twisted, trying to free himself, only to wind up on his back, his body half-in and half-out of the darkened room. All the lights that had protected them were extinguished now, making the bedroom pitch-black.

He pulled and pulled, trying to break free of whatever had hold of him. The more he tried, the more hands and claws he felt tightening around his ankle. The Se'irim were vocal; some cackling, some laughing, some whispering threats in Hebrew and Latin. With a tug, his body slid violently back towards the dark room.

"Grab his other arm!" Shimi yelled to the other boys as he tried to pull his friend back from the brink.

Yakov and Omri joined him, taking hold of Jacob's arms, shirt, whatever they could. All three strained to pull him away from the grasp of the Se'irim in a tug-of-war that was as painful as it was frightening. Joseph could feel the skin around his robust stomach begin to tear.

Shimi had one last trick up his sleeve though. The smartphone was still in his possession and it had a camera, but more importantly, a light source. He let go of Joseph's arm, pointed the phone towards the doorway, and began taking photos in rapid succession. The flashbulb popped again and again, winning a chorus of cries and howls from the darkness. The grip on Joseph's ankle relented, allowing Omri and Yakov to easily pull Joseph out of the shadows and into the light of the hallway.

"Are you okay?" Yakov asked his brother.

"I ... I ... I think I am. My leg hurts though," Joseph answered, clutching at his ankle.

His white sock was charred black, smoke rising from a litany of blackened fingerprints. The heat subsided within moments but the pain lingered. Joseph wiggled his leg a few times, trying to shake away the anguish.

The four boys sat in the hallway, their brows glistening with sweat, their hair plastered to their heads underneath their yarmulkes, all waiting to see what the room offered up now. It was silent. The doorway sat open and empty.

As if waiting for the right moment, the blackened doorway filled with a dozen deranged faces, the fleshy masks of the Se'irim straining against the barrier. The grotesquery could be clearly seen now: the oval shaped head of the tallest, the goat-like horns and hairy face of another, the hooked nose one, the gnome-sized tormentors, and even the giant spiral face, all cramming the doorframe like rats trying to squeeze through an open hole in the wall.

"They can't get to us," Shimi noted. "The hallway is too bright. We need to get out of here."

Joseph seconded his sentiment, "You don't have to tell me twice. Let's go!"

♦

The upstairs hallway was well-lit, but Omri knew the rest of the house, especially at this late hour, would be dark once they hit the stairwell. It was around the corner from his bedroom, but the switch to turn on the lights downstairs was on the wall at the bottom of the stairs. He didn't know whether or not the Se'irim's mastery of the dark extended beyond his bedroom, but just in case, he'd make sure he turned on every light he could in the house.

It would not be necessary. As the boys turned the corner for the stairwell, they were greeted by an abundance of fluorescent light. The ceiling lights, desk lamps, the kitchen lights, dozens of candles, all flooded the entire home from ceiling to floorboard.

While it was a surprise, they boys quickly rationalized that Omri's parents had taken these precautions to protect themselves from the Se'irim. Their reach clearly extended beyond the boy's room. What was more distressing to Omri's friends was the obvious fact that his parents cared little for their son's safety, knowing he was being tortured night after night, but caring more for their own protection than his. Sweep it under the rug. Pretend it doesn't exist.

"What really happened to your brother, Omri?" Shimi asked.

"He left, I told you."

Yakov didn't accept the answer, "Did he leave or was he killed?"

"I don't know."

"I bet you his parents know," Joseph said.

As they carefully made their way down the creaking wooden staircase, a faint sound could be heard coming from the living room just adjacent to the stairs. It was a woman's voice, a woman's hum more specifically, peacefully reciting the Bedtime Sh'ma. The song was familiar to the boys, but in this setting, trapped between the hive of demons upstairs and the callous adults downstairs, it took on a different tone entirely.

May my bed be safely guarded in your presence.
And may you give light to my eyes lest I should not wake.

The words floated out of the living room and through the rest of the house. Her voice was both beautiful and haunting.

I lie down. I sleep. I awake.
I lie down. I sleep. I awake.
Blessed one. Dear one. My God

On the last step, Omri swallowed hard before daring to look around the corner. He had no idea how his mother would react. She could be angry with him, she could be fearful of him. Deep inside, he wished she'd be comforting. Was it not her natural calling as his mother to protect him from such nightmares and dangers? Yes, she would. She had to.

That you help me to lie down in peace.
And you help me, to arise in peace.

The song had reached its end and all was quiet. It was the perfect time. Omri rounded the corner and entered the living room, the other three boys right behind him. There his mother sat in a rocking chair, gently knitting away at a blanket while staring off at the walls of the room. Every lamp was lit in the room, the lampshades removed from each one.

"Mamelah?" he said quietly.

She didn't respond. Perhaps she hadn't heard him, so he tried calling to her again, this time a little louder. He didn't want to wake his father who he knew had returned home and was likely asleep. Omri didn't care that she had been complacent in his abuse, had turned a blind eye and a shut mouth to what her husband had done to her two boys. Right now, Omri just wanted to be protected by her.

He approached her slowly. She had to know he was there. How could she not? Yet she still stared at the far wall in a trance, her hands knitting away as if on autopilot.

"Omri," Yakov whispered to his friend. "I think we should just leave the house."

"Wait please," Omri said.

"Omri! I don't think this is a good idea. Let's just get out of here."

"He's right," Joseph said, "I don't want to stay here any longer than we have to."

"Just one second!"

Omri placed his hand to his mother's shoulder and finally she responded. Her head turned slowly towards him, her eyes wide and wild. He didn't want to accept it, but at this point there was no choice: his *mamelah* was not herself, a husk sitting in a chair knitting away, unable to recognize her own son.

"Mamelah, we must leave. You hear me? We must go!" he pleaded with her.

She stared blankly at him for a moment. Then, her lips quivered into an uneasy smile. It appeared as if she was trying to form words, but some force, whether internal or external, was preventing her from doing so. A tear then fell from her eyes as she started the Bedtime Sh'ma again.

"Mamelah!" Omri cried, clutching his mother's hand, trying as hard as he could to yank her from the chair.

He couldn't move her. It was like trying to pull a boulder.

Shimi interjected and pulled a sobbing Omri from his mother's side. "She can't hear you," he said. "We have to leave. We have to get out of here."

"The door won't open!" Joseph shouted as he tried with all his might to twist and pull at the door knob. "Is it locked?"

"It's jammed," bellowed a male voice from behind them.

The boys all turned towards the stairwell, frightened and

startled by the figure descending the steps. As terrifying and deformed the Se'irim were, none of them matched the horror that Omri's father presented. He was a tall man with broad shoulders and a rough face. His beard was long and frizzy, his eyes solid black. Shimi had met Omri's father before, but this was not how he had remembered him. This was a man who looked possessed by something even darker than the spirits in the bedroom.

"We always jam it at night," he continued as he reached the bottom of the stairs. "So, I see you have the neighbors' children here, Omri. I'm glad you still have friends. They clearly have helped you get over your delusions about monsters in the bedroom."

"Delusions?" Joseph scoffed. "Have you been in his bedroom?"

"Bad question, Joseph," Yakov observed.

Omri's father conveniently ignored the comments of the children and continued on into the living room. He put his hands to his wife's shoulders, kissed her on the forehead, and then sat down on the sofa. How could he be so comfortable? He knew what horrors his son had awakened. What other reason would he have to keep all the lights in the house on in the middle of the night? At this point, his arrogant avoidance of the demons, his molestation of his son, and whatever he had done to his wife, were both equally frightening and insulting.

"Can you let us out? Please, Mr. Rabin, we just want to go home," Shimi pleaded.

"Of course, you can go home," Mr. Rabin responded plainly. "I can unlock the front door for you..."

"Thankfully!" Joseph said.

"... under one condition. You do not mention any of this to your parents, they don't need the worry."

Yakov and Joseph nodded to one another. Ultimately, there was nothing they could do to help Omri. Even if they told their parents, they knew that nothing would come from it. No, it was best to cut their losses and leave. They'd have to fight another day for their friend.

Shimi was not so easily swayed.

"I'm sorry but no, Mr. Rabin."

With a deep sigh, Omri's father rubbed the top of his head in frustration. He casually crossed the living room to stare down at Shimi. This boy, their neighbor's child, was always a troublemaker. Now here he was defying an adult. It seemed that he would need to be taught a lesson too.

"Now, I'm going to say this again, Shimi," Mr. Rabin spoke in a low, measured tone as he knelt down to put his face closer to the boy's. "You may leave this house but you must not speak of what you've seen here to anyone. Do I make myself clear?"

Shimi swallowed hard, trying not to show how freaked out he was at this moment. He bit his lip and answered coldly, "And I said no. Is that clear, Mr. Rabin?"

He was asking for it, Mr. Rabin thought. This boy needed some discipline as his parents clearly had not instilled it in him. How dare he talk back in such a way?

As Mr. Rabin's mind spun through the ways in which he would handle this problem, as well as how to explain the results of it to the boy's parents, Omri came in between the two.

"Get out of the way, Omri. Now!" Mr. Rabin barked.

"You're not going to touch Shimi. You're not going to touch any of us. Not anymore," he snapped at his father. "I can't do this anymore poppa! Not anymore! They came because of you, not me, you!"

"Go to my room now, Omri, I'll deal with you later."

"No! No more, poppa."

"Omri! Go now!"

"No!"

Shimi pulled his friend back out of his father's reach as he saw Mr. Rabin's hand raise above his head, ready to strike his son.

"Our parents will find out what happened. How do you think they won't? You really think we won't tell?" Yakov said, finding the bravery to speak up now.

"And what if you do? You'll pay the price, not me. What I do with my son is my business. They mind theirs, I mind mine. That's the way it is."

"I can't believe my parents would turn the other way while you molest your son," Shimi countered.

"*They* won't do anything!" Mr. Rabin yelled. "They don't know but they suspect, but they won't help. What does it matter? He's brought those things into this house and I haven't been anywhere near him since he did. It's over."

Shimi cracked a smile that caught Mr. Rabin off guard. What in the world could this kid find amusing right now? It wasn't until Shimi pulled his hand from his pocket and showed his smart phone that he realized. The little nebbish had been recording this the whole time.

"All I have to do is hit send," Shimi said as he held it up as though it was a grenade he would set off, which, for Mr. Rabin, wasn't too far from the figurative truth. "Someone out there will do something about it. You were right though, it is over. Omri is not staying here, not with you."

"Clever boy. You always were quite bright, Shimi. I knew that," Mr. Rabin turned to the coffee table and grabbed a letter opener. "Well, we'll see just how far you get with that. Now, hand me the phone or else. This doesn't have to be messy, just hand it over."

The flaw in Shimi's plan had been exposed. The door was still locked so he could not escape this house. The windows were barred, the back door was compromised and the last thing he wanted to do was go upstairs. From the look in Mr. Rabin's eyes, he'd rather kill them before he would let the outside world know what he had done to his sons.

He and Omri backed up from Mr. Rabin but the man was determined, luxuriating in the chase. The letter opener gleamed in the bright lights of the house. The molester held it tight in his fist as he raised the weapon above his head. Such a plainly decorated house holding such horrors, both supernatural and paternal; the spirit of evil set against the dullest of decors.

Shimi turned to look for an exit and saw nothing but picture frames of the Rabin family, the false pose he noted earlier in the day more profound now than ever. A glass cabinet reflected the scene, four boys cowering from a sick man who would threaten them.

"You can't kill us," Yakov said.

Mrs. Rabin's started singing again in the other room.

"I'm not. But you will be disciplined," Mr. Rabin answered, his teeth grinding against each other now. "And your parents will do nothing. I gave you the chance to leave this between me and my son. You wanted to know what was going on with him? Well, now you will."

And may you give light to my eyes lest I should not wake.

"No, they won't," Omri said, no longer backing up but standing his ground between his father and his friends. "But you will."

Mr. Rabin stopped his advance, puzzled by the words. It was long enough for Omri to lunge past him to the wall. The light switch! Before his father knew what was happening, Omri had turned the lights off in the room, plunging all of them into darkness.

Without missing a beat, the room filled with the Se'irim. It was the first time Mr. Rabin had witnessed this menagerie of monstrosities that plagued his son's bedtime for some six months. Was this what Omri had faced every night? This boy cowered as these demented and demonic faces surrounded his bed all just to keep him away?

A great swell of emptiness filled Mr. Rabin's soul, fueled by a shame he had not felt about his actions until this very moment. The children were right. These were his conjurations, and as malformed as the bodies and faces that crowded the room were, they were dim to the raging light of horror he had shined in his son's eyes.

The boys moved back to where Mrs. Rabin was sitting, still knitting away and singing to herself. There was enough light around here from the lamps to keep them out of the shadows. Even with all the shouting and screaming she was still in a trance.

From the other room, they could only hear the voices of the Se'irim repeating the same phrase over and over again in Hebrew: *you promised us, you promised us*! Unlike before in the bedroom when they heard this phrase, it sounded more accusatory. It was not Omri who had made a promise to the devils in the shadows, it was in fact his father.

Mr. Rabin protested and pleaded, his whimpering a pathetic change from his aggressive posture just a few minutes earlier. He begged and sobbed, cried and bargained, but none of it would save him. His cries grew increasingly desperate to the point of jabbering. Without warning, they struck. Glass was broken, wood splintered, walls pounded, all to the backdrop of the molester's painful screams.

Omri turned to his mother one last time. He held no anger towards her, it was near impossible for her to go against her husband in such a way. He suspected she didn't want to believe he was such a monster. The pain and shame of what he had done to her children was too great to face. Best to leave it under the rug, to blind herself from the truth given there would likely be little help for her or Omri.

Just as he went to speak to her again, his father's screams were suddenly ended by one last gurgling cry, then nothing.

"We have to leave," Shimi said. "Omri, is there any other way out of here?"

"No, and I'm not leaving without Mamala."

A jingle came from the darkness of the other room. The boys expected it was their turn. The Se'irim would not be satiated by just one body. Why would they be?

One of the smaller demons, the impish ones that had tried to unplug the lights in the bedroom earlier, shuffled to the edge of the shadows, just keeping itself out of the light. In its small hands was the key to the front door, its metal spotted with blood. The monster dropped it with a snicker to the floor and kicked it towards the boys.

Joseph took the hint and grabbed the key from the floor and unlocked the front door. The chill of night rushed into the house, knocking a few of the candles onto the carpet.

"Let's go!" Joseph yelled.

He and Yakov crossed out into the front yard, followed by Shimi who was dragging Omri by the arm. The boy still wanted to save his mother. She had not moved despite all of her son's pleas.

Then the fire started. The spilled candles ignited the rug. Flames spread throughout the main floor, engulfing the furniture and dissolving the drapes. The Se'irim could be heard over the flames laughing in celebration. From outside, Yakov and Joseph witnessed them through the window, their deformed silhouettes dancing in joy.

Omri continued to fight Shimi, despite the flames and the heat. It wasn't until the spiral-faced demon appeared in the doorway that he backed away. Shimi and Omri stared up at the creature, their mouths open in astonishment. It was female in form, naked and raw. There were no details to its body just a mass of solid black against the encroaching fire behind it, the stringy hair flowing in the night air. Its spiral face was still spinning; a white oval with red swirls going around and around. A single word echoed in the boys' heads as they watched the Se'irim. Not a word, no, it was a name. A name they had never believed before and would never forget in the future.

Lilith

The demon raised the severed head of Mr. Rabin high above, a fistful of hair as streams of blood poured from the jagged wound where neck had been ripped from torso. Even more gruesome than that was the expression on the molester's face. His mouth was frozen in a wide insane smile, his eyes drained of all color except for his pupils which were now small dots.

The door slammed shut as the fires raged on and the silhouettes of the monsters dissolved into the orange and red light of the inferno. Omri collapsed in anguish in his front yard. He put his hands to his face to cover the sobs as the flames continued to engulf the house. His friends consoled him, or did their best to. There were no words for this, no prayers or affirmations that could ease his pain.

His mother's voice still lingered in the air, calmly singing the Bedtime Sh'ma before fading into silence just as the fire trucks arrived. He almost wished they hadn't, wanting to hear her sing for as long as he could. Even though he was relieved that he would not have to spend another night of his life either terrorized by Se'irim or his father, the cost was too high.

The firemen moved the kids away from the flames as the police entered the house. Shimi looked down at his phone with its cracked screen and noticed the time was still 2:22 am. The number six again. As if to mock his realization, it changed to 2:23 am.

◆

It would be a week before the police finished their investigation of why the fire had started. Many in the community would speculate, gossip, theorize, blame, and fabricate much about what happened that night. The boys knew they couldn't tell the whole truth and kept it to what they could prove with Shimi's phone recording. They knew without it that their accusations about Mr. Rabin would have been dismissed and ignored.

Omri spent the next few weeks with Shimi's family until other arrangements could be made. While a comfortable setting, he found sleeping difficult. Even though he knew the Se'irim wouldn't return, Omri could not sleep for three weeks. Bedtime would haunt him with sounds and images of that night. One hour would pass at the most before his mind flooded him with intense reminders, waking him in a cold sweat.

It all ended one night when he lit a candle next to his bed at 2:22am. He didn't know if it was imagined or not but he heard a voice again, faintly on the air. The windows were shut and the only other person in the room was Shimi, but he heard a female voice inside the room. It was his mother's, he could swear it was her, gently speaking as if to only him in the silence of the night.

May my bed be safely guarded in your presence.
And may you give light to my eyes lest I should not wake.

Omri caught his first full night of sleep in months that

night. Shimi blew the candle out once he heard his friend start to snore. Before going back to bed himself, he grinned and reached under his bed to turn off his phone.

Postmortem I

"So, you get the father and the mother?" the angel asked, her voice suggesting a bit of suspicion over the tactics her opponent was using in this game.

"Nothing against that," the demon countered. "It was fair. She had a choice in the matter and decided to retreat into her mind. Don't start with the rules again."

"I was just asking. I got the best out of that round, anyway. The four boys will come to us when the time is right."

"They're still available for another game."

Omar couldn't believe what he had just seen. These two entities had just completed a hand of a card game where lives had been traded, bargained for, influenced, and collected with as little sensitivity as possible. While his sense of morality was shocked by the utter lack of compassion shown for the souls they were playing with, Omar couldn't help but marvel at the exquisite nature of the game.

A deck of cards was selected from one pile that each player

would draw five cards from. The cards could represent a person, a situation, some form of natural or supernatural event, and various other manipulations that were limitless in scope. With the hands drawn, the winner of the previous hand would go first and play a card. The first move was to take a card from your hand that represented a soul place in the center of the table. Both players had to choose a soul to place in the middle, at which point they would start playing other cards that would manipulate what situation those souls would be involved in. It could be anything from afflicting a person with a disease to ending a relationship to more supernatural events like an encounter with a cursed object or, in the case of the prior hand, the ability to conjure demons. They would then watch the cards as the souls they had chosen responded to the situation.

With each response, the demon and angel would place chips next to each card—a bet of sorts—proclaiming the likely outcome of that soul during the hand. Other cards could be drawn from the deck and added to increase the likelihood of a particular outcome. In the case of the Jewish children, the angel had placed a heavy bet on Shimi using his smartphone to influence the outcome while the demon had bet heavily on the boys and the parents dying at the hands of the Se'irim.

The demon lost most of the hand but gained two souls, which made him the ultimate winner. While the angel had bet the boys would survive, she could not claim them in her pile for none had sacrificed anything or saved a life in the process. The demon, on the other hand, could claim the father and the mother, although the mother was in dispute for some time as to whether or not her death was a sacrifice or just merely the result of inaction.

"You can keep it," the angel finally conceded. "It's indeterminate what her motive was. Mental collapse puts it in your territory, anyway. The rules are clear on that, at least."

"Like I said, it was fair," growled the demon.

"Are you learning anything so far over there?" the angel asked Omar.

Omar was at a loss for words. *Find something to say so they don't think you're an idiot!* he thought. If they could do this to souls playing a game, what would they do to him if they didn't find his company useful?

A question would show his interest. "W-what is the name of this game?"

The angel smiled, her wings flourishing involuntarily as she answered, "*Cluichi.* It's that simple. Cluichi."

"And how long have you been playing?"

"Time doesn't matter here. You're inside the game now. From outside of this table, it looks like a blur, doesn't it? You saw that, right? To anyone not at this table, time is different, slower. We have played nearly three hundred hands at this point, which would be minutes to you out there."

"What does he need to know the rules for?" the demon argued.

"If he's going to watch, he should know what he's watching."

"If you say so."

Omar thought to profess his desire to learn, but it would be a lie. While that may have been a smart move in any other situation, these were ethereal beings, and any lie he told might be sniffed out and result in an unpleasant ending to his spectator status. It was best to keep his mouth shut and not disturb the thin ice he was treading by just being here.

"Next hand?" asked the angel as she grabbed a new stack of cards. "I'm dealing this time. That last hand was heavily in your favor calling on the Se'irim. I doubt you'll get to use your cousins this time."

Man of the People

"We are back on WXMN 660 AM, and this is *The Shawn Levine Show.* I am your host Shawn Levine, and this is *Man of the People.* That's right, folks. We're taking back the airwaves, taking back the culture, and taking back the country one day at a time, one night at a time. Of course, you can call into our hotline at 1-866-MAN-O-PPL. We'd love to hear your comments and questions right here on the air. So, pick up your phones and dial in."

Since the day he had understood the nature of politics in

the United States of America, Shawn Levine had proudly and boastfully declared himself a Conservative. From school elections in grade school to running different political action groups in college to interning for senators and congressmen in Washington, to even running for political office himself in his home State, Shawn had an iron-clad ideological worldview that no emotion, logic, fact, or fiction was going to sway. After fifty-six years, he found himself with a mid-level AM radio show, a gracious salary, and an audience of tens of thousands who listened to his late-night broadcasts Monday through Friday.

He had been slotted in the 10pm to 2am shift a few years ago which, oddly enough, was a popular timeslot for AM Talk Radio. He had gone up against others at the time, the Savages, the Great Ones, and although he didn't rule the nationwide ratings, he could claim six number one spots in particular states. *The Dawn of Shawn* was a catchphrase that had caught on with his audience, and he saw it repeated in hashtags online and t-shirts at rallies and town hall meetings. His name was getting out there, more so than it ever had when he was running for office. In a sense, Shawn knew he held more power behind his microphone than most senators and congressmen behind a desk in the middle of the muck that was D.C. politics.

Without the filters he had while running for office, he sat in an excessively expensive leather chair behind a thick wooden desk. His engraved microphone arched towards his mouth; the mouth that had, for five years, brought his views to the ears of many like-minded (and some who were listening just to record any violation of *their* beliefs) citizens of the country. Curtis, his engineer, sat in the booth just to the right of the studio, occasionally peering through the rectangular slit of glass that overlooked Levine's workspace. They had a business relationship founded on their mutual tastes in politics, humor, affinity for Italian wines, and, most importantly, the smoking

Man of the People

of large cigars which had become a post-show ritual.

On this night, what had been a routine show highlighting the excessive protesting of Liberal America and reciting handpicked news stories was about to be saddled with a segment he'd later find the most important of his career as a broadcaster.

Sitting in the Green Room was his guest for the third hour of the show, Chad Ortiz. Born to a German-American mother and a Puerto Rican father, the young man had been an activist for the last six years of his life following an unexpected, and beneficial, feature on the major networks as an advocate for gay marriage. What had caused his fifteen minutes of fame? A statement he made about homosexuality being as natural as being left-handed. That statement had been chronicled and recycled in the press for years. Many felt it had changed the minds of enough people to sway the votes in favor of new protections for same-sex married couples.

Chad also fit into part of Shawn Levine's audience: someone who listened to hear what the opposition was saying. It was a tedious and agonizing task for Chad, night after night listening to the drivel from this middle-aged man who had few, if any, inclinations about what it was like to be a minority, a woman, a homosexual, an immigrant, or any other number of disadvantaged people living the good ol' U.S.A. But politics had become tricky in the last few years with people becoming coy in what they said and how they said it. The real meaning was between the lines, under the words, within the tone and inflection of what was being presented, not so much in blatant bias.

The goal for tonight was simple. He'd rattle Levine's cage, something no one had been able to do, although many had tried.

"Coming up next after the break, we have a young man who disagrees with me on a variety of topics, most of all the pending law your representatives are going to pass in a few days. That and much more coming up after this brief but obscene profit segment."

Levine muted his mic and got up from his desk for a brief trip to the control room. He needed coffee and a candy bar, in that particular order, before he could continue with his show. A simple but comforting ritual he had before conducting interviews.

"So, is he here?" Levine asked as he unwrapped his chocolate treat.

"The gay protester? Yeah, he's been here for a while," Curtis responded through a haze of cigarette smoke. "Boy's been sitting in that room for almost an hour, listening to every word you say. You know he's gonna try and get you mad, right? His little gay friends are going to record it, chop it up, make you sound like an asshole, and it'll be all over cable tomorrow night."

"First off, no one rattles me. Secondly, that's the whole reason we're doing this interview, for the cable exposure. Another year of this and one of those channels will come at us with a decent price to host a show. Not the pennies they came with before. Third, stop smoking in the booth, you'll ruin the equipment."

"That's a myth," Curtis spat as he coughed his words out, then immediately inhaled another lung-full of tobacco smoke. "I've been smoking for thirty years and ain't nothing happened to me yet!"

"You sound like it," Levine mused. The joke went over Curtis' head. "When he's ready, send him in, okay? I'm going to go get ready."

"Right."

"And Curtis ..."

"What?"

"Don't insult the kid, alright? We need him to actually want to be on the show. No gay jokes."

"Whatever," Curtis huffed as he extinguished his cigarette before fetching Levine's guest.

The studio was circular with the desk in the middle, creating the feeling of a coliseum where these two men were to do battle, only with their wits instead of weapons. There was no doubt though that this was Levine's Coliseum and he held court here. The chair for guests was noticeably lackluster in comparison to the leather seat of the show's host.

"Tonight we have Chad Ortiz in the studio. Many of you are probably familiar with him, he's been associated with La Raza and the New Family Initiative, among about another dozen liberal causes and organizations around here in Northern Virginia and in Washington D.C. Good evening, young man."

Chad smirked at the introduction. "I certainly hope it will be."

"We're only looking to get to the truth here, Chad. I must start out though by asking you a very simple question: what is the biological definition of the word 'family'?"

Already, this was off to a rocky start. Chad saw the trap set and was frankly surprised that Levine would put it out there so blatantly.

"Well, the definition of what a family is can be different for many people. The population of the United States is made up of different kinds of families, some extended, some with multiple fathers or multiple mothers or no mothers or no fathers. The real definition of a family is the people who love you and are there for you, that's about it."

"I see you sidestepped my question and went into a speech."

"Perhaps," Chad grinned.

"All right, let's not insult each other's intelligence or that of the audience. I asked you a very simple question, and you didn't answer it."

"I feel I answered it the best way I could," Chad responded, noticing he was being put on defense already. "But, let's not insult your audience's intelligence any further by trying to pretend that your question was not bait. We all know how this works. Let's just put it on the other foot, since I am not answering the way you want. What do you think the biological definition of family is?"

"Do I have to pull up a dictionary for you? I think I do. This isn't a hard question, Mr. Ortiz." Chad noted how Levine had now stopped using his first name. "And come on, everyone knows what the definition is. A family is people who are related by blood, meaning a man and a woman give birth to a child, and they are related to each other and all other people who share that bloodline."

"That's one definition."

Levine had expected that response. "It's the *only* definition if we're going by what words are and not how you or anyone else on the Left wants to feel they should be. And this gets at what my major issue is with what you and your peers do. You go out in the public arena and distort the definition of words to engender sympathy. Since the word was invented, everyone has known what a family is, but in the last ten years you have all sought—and in some precincts achieved—the redefinition of that word, among others."

The boldness of the statement, and its certainty, chaffed Chad's sensibilities. He couldn't help but let out a small laugh as he shook his head in disbelief.

"Did I say something funny?" Levine asked, feigning outrage as he did.

"Look, I'm not here to argue with you, Shawn. I actually kinda like you."

"I find that hard to believe."

"No, you shouldn't. You're a person, a human, just like me.

I don't have any ill will towards you, just the rhetoric you put out on the airwaves."

"Rhetoric?" The word offended Levine. "I'm telling the people the truth of what's going on out there. We've just established how people like you use word games to emotionally manipulate people to accept things that aren't natural. Whatever your sexual orientation or gender identity or whatever it is ... it's fine for you. Most people don't have those conflicts."

"Is that society telling them what to be or them knowing who they are?"

Levine had heard this argument a thousand times, and it never held any weight with him. They were both playing their own word games. A chess game of verbal manipulation where each one of them knew what was underlying the phrases they threw at each other like little jabs.

"Even if it is society, it's society through nature. Naturally, men and women are needed to create a child, that's what is known as a family. I get your expansion of the word to include friends who are tight with you but honestly they're not a family in the biological sense."

Chad ceded the point, "I understand that. I think most people understand that. We're talking emotional connections, though, when we bring up the word family. But that's not even what I'm here to discuss."

"But it is related," Levine countered. "The Universal Family act has many people concerned about the deterioration of family in this country. For those of you who do not know, it's an attempt by lawmakers to redefine the family to include non-blood related relatives."

"More or less. But you're leaving out some significant parts of the measure."

Levine sifted through a stack of papers on his desk. His show had received plenty of criticism over the years for its presentation, but the one thing that was universally praised was the accuracy of the research. You would not win a game of facts with Shawn Levine, and he made sure of it by hiring a very young, but extremely thorough team of researchers and investigators.

With a sly smile, he lifted a sheet from the stack and held it out in front of him as he spoke. "Individuals seeking benefits will be allowed to name up to four non-blood related persons as members of their family, thus providing all previous benefits, rights, and legal privileges that were not covered under current state law," he read.

Chad knew the document well. He helped craft much of the measure along with lawmakers. It was an attempt to extend legal rights to those who considered each other family but did not share a bloodline because of how commonplace the non-blood related family had become in the community. It was something he had worked on for years and what he saw as a shining achievement in his career as an activist.

"What could possibly be wrong with that, Shawn? You're allowing people who already consider each other family to be able to have the same rights and benefits that other people do. Many who are blood relatives don't have close bonds but still gain benefits from it because of the family designation."

"I may be old-fashioned, but a friend is a friend, family is family; they're totally different things. Not to mention there's another benefit to this, isn't there?"

A bewildered look crossed Chad's face.

"What other benefit?" he asked.

"Everything has an agenda behind it. If this became law, it'd be an easy way to give benefits to illegal immigrants, for starters. It also changes the definition of family, much like we've changed the definition of marriage."

"So you fear change?" Chad countered.

Levine's hand balled into a fist around the piece of paper,

hinting at the irritation he was beginning to feel from his guest. Something about the kid's smug attitude struck Levine as slick and greasy, like an oily coin stuck to his finger that he couldn't shake off.

"I don't fear change. I do suggest you fear the law. I suggest you fear that what you are is not considered natural, and so you want to say it's natural over and over again to the point where people just accept it. I suggest you fear an honest debate about the issue," countered Levine.

"So, what do you want us to do? You want us to hide in the shadows again? You want the Mexicans and my fellow Latinos to just go back home? You want the gay community to stay in their little corners of the world, sectioned off like we have the plague or something? What is it that you think should happen?"

"I think people should follow the law, if you're asking me honestly. Illegal immigration is, in fact, illegal."

"A person can't be illegal."

"Don't give me that garbage," Levine's voice started to rise. "Again, another word game. No one is saying *people* are illegal. It's their status as immigrants that is illegal given the laws of the country they are in. What about that do you not understand?"

"What about people's lives do you —"

"No," Levine cut him off, "don't dodge the question. What about breaking the laws of the country do you not understand? What about the fact that a sovereign nation and its people have rights, and one of those rights is to determine how someone becomes part of that nation? You want to talk about how I disrespect immigrants? How about how they disrespect the people who are already in this country?"

"You can go on and on about respect, Shawn, but you show no compassion for anyone. But then again, you're a rich white man —"

"I'm far from rich."

"— a rich white heterosexual American male, to be exact. You haven't had to face oppression or desperation or isolation as I have, or my people have, or my friends or family have. You have all of this and, like a spoiled child, don't want to share it."

"I earned whatever I have!"

"You didn't earn the land. Your forefathers built a nation on top of another nation."

"This is going nowhere. You realize this, right? You're not going to even consider the universal right and wrong, you're just concerned with people like yourself gaining whatever you want, whether you deserve it or not, at the expense of people you feel don't deserve it."

Chad had reached his point with Levine's ranting and pulled out his ace in the hole, "Yeah, we don't deserve it. Like how your sister didn't deserve to be a part of your family anymore, right?"

It was as if a collective gasp could be heard in the studio and throughout the airwaves. The argument had gotten personal very quickly and no one, not even his most confrontational guests, had ever gone to such a level with Shawn Levine. Even Chad was taken aback after the words had left his lips. It was done, though. No going back now. Might as well double-down.

"Your whole family disowned her, right? And what happened to her? Do you want to tell your audience?"

Levine's response came back measured but with a noticeable menace underscoring it. "This interview is over."

"Why? Come on, Shawn. Tell your audience! Tell your followers! Tell your devoted people what happened to your sister."

"Cut his mic," Levine instructed Curtis.

Chad continued his verbal lashing, but the mic was no longer working. At the glass doors of the studio, the radio station's staff were gathered, watching the two debaters in anticipation of what possible retribution would come. Shawn was not known to be a violent man, but he certainly had an imposing presence. At 6'4" and being a former football player in college, he had a physicality that was enough to intimidate anyone without him laying a finger on them. If there was ever sufficient cause for him to do so, this exposing of his dirty family laundry on air would be it.

Commercials were playing in the background as they went off the air. Levine slammed his headphones down, stood from his desk, and swiftly approached the young man. Chad got out of his seat to meet his adversary, but before they could reach each other, the security personnel of the radio station intervened.

"I'm not going to touch him," Levine said calmly, though his eyes showed a fire that told a different tale. "I want him out of here. Now!"

"It's funny what happens when someone brings the truth to your carefully constructed image," Chad snipped again at Levine.

"Boy, if you don't get the hint that it's time to leave, I'll be more than happy to show you out the door myself," Curtis said. "Trust me, you'd be better off leaving now."

"Is that a threat?" Chad shot back, his cockiness getting the better of his common sense.

"You little faggot!" Curtis shouted as he lunged at Chad.

Security was still keeping the boy protected from being assaulted. Shawn grabbed his studio producer's shoulders to hold him back, not wanting this to escalate any further.

"Just get him out of here," Levine ordered. "You need to calm down! He's trying to bait us into attacking him. Think about what he'll do with that," he turned his attention to Curtis, forcing him back to the opposite side of the studio.

"Face yourself, Shawn! Face yourself!" Curtis shouted as the security team took him from the studio and down the hallway.

A couple of other employees of the station stood in shock at what they had just witnessed. Never had they ever seen something come so close to an actual physical confrontation. Sure, there had been several guests that sounded like they would go toe-to-toe with others—some of them theatrical, others real—but this was something altogether different.

Realizing there was another thirty minutes left on the show, Levine took on the role as leader and got his staff back to work. Curtis was directed to get back in the booth and to not take any calls. The last thing Levine wanted to do was be questioned by his audience or have to get any further into the issue. He'd seek other means to deal with Chad Ortiz, that was for certain, but it wouldn't happen tonight, and he wouldn't diminish his show to do so.

After five minutes, he was back on the air, explaining briefly to his audience how what Chad Ortiz had said crossed the line and he was not going to entertain such cheap shots at his family on air. He then changed the subject to another hot topic, a scandal involving the NSA and spying on members of the Supreme Court, before ending the show with a monologue on the desire for law and order in the United States.

Friday morning saw Shawn Levine's email box flooded with listener emails. Many were in support of him, some using the most despicable language to describe Chad Ortiz, others just upset that the young man would do something like that on the air. Levine found the racist and homophobic comments unsettling. While he wasn't extremely sensitive to the issues of many of the "protected classes", as he referred to them, he didn't have a hatred for them. Such vileness went against his beliefs as a Conservative, which weren't focused on racial makeup or sexual orientation but whether or not a person held up the ideals of Americana: family, community, God, productivity, and nationalism.

After answering a few of the more sane emails, he saw that it would be futile for him to spend the morning trying to answer all of them and sent the task to his intern. His secondary email account, which was for business, required his immediate attention.

Various colleagues had corresponded with him overnight expressing their well wishes and some even providing ways in which he can minimize the damage done to his image after the interview with Chad Ortiz. One broadcaster, known for being on the Fox News Channel, had even offered him a spot on his prime-time show as part of a story called "Attack on the Family": an ongoing series that highlighted how the traditional family was being devastated by social changes in America.

He'd answer them later, even though the offer from the TV show commentator would be highly beneficial to his own show's national exposure. Right now, he had other matters he wanted to attend to. The one weighing on his mind the most was visiting his sister's grave.

That was a history he had left well in the past. Given recent events, it had been thrust back into the forefront of his mind, and there was nothing that would shake it but to see her tombstone and try to move on with his life.

Michelle Levine's story was not known to the public, but it resonated throughout everything Shawn Levine had done since then. He didn't want to think about it in detail. She was dead. What good would it do to mill over this and rehash every sad moment, every dropped tear, every disappointing choice and consequence? Pay your respects and leave.

His visit didn't last long. He took the subway down to the cemetery, spent a half hour there, and was quickly on his way back to his condo. While the visit had made him more sympathetic, the ride back on the train reaffirmed many of his social and political stances.

The last car of the train was filled with Latino immigrants, many of whom he prejudged as being in the country illegally, speaking Spanish while observing the females in the train car. Levine knew enough of the language to decipher what they were saying, most of it crude observations about every female in the car that, if it were in English, might have earned them a slap or two. They exited at one stop only to be replaced by a young black man who seemingly didn't understand how headphones worked; his profanity-laced music blaring loudly enough to be heard over the grinding of the train's wheels and anyone else's conversation. Oh, he was so cool, Levine thought sarcastically. So insecure in his own skin that he needed everyone around him to know he was part of *that life*, as it was called. So obnoxious. So inconsiderate. But he would do as most white men in his position did when they encountered this at the bus stop or the gas station or in line at the grocery store: pretend that it didn't bother him. He was in no mood for a confrontation today. The last thing he wanted to do was draw attention to himself as "that guy from the radio show".

The fourth stop held a surprise. Malcolm Johnson entered the car with two very obvious security guards who were trying to act as if they weren't protection. Johnson was a young black man and an up-and-coming member of the local Republican Party until he switched his affiliation to be an independent last year. The move was well known in the city. Even on the subway at this awkward time of the day he was greeted with stares and whispers. While the rest of the Conservative movement had given up on him, the would-be future ethnic star that could show the Republican Party was not racist, Levine had a long history with the man and appreciated his practical approach to politics that was based on common sense and fairness, but also relied heavily on the old American Dream.

"Well, you're the last person I expected to see today," Johnson greeted him as he took the seat next to Levine. "Porsche in the garage?"

"Yeah, right next to your Lexus," Levine responded with a grin. "Do you mind telling me what the hottest rising star in local politics is doing on the subway?"

"It's not a publicity stunt," Johnson answered. "If I'm going to run for office I need to know the people."

"We're not in the city," Levine pointed out. This subway line ran from the county and ended only a few miles into the city which they were several stops from. "None of these people can vote for you, you know."

"That would be a concern if I were only concerned about being mayor," Johnson said.

"Governor?"

"One step at a time, but yes, someday."

"I get the exclusive interview when you announce."

"We'll see about that," Johnson put his hand in his pocket to retrieve his buzzing cell phone. He answered the text message that was demanding his attention and then turned the phone off. "You see, I have interviews lined up as it is. Speaking of which, what happened last night?"

"You heard that?"

"Who hasn't?"

"Most of the people on this train."

"I mean, who in our circle hasn't? It was all over the blogs and Twitter today. You don't want to know what they're calling you."

Levine's face wrinkled in anger, "Do you really think I give a fuck what those assholes say?"

"Public perception, Shawn. It's important. I assume you have a response for your next show tonight."

"I was thinking of taking the day off," Levine admitted, something he had been considering since he left his sister's grave.

"That's not a smart play. You should capitalize on this. I'm sure the cable outfits will be calling."

"They already have."

"Tucker?"

"Hannity."

"The big dog?" Johnson mocked, puffing his chest out to emulate the television show host. "This is bigger than I even thought. You're taking him up on it right?"

"It's for Tuesday. His staff said that's when he's continuing that series about the Attack on the Family."

"Well, you certainly fit that. To be honest, I don't have much use for some of your more sensational stories, but that kid was out of line. You don't bring family into this stuff. He clearly dug up information on your sister, I'm just glad he didn't go any further with it."

"So am I, Malcolm."

The boy blaring his music had moved from his original seat to stand in the center of the car. Holding on to overhead bars he wobbled back and forth as the train continued down the tracks, his eyes catching sight of both men with a curious look on his face. It wasn't the look of someone who recognized celebrities, it was the look of someone who saw a target.

"What is going on in this world today, Malcolm?" Levine asked his friend as he peered out the passenger window. "It's like if you're a decent person, there's a license to treat you like absolute shit."

"The world isn't the place we want it to be. But it is the place we have to live in," Johnson replied with a wisdom and poise that far exceeded his age.

"I can see now why you want to run for office. Even though you left the party, I have to be honest, I'd vote for you over any R.I.N.O we put in place. That's for certain."

The young boy made a move towards the two men, slipping his hand in his pocket. Before he got any closer, Johnson's security team was on him, wrestling the boy to the floor. He howled in pain as they wrenched his arms behind him. Some of the passengers started filming the incident while others decried the scene, claiming racism as the reason for the two men detaining the boy.

Johnson and Levine sat casually in their seats and watched as the security officers pulled the boy to his feet and warned him from making any other advancement towards Johnson. At the next stop, the doors to the car opened and the boy rushed off of the train, cursing the security officers as he went and throwing up his middle finger in protest. Some of the other passengers joined him in their cursing of the guards.

"You have to understand one thing about what the world is now, Shawn. People do not care about what really happens, only how it looks. Is it fair? No. Is it what we have to deal with? Yes. You better get a handle on it today. Do your show and deal with it."

That evening the radio show went on as planned. Levine had prepared a statement to open the show, addressing the incident that happened the prior night. Malcolm Johnson was right; he had to tackle this and change the narrative before it solidified itself for him. It was Friday, so this was the last show of the week, and he wanted the audience, which would clearly be considerably larger than normal, to hear what he had to say. Other news outlets would be listening to for quotes to run with for the weekend news cycle.

He would make this right. He would undo the damage done to him by that little bastard and make Ortiz the bad guy.

"I wanted to start out tonight's show by addressing what happened last night. Of course, you all have seen that it's been all over social media and cable news. People are talking, and while it is good for my ratings, it's good for Mr. Ortiz's standings with his people, it is not good for my family or me.

"I keep my personal life just that: personal. It is for a good reason of course. Not to hide anything or to pretend I am something that I'm not, but because there are things that happen in life between you and those closest to you that shouldn't be subject to the public's short attention span and often overly critical eye. Every single person listening to this broadcast knows that feeling. We have loved ones who may have committed a crime or friends who cheat on their spouses or co-workers who you know have screwed over other people in the company, whatever it is, there are things about our private lives that should be kept private.

"My sister, Michelle, was a lesbian. She made choices in her life that sent her down a different road than the one I am on. She and my parents had a strained relationship, and she left home at a young age. Two years after leaving she was found dead in an alley.

"Now, I tell this story to the public because I know people will find it. They'll look up records, post it online, and spin it to make me or my parents look bad. They'll carry it around like a badge of honor, patting each other on the back and saying 'We got him!'.

"To those people, enjoy yourself. You've used the tragedy of a dead woman to score political points. You should be proud of yourself, truly.

"To the sane people out there, many of you who have listened to this program for years and have already sent your well wishes to me, thank you for letting me take this time to stop this before it gets any worse. Now, I don't know why Mr. Ortiz decided to throw that out to the public, I'm sure he has his reasons, but tonight will be the absolute last time his name or the name of my sister will ever be mentioned on this show again. I appreciate, in advance, the respect of this audience and others for honoring my family's privacy."

He delivered this monologue with enough class and humility that it might have just done the trick to swerve public opinion in his favor. It was a tactic he had seen used against him so many times that he could adopt it, beat for beat, to his own whim. Connect with people on a personal level by addressing flaws in character and loss, and it makes it very hard for anyone to wag their finger at you.

There would be those that would still dare to point a finger of blame at him and rip him apart regardless of his personal tragedy. Curtis informed Levine during the first commercial break that there were a couple of individuals and groups on social media that had seen fit to speak ill of him, but overwhelmingly there was support.

The rest of the show went on as it usually did. Levine returned to his format of discussing the topics of the day in the first hour, spending the second hour with two interviews—the guest were friendlies and not combative this time—and then the third and final hour taking calls from listeners.

Everything was going swimmingly. The only strange thing he noted, which was confirmed by Curtis, was that Chad Ortiz had started tweeting negatively about him at the beginning of the show but had gone absolutely silent on all social media channels fifteen minutes after Levine's monologue had ended. A few of his callers mentioned it, speculated as to why, but

Levine didn't seem all that interested in what Chad was saying about him anymore. The boy was banned from the show for life, and hopefully, in a few weeks, he'd never hear his name again.

One caller was able to completely turn things around. An older woman called the show by the name of Margret. She was a long time listener, first-time caller, who was a member of an organization called *First Patriots*. Levine had heard about the group and their considerable donations to many Conservative mouthpieces, sponsoring books and tours and speaking engagements. It was an aspect of his career he had slacked on.

"I can speak for the others when I say we do so admire your bravery today," Margret's voice was warm, southern, and polite. She spoke like a grandmother who had raised many men from boys, stern but sweet simultaneously. "If you wouldn't mind, we would love it if you came to visit us this weekend at our retreat. There will be speakers, entertainment, and a fine banquet. We'd be honored if you would attend."

"Well, that's extremely generous of you," Levine replied, trying to play it Bogart. "I have heard of your organization. This is short notice, however."

"Sweetie, trust me it will be worth it to ya. All expenses paid, of course. You can come back on the air Monday and tell your listeners what a great time you had, that's all we really ask in return. How about it, sweetie?"

"You know what, I can't guarantee anything but you can speak to our producer Curtis, and he'll get all the details. I'll contact you after the show. How does that sound?"

"Perfect! I look forward to talking to you soon."

♠

Travel arrangements were made before Levine woke up Saturday morning. By 10am a luxury sedan pulled up to the front of his condominium ready to take him to the airport in style. It would be a short flight, two and a half hours down to North Carolina, and he the itinerary he received via email had him scheduled for a long drive from the airport to the retreat.

Career advancement was the main goal here. Levine knew very little about the First Patriots outside of rumors, but he did know they had contributed massive amounts of cash to any public personality they felt was in line with their worldview. Their headquarters in North Carolina didn't surprise Levine either despite his slight resentment towards the south. That was usually where the more racist members of his political party came from with their outdated arguments and severe lack of social graces when it came to discussing minorities and homosexuals. Backwoods fucks, all of them, he thought. But, if they were going to funnel a few million his way over the next few years to expand The Shawn Levine Show's reach along with more appearances on the national and cable television shows, a weekend in North Carolina would well be worth it.

After landing in Charlotte, he was escorted by SUV to a location south-east of the airport off the beaten path from route 601. Not being familiar with North Carolina at all he became somewhat concerned that he'd not be able to find his way back to a heavily populated area if need be. They were deep in the woods, the places where he had only heard about and was, quite frankly, distrustful of. Sure, they had sent him a classy car, but he knew very little about this organization.

Stop being biased, he told himself. A group with such funds would not be comprised of toothless rednecks drinking moonshine in the deep woods of North Carolina. It was a media stereotype that was working on his mind right now, no need to let it color his thoughts.

"We're almost here," the driver told him as they crossed another patch of dirt road. "I know it must be different for a feller like you to be down here this far out. You a city boy, ain't ya?"

"Suburbs, but I guess it's all the same," Levine admitted, seeing no reason to lie to the man.

"Yeah, might take ya a minute to get used to it. But, you will. They all do."

Levine wasn't interested in small talk with this man, but something about how he turned a phrase unnerved him. It had nothing to do with his thick southern accent or the amount of sweat that trickled down the back of his fat neck. There was a confidence about this man that didn't set right with him. He was almost too confident, the kind of assurance that someone held when they knew something you didn't.

"And here it is," the driver said as the car turned one last corner.

This was a mansion, not a row of trailers or some broken down shack. Correction, it was an old plantation, something right out of a civil war era picture book. The wide porch, the tall white columns, the arched windows, all of it not only spoke to a certain way of life but a certain amount of wealth. Levine started to get a sense of why they called themselves the First Patriots, this was an old and forgotten side of America, a side many pretended no longer existed.

It didn't take long for Levine to be greeted by one of the founders of the First Patriots.

"Shawn Levine, it is our pleasure to have you here sir! All of us have been keeping an eye, or shall I say, ear on you for the last year or so. Your show is truly an inspiring piece of auditory exhilaration for those of us who know right from wrong. I'm Cecil Spaulding. I sit on the committee for the First

Patriots, mostly in charge of recruiting new folks and the like, but I do so enjoy these monthly get-togethers. A glass of champagne?"

This rotund little man talked with the smoothness of a classic southern gentleman, but his pudgy face was so flush that it looked like a red balloon that would pop if you pricked him with a needle. He clearly was an avid drinker as well, holding two glasses of champagne, neither of which was what he was offering to Levine. He downed one and then set the glass on a nearby ledge.

"I feel a bit underdressed," he said as he looked into the large foyer, everyone else attending dressed in tuxedos and sparkling evening gowns.

"Oh, don't you mind that right now," Cecil reassured Levine, smoothing his greasy strands of hair over the ever-growing bald spot. "You'll have time to get changed. Most of these people are just early and want to get in on some of the festivities before the entertainment this evening."

"Entertainment?" Levine questioned.

Cecil gave a look as if he had said too much, but then waved it off and smiled reassuringly, "You'll see later tonight. Nothing to get concerned with now. Just a little thing we do especially when we welcome new people in."

Levine was presented with a glass of champagne by a butler. He smiled nervously as he toasted with Cecil. The bubbly went down smoother than he had expected. It even had an aftertaste that was a mix of sweet and bitter, lemon perhaps? He was no connoisseur and didn't want to question it for fear of looking less sophisticated than his hosts. How funny, he thought, that he was expecting trailer trash and now he was the one who wondered if his status was high enough to rub elbows here.

"That's him! I knew it," came a high-pitched voice, feminine and assertive. "Y'all didn't tell me he was handsome!"

"A pleasure to meet you, Mr. Levine," the man at her side

greeted Shawn, shaking his hand with the strongest of grips. "My name is Luke, and this is my adorable wife, Cheryl."

"Pleased to meet you both," Levine said. "This is an amazing house. It's yours I assume?"

"It belongs to the family actually," Luke answered, now taking time himself to look around at the majestic opulence of the foyer. "All of these paintings, all of this artwork, from the 1800s. Most of the decor of the house has gone untouched. We have updated the rooms, electricity, plumbing and such. You'll find a room for you upstairs. Cecil can show you to it."

"Thank you," Levine smiled. "I didn't bring a tuxedo though."

Cheryl waved off his concern, "Oh, honey we've got you all set up upstairs. We have the most talented tailors in the Carolinas. They'll measure you up, stitch it up, and suit you up right quick! Just go on upstairs, and we'll see you later this afternoon."

Levine took the next two hours to get fitted for his tuxedo, enjoy some of the fresh pastries that the kitchen staff had prepared for him, watch some television, and take a nap before dinner.

Not as bad as he thought it was going to be. The room was elegant but not garish in its decor, the staff at the mansion came across as polite and genuinely happy to be there, and everyone who had stopped by from the First Patriots treated him like a celebrity. Networking wasn't really something he was experienced with. Being waited on, indulging in the finer things in life, yeah he could get used to this world.

By sunset, Shawn Levine was ready to play socialite. The mansion's main ballroom was a splendid sight from the polished marble floors to the sweeping arches and high ceilings. Paintings hung from the walls that were worth more money than he could imagine any sane person would spend on art, hung in perfect alignment, spanning from Art Deco to Romantic to Existentialist. The centerpiece of this room was an enormous table covered in a buffet of meats, cheeses, wine, fruit, and an enormous roasted slab of meat. The animal it was from wasn't recognizable but the aroma of its husk, sautéed and accented with herbs, spoke to his stomach.

What he presumed were the key members of the First Patriots were already seated around the table along with other dignitaries. He recognized a few faces, politicians he knew from television, businessmen and women from companies endorsed by the First Patriots, and two men he could only assume were religious leaders. All of them dressed for an evening of dining and, according to his hosts, entertainment.

"Please, have a seat wherever you like dear," Cheryl whispered in his ear.

She seemingly appeared out of nowhere, sneaking up behind him with the cunning of a snake and placing her weathered, sunspot marked hands on his shoulders.

He nodded and took a seat near the center of the table. The staff immediately began to prepare a plate for him, starting him off with an amuse-bouche perfectly centered on the most expensive plate he had ever seen.

"None of them are really that expensive," a portly man with a spotted bald head was in the middle of a conversation with Luke who sat at the head of the table. "Once they come in from the border, we've got enough people to snatch up a handful here and there. Everyone is so preoccupied with catch-and-release or sending them back to whatever God-forsaken country they came from that no one really misses one or two."

"They paid a price for coming into the country, Bishop. As long as they are worth the money you spent to get them here I see no harm in allowing them to stay for a while," Luke said, promptly taking a bite of his dinner as he did so.

"Well let me tell you this, they are certainly special. All this talk from some of us on the Conservative side about deporting them. I swear to you, Luke, they don't know what they're missing."

"I can only image," he replied. "Not my cup of tea, per se, but I understand your stance on the issue. But I'm sure the congressman would disagree, no?"

All eyes of the table turned towards the only guest at the table that had a hint of color in their skin. Congressman Garza was one of few Latino Republicans in the state, and he had been against much of the immigration reform sought by his peers. Levine was genuinely surprised to find him here though as he wasn't known for being much of a Conservative socially, more of a business-minded man.

"I cannot look down on Bishop anymore than I could look down on myself," the congressman conceded as he took a bite of his meal, taking a moment to close his eyes and savor the taste. "You shouldn't think I have any allegiance to those people. They are peasants where my family is from. If anything, America treats them too well."

"And how about you Mr. Levine?" the portly Bishop grunted.

Now, the eyes of the table were on Levine which took every ounce of comfort he had found in this situation and flushed it down the drain. He didn't want to be the center of attention here, but it was something he should have anticipated. He'd have to make his case here and show them what he was about.

"I'm not sure what you're asking," he said.

Cecil interjected, "Shawn is new to the group, Bishop. This is his first dinner with us."

"Oh, I see," grinned the bald man. "Well then, I guess I should rephrase my question. What do you think is wrong with this country? I mean, speak honestly now, you're not on the air. You don't have to mince your words with us."

It was a question Levine had been asked numerous times in various situations. Here, he could be less mindful of offending anyone or having his words taken out of context. These people knew what he knew, and they felt what he felt.

"We've lost our way," he said flatly after taking a moment to choose his words. "I believe in America. I believe in Americana, I should say. We used to make things in this country, build things. We were great individualists who always wanted to see what was over the next horizon and then get there.

"Now, this culture is dominated by the extreme Left, the socialist liberals who make it a point to be against everything that is Americana. We used to want a family with kids and a nice house, now that's a bad thing to them. We used to honor a man and cherish a woman, now they've confused everyone as to what a man and a woman is. We used to be a nation of laws, now we're a nation where the law is if you're a minority you should get advantages and if you're the majority or successful, you should be ashamed of yourself.

"We've lost our way. Now, I don't know how you would ever counter that or change it. Things have been spun so far out from reason that I'm not sure how we can go back, or better yet, go forward. I can only hope organizations like this one can be a force to fight against the destruction of the ideals that I love."

It was unfiltered, but it wasn't mean-spirited, just the right tone Levine wanted to get across. The table of men and women all applauded his brief speech and toasted to him, raising their glasses of expensive champagne and nodding to him in unison.

"That young gay man who was on your show made quite the story for you didn't he?" Cheryl said from across the table.

"Yes, but I think we handled it well," Levine responded.

"Do you?" Luke asked, almost mockingly.

"It's the best I could do given the market. He's a gay man

and a Latino, and he has been a loud voice that many on his side listen to. I went for the sympathy game, something they always do."

"I think it was well played," Cheryl said.

"But, the problem still persists," Luke countered. "If left unchecked, people like him can continue to be a problem. He wouldn't stop, now would he?"

Levine thought briefly on this and saw the man's point, "You're right. I don't expect him to stop. Although, I did notice that he stopped tweeting since I made my statement on the last show."

Luke threw a sly grin towards Levine. What was that about, he wondered. Before he could follow up on the matter, the wait staff came in and cleared the table. It was rather abrupt how they rushed into the room and began rearranging everything.

The other guests stood, apparently knowing that this was part of the routine, and took their glasses of champagne along with them into an adjacent room from the dining area. Luke lead the way with Cheryl on his arm.

"I think that was well said," Congressman Garza whispered to him on their way into this next room. "I think you'll do well going forward. I could use your help on a few matters back in my district if you could present them on your show."

"Sure, that's not a problem. Anything to help."

"Enjoy the show," the politician said as he downed the last of his champagne.

The show? This must be the evening's entertainment he had been told about earlier in the day. The room they were all entering was considerably darker than the dining hall. The ceiling was lower, the lighting dimmed to an eerie yellow-orange that crept along the rocky walls. At the far side was an opening to a chamber below. From here you could look down to an even larger room that strongly resembled a dungeon.

What in God's name were they doing here? Was this some

sort of animal fight?

"Come closer, dear!" Cheryl called out to Levine, waving him to her side and then snaking her arms around his. "You'll want to see this."

The opening in the wall looked out over a pit below. It was as Levine had feared, worse even. This wasn't a battle pit or dog fighting arena, but a place of torture.

A woman in her twenties and as thin as a runway model quivered and sobbed in the middle of the pit, her hands bound together and her hair a ratty nest of dirt and blood. She looked up at the man standing over her who was dressed in a butcher's outfit. His black leather apron was stained with blood and tissue, his head covered in a black leather cap, his face protected by a clear plastic mask. A giant by any measure, the Executioner as the others called him clutched a machete in his right hand and a mallet in the other. These tools had seen years of use by their look.

"We have here a young Social Justice Warrior, or SJW for those of you who are so inclined to acronyms," Luke said to the audience. "She had three of our cops tried for excessive violence against some niggers in Charlotte. Smart woman, there's no doubt about it. Her career might have gone far as an attorney, but unfortunately, the cops she had on trial were some of our own Patriots."

This wasn't only an execution, it was a sermon.

"Mrs. Schmidt, do you admit to the acts we have detailed to you here?" Luke yelled down into the pit.

The woman let out a shriek, uncontrolled and primal. Reason had left her a long time ago and in its place was unbridled fear. The terror could be seen in her wild almond eyes as they stared up at the dinner party through a glossy haze of tears.

"Let me out! Let me out of here!" Mrs. Schmidt shouted. "I want to go home! I want to see my kids. I want to see my kids!"

Levine turned away from the scene, but his eyes were caught by Cecil. The look he got from the slimy little man suggested he better not show any disgust here. Get in line or else. The threat was subtle but clearly understood. Not wanting to draw any more attention to himself, Levine forced his gaze back into the pit and his face to show no emotion.

"Do you admit to it, Mrs. Schmidt?" Luke asked her again.

"I don't know what you're talking about," the woman sobbed. "I want to go home. I want to go home!"

"They don't even realize what they've done. That's the problem, isn't it?" Luke turned back to the audience to gauge their thoughts.

Nearly every member of the dinner party was indifferent to the woman's cries. She had wronged them by defying their circle, by going against what they thought should be the way of the world. Their authority would not be challenged by her, especially when it came to slighting their own.

"Mrs. Schmidt, you have been deemed an enemy of the First Patriots. As such, we cannot allow you to continue in this country. I cast a vote of *no more*. What say the other Patriots?"

No more came from the rest of the dinner party, all except Levine who was still in a state of shock over the experience. These bloodthirsty monsters were too consumed with their own condemnation of this woman to be bothered to pay him any mind at this point. What horror was to follow he could only imagine.

"What does that mean?" Mrs. Schmidt's tears were paused as a growing sense of worry filled her mind.

She looked up at her accusers again, but a blinding light replaced their silhouettes. White blotches clouded her vision as her eyes tried to adjust but it was too late. She felt the giant's hand against the back of her neck. As she started to cry out in protest, muttering a series of pleas, the brute bludgeoned the back of her head with the mallet.

There was a detachment about the way in which he committed this murder that turned Levine's stomach. He almost preferred if the Executioner had some joy in the act. That would make it more human. Nothing close to emotion was in this man's soul as he systematically pounded away at the back of Mrs. Schmidt's head, staining the rusted metal of the mallet with her blood as her skull was cracked open like a walnut. Gray matter oozed from the wounds in a stream of crimson, trickling to the filthy floor of the pit where so many others had met the exact same fate. He pounded and pounded, each strike ending with a wet thud until the woman's arms stopped twitching.

Next came the rest of the body, which the Executioner just as lackadaisically chopped into manageable pieces; arms, legs, torso, breasts, hands, all hacked, wrapped, and placed in a bin nearby.

That was enough. Levine didn't have the stomach to watch any more of this literal butchery. He asked for another glass of champagne to clear out the bile building up in his throat.

Cheryl tightened her grip on his arm as the Executioner finished up his work in the pit below. The smell was starting to rise up from the pit, and all of the guests took a few steps back, choosing to socialize while they waited for what was next.

"I would have thought you'd have a stronger stomach for this kind of thing," Cheryl said to Levine as he continued to down his glass of champagne. "Is that the first time you've seen something like that?"

"Like that?" he answered while gulping down his drink. "Yes, that was the first time I've ever seen anything remotely like that. How can you get away with this?"

"Come now, I know you're a Man of the People, but really, you know what goes on behind closed doors with those of us with the means and the ability. We're doing a good service here."

"What did that woman do again to be murdered like that?"

"*Cleansed*, that's what we call it," Cheryl corrected him. "You heard Luke. She put three fine officers on trial for ridding the world of the wasteful vagrants that pollute our inner cities."

"And she nearly exposed us in the process," Bishop added as he joined their conversation. "So, that was your first time seeing this, huh? Shocked, I'm sure. But I wonder, do you have any objections to what we do here?"

Bishop and Cheryl eyed Levine up and down. He had to choose carefully here. Suggest that they were sick criminals and there was no way he would escape. It would be his head bashed in with a mallet if he wasn't careful. At that same time, he couldn't be fake about this. These people could read anyone like a menu and select what was palatable and what wasn't. Measure your words, he thought. Be stunned but not judgmental. Allow them to think you could be swayed to their way of thinking.

"Well, I admit it seems excessive. No doubt the woman was a blight on the country, I'm sure, but how do you explain this to her family, her friends, her colleagues?"

"Suicide. Overdose. Home invasion. Any number of reasons the public will buy if it makes sense," explained Bishop.

"Even sometimes when they don't," Cheryl laughed. "Honestly, if you tell people what they want to believe about something, especially if it makes them feel better about themselves, it will work."

"Well, I'm sure Levine knows that. You are a talk radio host, after all, right?"

Levine bit his lip at Bishop's clever weaving of his work into what the First Patriots did here. Almost slipped there, he thought. Through grinding teeth, he managed a smirk and wagged his finger playfully at Bishop.

"Smart man, this one," Levine said.

Over his shoulder, Cheryl saw Luke waving to the group to assemble again. Excitedly, she took hold of Levine's arm to pull him to the pit. Again? Was this going to go on all night? He needed something stronger to drink if he was going to stomach another execution, so he asked politely if they had Jack Daniels on hand.

"You'll really like this one," Cheryl whispered to Levine. "Just you watch. You'll get it now."

What this woman could possibly be talking about Levine didn't know. He had just watched a woman literally beaten to death with a mallet and sliced up into pieces. Just get through this and then get out of here tomorrow morning. He regretted coming to this place alone and without anyone else knowing where he was. Too trusting. Once he assured them that he was part of their clique, he'd get home and find a safe way to alert the authorities to what was going on here. Just how he'd do that would be a thought for another time. Right now, he had to pretend he wasn't physically ill as the stench of body fluids flowing up from the pit.

"Shawn Levine!" Luke called out. "Please, step up here beside me. This one is for you."

Dear God, what was this?

"As part of us inviting you to join the First Patriots, we offer you this. You may recognize one of the two people down there of course."

It was Chad Ortiz, stripped of everything but his underwear, at the bottom of the pit. Much like the woman before him his body was covered in bleeding scars and browning bruises. He was shivering in the dark, muttering to himself as he tried desperately —and without much success—to undo the bindings around his wrists. Next to him was another young man whose hair was dyed various colors but in the muck of the pit had been stained with dirt and his own sweat. Both were forced to their knees by the Executioner, their heads turned upwards to the audience looking down on them.

This was why Ortiz had fallen off of social media during the show Friday. This was why the First Patriots had invited him here. For his loyalty, they would sacrifice the man who had embarrassed and humiliated him in front of the entire world.

Luke whispered in Levine's ear as the radio host tried to absorb what he was being shown, "You see, we make good on what we speak. The swine, the filth, the sinners of this world will be held accountable here, I guarantee you that. But this one ... this one Shawn, is for you."

Below, the Executioner was wiping off the mallet with a dirty rag, discarding it on the ground when he was done. Chad's eyes darted back and forth at the silhouettes above but Levine knew in his heart, he felt in his soul, that the young man was looking directly at him. His brown eyes blinked accusatory and sorrowful at the same time.

"What we have here is Chad Ortiz and his lover Devon Tripp. Both of them Latino illegal immigrants! Both of them homosexuals! Both of them the worst of sinners, spraying their mental poison to the youth and flaunting their disgusting sexual choices for the world to see," Luke sermonized to the rest of the dinner party.

"Chad," Devon called to his lover. "We'll get through this. Trust me, we will get through this."

Chad continued to mutter to himself. His mind wasn't in the pit but up at the people looking down at them. His anger was growing by the second, replacing whatever fear he had before. Being entertainment for a bunch of psychotic rich people was not how he was going to go out.

"Chad!" Devon yelled. "Snap the fuck out of it! We need to do something."

Chad's muttering stopped. "What do you suggest we do? They're not going to let us out."

"Don't say that! We're going to get out of here."

"No, we are not."

Devon, clearly the more sensitive of the two, shifted his body to get closer to his partner. Chad watched him and tried to fight back his tears, but they were coming in rivers. Why was he doing this now? Damn him, they needed to be defiant against this evil, not showing weakness. That's what they wanted.

"I love you," Devon sobbed as he finally reached Chad, laying his head on his shoulder. "I love you so, so much."

"I know," Chad said, trying his best to pull himself back into his anger. "I love you too, Devon. I'm so sorry for this."

"This isn't your fault," Devon responded, his anger now showing through the tears. "It's those fuckers up there! I hate them. You hear me! I hate you! All of you fucking assholes! Why don't you come down here and do this yourselves instead of having this freak do it? Cowardly pussies! Come down here!"

"That's quite enough of that," Luke shouted back. "Let's get on with it, shall we? Chad Ortiz, do you admit to being a devoted enemy of the First Patriots, an illegal immigrant to the United States, a lover of sodomy, and an opponent to all that we hold dear about the American way of life?"

Devon shook his head for his partner not to answer. This was all theater, and both of them knew it. His answer would have no effect on what would come next. They were going to be killed no matter what he said.

Defiantly, Chad refused to answer and instead turned his head away from the Executioner. He waited for the blow to fall but it didn't. Devon continued to plead with him to answer, but he wasn't going to do it.

"Please answer," Luke demanded. "The consequences will be worse if you don't answer."

"Chad, say something. Even if it's our last words we have to say something," Devon said.

"Do you, Chad Ortiz, knowing your crimes against humanity now pledge to leave behind all of your prior sins, your prior blasphemies, and your unnatural lust for the male figure?"

He knew it! That's why he didn't want to answer in the first place. These jackasses wanted him to confess that he was wrong to be who he was. For them, it was an even greater victory to have him renounce his life than to simply take it. The arrogance of these people had boiled his blood to the breaking point.

Summoning as much energy as he could Chad slowly got to his feet. The Executioner eyed him cautiously, gripping the mallet in his hands and preparing it in case the boy attacked him. Chad didn't have any such thing in mind. He wanted to die on his feet, not on his knees.

"So, you want a confession?" he said to his accusers above.

"In so many words," Luke replied.

Now that he stood up he could see more of who was above him in the chamber, and his gaze fixed on Shawn Levine. Unbelievable. He knew the man to be a right-wing soldier but this barbarism he never expected. The two stayed fixed on each other for a few heartbeats, one defiant and the other falsely stoic. Chad snickered, brushed the sweat from his face with his bound hands, and offered up the only answer he could.

"I confess my love to Devon Tripp. Here, in this pit, I ask for his hand in marriage."

Amid the various gasps and scoffs at Chad's reply, Levine couldn't help but have a small chuckle in his core. The bastard was bold, he'd give him that. It would cost him his life, and he knew it.

"Very well then," Luke replied coldly. "Then as they say: til death do you part."

Luke nodded to the Executioner who prepared to carry out

his orders. Chad closed his eyes, content that he had stood as strong in facing death as he had in facing life. He whispered one more "I love you" to his partner and waited to the blow to strike. What he felt instead was a warm spray across his legs and back. His mind worked quickly through the scenario, and once he realized what had happened, it was too late.

The Executioner had smashed Devon's head in with the mallet. The lover's teeth and blood erupted across the pit, speckling every inch of floor and wall it could. Devon was still alive however which made it ten times worse. His jaw hung by strands of flesh, dangling below his upper row of remaining teeth. The impression of the mallet was tattooed across the left side of his face, his orbital socket a crater of black where his eye once was, his nose twisted at an unnatural angle. The only sound Devon could manage was a whimper as he tried desperately tried to reach out for Chad.

"No!" Chad howled, lunging towards the Executioner.

It was a silly attempt. The man was nearly a foot taller and a hundred pounds heavier. He effortlessly pushed Chad away. Two other men appeared from the shadows of the pit to restrain Chad as the work of the butcher continued. The head must be smashed in until the brain no longer works. Devon didn't go quickly though. Seeing his work incomplete, the Executioner continued the methodical process of bashing Devon's head in. Like a blacksmith pounding away at a molten piece of metal, the giant raised his mallet high and brought it crashing down with a sick, moist thud. And again. And again. The process continued while Chad was forced to watch the face, the smile, the lovely eyes of his partner reduced to a mangled lump of meat.

"I'll kill you! I'll kill you all!" he howled as the two men restraining him dragged him away.

"They are so dramatic, aren't they?" Luke quipped as the scene ended.

The dinner party slowly dispersed back into the dining room as the wait staff rushed to prepare their seats. The entertainment, thankfully, was over. Levine stood shocked for a few moments before the tug on his arm from Cheryl brought him back to reality. Remain in character.

"I told you that you'd like it," she said, completely misreading his expression.

"That was all for me?" he asked nervously.

"Of course! We want you to know that you have the full support of the First Patriots. Don't ever doubt that honey. I know you won't now. Come back to the table, dinner is about to be served."

"Yes, just give me a moment."

"No stomach for it, Levine?" Cecil asked as he sauntered over to the two.

The man was still giving Levine a questionable stare, but that would pass if Levine said the right thing. As pathetic as he had first thought the little man, it was becoming clear to Levine that Cecil had a keener eye than he let on.

"I've just never seen that before," he answered.

"You disapprove?" Cecil asked.

"No, it was brilliantly done," Levine lied.

"Good," Cecil said, taking a moment to observe Levine's expression and eventually accepting that this newest member was on board. "Good."

Levine was slowly losing it. The sights and sounds of what had just happened were beginning to press in on his head. Was this what he had inspired in others?

"Now, it is time for the main course. I believe most of your meals are ready," Luke announced to the table.

The wait staff brought out several trays of smoldering meat, accented with the rich woody scent of rosemary and just a hint of garlic. Levine did not get a plate, and neither did Cheryl or Luke.

The roast looked delicious. Those who had a plate savored each bite, carefully slicing each piece of meat apart with their knives and gracefully taking bite-sized pieces to their mouths with a fork. Levine wasn't so sure he could hold down food after what he had just witnessed. He had to keep up appearances though. In an hour this would be over.

"So, what can we do to help our newest member?" Luke asked Levine as they watched the rest of the table consume their meals.

"I think you've done enough," Levine replied. "I couldn't ask for anything else."

"Nonsense dear!" Cheryl chimed in. "The whole reason we brought you here was to give you aid. What you've said on the radio for years has inspired me in particular."

"Yes," Luke added. "She is a huge fan."

"Your biggest fan!" Cheryl corrected. "I've always said that you should have your own national talk show on the television. You can replace the hacks they have on at 9pm."

Levine couldn't tell whether or not this woman was flirting with him right in front of her husband. Luke didn't seem to mind at all. His focus was more on whether or not Levine was all in with the First Patriots.

"That would be nice, of course. A national television show is what I've always wanted to do with Man of the People."

"We'll make a few calls next week," Luke assured him. "It might take a month or so, but we certainly can get the wheels in motion on that. All we ask in return is for you to report some of our stories, select a few guests we'd like featured from time to time."

"Members of the First Patriots I assume?" Levine asked.

"Well, yes. A few others as well. We have friends all over the country. Ah, here comes our dinner," Luke smiled.

Levine was presented with his dish, the same as Luke and Carolyn. It was artfully presented—or *plated*—with a dollop of mashed potatoes, steamed vegetables, and several slices of meat with a few sprigs of thyme on top for garnish. The aroma was mouthwatering, to the point where it restored his appetite. His stomach growled now, forgetting its previous desire to push out its contents, now wanting to be as satisfied as his nose was.

"I hope you don't find what we've done here to be too harsh for your tastes," Luke said to Levine as he cut into his meal. "There are so many things that go wrong out in public, and none of it happens to deserving people. Just the other day there was a Jewish family who had their house burned down. The media reports that the circumstances were mysterious, but it very easily could have been a Muslim attack from some Jihadist living in the country undetected. We seek to remove those who would terrorize us or promote anti-American thoughts. It's crippled the nation's core."

"I understand why you do it," Levine said as he swallowed his first bite. "I've never seen anything like this before. But, if you're worried I'm going to go running to the police or anything, it's not something you should concern yourself with."

"That's good to hear," Cheryl smiled.

"Then, we have you as our newest member I assume?" Luke asked.

Levine was too consumed with how fantastic this dinner was. The mashed potatoes were perfect, the aroma was intoxicating, and the meat was so tender that it nearly melted in his mouth. He still had to find a way out of this nightmare scenario, no matter how great the food was, these people were insane. He'd just have to finish dinner and get out of here in the morning.

It was then that he looked down at his plate and noticed

something strange about the meat. What was that discoloration? It looked like a pattern. He pushed aside the sauce and garnish to reveal a symbol, a tattoo. He recognized it immediately as the same tattoo that Ortiz's lover had on his midsection. Could this possibly be? No. They wouldn't dare.

"It's ..." is all he could say as he continued to observe his meal.

There was no doubt. This was the same tattoo. They had fed him his enemies, literally. Panic started to take over as his eyes darted around the dinner table. All of these people were gobbling up the flesh of their enemies. With all of this finery and extravagance, the First Patriots were no more than dressed up cannibals, indulging their sick fetish under a mask of righteousness.

"May I be excused," he asked.

"Sure," Luke replied.

Levine had already left the table before Luke could answer. The rest of the guests ignored him, consumed by their own conversations. Cecil and Luke threw concerned stares at one another as if to question how dedicated this new recruit would be to the organization. Luke lowered his head and then shook it subtly. Cecil clearly wanted Levine to be dealt with, but Luke was not in agreement. The radio host could be very beneficial to spreading their forward-facing message, he didn't want to give up on him so quickly.

After five minutes of regurgitating every scrap of food that was in his stomach, Levine washed his face with cold water, gargled three shots of mouthwash, and took a moment to look at himself in the mirror.

"Ah, that wasn't good. Not at all. Not at all," he muttered to himself.

He had tried hard to keep them from knowing what he really thought. With that little display at the dinner table, he may have just given himself away. He'd have to find a way out of here, but that was going to be harder now. He didn't trust their drivers to take him back to the airport safely. He'd have to get his hands on a set of keys and get out of there. But how?

Over the next hour, Levine packed his bags. Fortunately, he had brought very little with him, and much of it could be put in his pocket. Wallet, keys, cell phone (he didn't dare use it here, there was no telling what surveillance technology surrounded this plantation), and his plane ticket were small enough to fit in his pants pockets. The rest of the clothes he'd brought with him were in his travel bag and that he could pick up later.

"Shawn," a voice came from the other side of the door.

"Just a minute," he said as he pushed his travel bag under the bed.

He opened the door to see Cecil's fat face staring back at him. The man had the most unnerving of smiles, something that made Levine's skin crawl. What could he possibly want with him?

"I just wanted to check in on you," Cecil said.

"I'm fine. It's just ..."

"The food, we know. Not everyone can handle it. But, it is necessary for some of us. Eat our enemies, as they say."

"I don't think it's meant to be so literal."

"Oh, but it is," Cecil welcomed himself into Levine's room. He took a good look around, what he was hoping to find here Levine didn't know, but his nervousness grew as Cecil continued to examine everything from bedsheet to closet. "We don't expect you to jump right into this of course. It takes some a few months or even years to understand what we do here. I do hope we have your loyalty though."

"You do," Levine lied again.

"I want you to come for a walk with me."

There was no other answer to this request besides yes. Levine left his room in the mansion and followed Cecil on a casual stroll through the rest of the building. Whether he was being led to his death or to another grand reward from the First Patriots that would turn his stomach was unknown. The one benefit he immediately got from their walk-and-talk was an understanding of the mansion's layout.

The top two floors were mostly bedrooms where the guests stayed. Each floor had ten to twelve bedrooms with a laundry room, and storage area sandwiched between them. The bottom floor he was already familiar with: the foyer, the entertainment room, and the infamous dining area. Attached to the dining area was the kitchen where he had not been taken before. It was massive in size and looked more like a kitchen from a five-star restaurant than a residence. The staff was still scurrying about cleaning pots and pans, prepping food for tomorrow, and managing inventory lists.

"Do you host many events here?" Levine asked.

"About twice a week. Luke likes to keep the place alive with souls, as he would say," Cecil answered as he surveyed the staff's work.

As off-putting as Cecil came across, it was clear he really ran the house. Luke may be the master, but Cecil was the workhorse. He knew every name of everyone on staff, what their job was, and how they should do it.

During their walk, Cecil continued to divulge more information about the First Patriots. Levine knew this wasn't everything, but this was enough for him to know how influential they were, which was extensive. It was a behind-the-scenes look at one of hundreds of cells like this throughout North America and Europe, all devoted to the advancement of the Natural Order, as Cecil described it. Their prejudice stemmed from biology more than race or gender. If it wasn't in line with what they perceived as the advancement and continuation of humanity, then it was an abomination and should be dealt with. The cannibalism was their way of personally eliminating the unworthy: consume the corrupt and shit them out.

After a half hour, their journey stopped in front of an old rusted door. It's lock was from another century which suggested this was part of the plantation's original structure.

"What is in there?" Levine asked, his posture defensive.

"It leads downstairs," Cecil grinned politely.

"I'm not sure I need to see that, Cecil."

The short man laughed, "You think I'm going to have you murdered or something? Come now! You are part of the First Patriots. You need to get over your fears. I know this is new to you, but I'm giving you a grand tour, not your last rites."

Levine didn't trust that this was the truth. Cecil had been eyeing him the entire evening, and they were alone. If he had a trap set up down here, there would be little Levine could do about it. He had to go through with this though. To back out would certainly put an end to this game if they were, in fact, playing one. Levine couldn't tell whether Cecil knew he was lying to them this entire time or not, but at the same time, he knew just as little about Cecil's motivations for bringing him here. He'd have to risk it.

"Of course," Levine said. "Let's have a look."

"More than a look," Cecil said as he unlocked the door. "I know you want to talk to him."

As Cecil leaned back to get enough strength to open the door, Levine realized what he was doing here. They wanted him to talk to Chad, the prisoner, the man who had ruined his life, as a last form of mental torture. They had no intention of killing him earlier. This was still for his benefit, to give him what they thought he wanted: revenge.

"Mind the last few steps," Cecil warned Levine as they descended into the basement level. "We've meant to fix them for a while now. A bit loose there."

"I've got it," Levine said, taking care to not put too much

weight on the last few steps.

It smelled like mold and death here. Leaking pipes could be heard from the far corners as well as the low rumble of the building's heating and cooling system. There were no windows here, but the fluorescent lights above did their job to keep the place from complete darkness. The white glow of the bulbs made the room feel sterile.

Cecil led Levine around a few corners to a small area near the back of the basement. It was here that four cages crowded against each other, their bars extending from floor to ceiling, hay on the ground and a small hole in the floor that looked to be the only toilet for their prisoners. Levine couldn't make out who or what was in the other cages, but he knew the face in the first one. It was indeed Chad Ortiz, his skin beaten and covered in a glistening film of sweat.

"I'd keep it quick," Cecil said to Levine as he pocketed the keychain. "He was given a sedative earlier but he's awake now. He's due for another shot soon."

Levine turned to Cecil, hardly able to keep his eyes on Chad. "I'm not so sure about this."

The short man's lip curled, "Well, I can take you back to your room if you want. I figured you'd want to talk to this queer before tomorrow."

"Of course," Levine replied, remembering that he still needed this man's trust. "You've been helpful, for certain. I'll make it quick."

"Alright then."

With that, Cecil left the cell area. Levine wasn't alone, there was a guard nearby, plainly dressed in a white t-shirt, leather jacket, and blue jeans. In his hands was a shotgun with a Glock nestled against his waist.

"Fuck you, Shawn," Chad's graveled voice spat from the cell. "I knew you were a piece of shit, but I never suspected anything like this."

"Keep quiet," Levine said, trying to sound adversarial for the guard who was listening. "I have a few things I need to say to you."

"And I don't want to hear them," Chad replied with a cough. "You want me to confess something like your sicko friends? You killed Devin! Bashed his skull in!"

"I didn't kill him," Levine protested.

"You might as well have. This is your group, isn't it?"

Levine turned to the guard who had no interest in the conversation. In fact, he had turned his back on them and walked further away from the cells. Clearly, nothing about Chad appeared to be a threat to him. Instead of keeping watch, he took this time to light a cigarette and relax.

"You have to listen to me," Levine said, finally able to speak freely and honestly. "I'm getting you out of here."

"What? Don't fuck with me, Shawn."

"Shut up and listen! I'm trying to save you. If you hadn't noticed, these people are fucking insane!"

"You're serious?" Chad said, his eyes lighting up now. "Then what the fuck is going on if you didn't send these people?"

"They wanted me to join their cult or whatever this is. The show from last week ... inspired them I guess."

Chad smirked sarcastically, "So, you finally get that the rhetoric you use on the air is dangerous."

"I didn't say that. These people were crazy before they listened to a word I've ever said. Not to mention, it was what you said that motivated them to do this. They're using you so they can use me."

"Wake the fuck up, Shawn. I'm in a cell, you're in a fucking tuxedo! Who's getting the worse end of this deal?"

"Just ..." he couldn't argue the point. "I'm trying to figure this out. Are you hurt?"

"If you're asking physically, I'll heal. If you're asking about how I feel ..."

The words lingered and didn't require Chad to finish them. Levine knew the pain Chad felt at losing his lover. It was the first time he had ever acknowledged that despite his views on homosexuality, they were in fact human. It was a moment of revelation that he didn't have time to process but absolutely noted.

"We should take his body with us," Chad said. "I don't want to leave it here."

Levine didn't have the heart nor did they have the time for him to explain what had happened to Devin's body. He certainly didn't want to admit that he had unknowingly eaten Chad's lover.

"We'd be lucky to get out of here with our own bodies. We'll get the authorities here afterward. They can find it," he rationalized. "Can you walk? Cecil said they gave you a sedative."

"Injected it," Chad said, tapping at his shoulder where they had inserted the needle. "So, that's that little fucker's name, Cecil? He looks like a Cecil."

"You sound delirious. Can you stand?"

"I'm not delirious. I can stand."

Chad stood up in his cell but swayed back and forth a bit before steadying himself. It would have to do.

Now came the hard part. Somehow he'd have to get past this hired thug with the guns and make their way out of the basement. After that, they'd have to improvise.

"Stay here," Levine told Chad. "I'll be right back."

"You're not going to attack that guy, are you? He'll kick your ass."

"Not if he doesn't see me coming," Levine answered and revealed to Chad that he had a steak knife from dinner in his coat pocket.

Five months in the army before his honorable discharge was enough time for Levine to know how to use a knife. Or so he hoped. He had never attacked anyone before in his life, but all the tough guy talk from his radio show was about to be validated or made into a joke. The guard puffed away on his cigarette without a care in the world and clearly had no idea Levine was sneaking up behind him.

"Say nothing. Just hand me the guns," Levine whispered as he stealthily slid the steak knife against the throat of the guard.

The guard didn't flinch. As if Levine wasn't even there, he took another deep drag of his cigarette, exhaled a plume of grey-blue smoke into the air, and then casually dropped his guns to the floor.

"I'm not going to try to stop you. This isn't even my shift," the guard said while raising his hands in the air. "As long as you don't do anything stupid like trying to cut my throat, we're cool."

This was unexpected, but Levine didn't have time to think about it. He let the guard go, grabbed his guns, and then watched as the man casually walked out of a nearby exit where he stood and lit another cigarette, making no attempt to escape, warn anyone, or sound an alarm.

"You take the handgun," Levine said as he handed it over to Chad. "Have you used one before."

"I started hashtag Fuck the Second Amendment," Chad replied.

Levine smirked at the irony and couldn't help himself but respond, "I think you'll be rethinking that one today. Just keep your finger off the trigger unless you are aiming at someone you want to shoot. Be sure to take off the safety."

"What's the safety?"

"Forget it," Levine grumbled as he snatched the gun back from Chad. "Just keep an eye out then."

With the shotgun in hand, Levine started a slow walk out of this dungeon and back to the stairway that led him here. Cecil wouldn't be too far off, but a fully cocked shotgun aimed at his skull would keep him in check. There he was, at the bottom of the stairs reading the newspaper. It'd be easy to kill him right now, shoot him in the back and be done with it. But they needed to keep quiet. The house was still full of staff and guests and who knows what else. The only way they'd get out of here was keeping a low profile.

"Hands up," Levine said as he jabbed at the back of Cecil's skull with the shotgun. "Don't say a word."

Cecil did as instructed. This was going easier than Levine had anticipated, a bit too easy. He didn't expect Cecil to fight him while he held a shotgun to the back of his cranium but the casual way in which everyone was reacting to him breaking a prisoner out of their makeshift dungeon didn't sit well with him. Better hurry this up.

"You know, I figured you didn't have the stomach for this, literally and figuratively," Cecil quipped.

"I think you're right," Levine replied. "But you can talk bad about me after I leave. I need your keys right now."

"Keys?"

"To the car."

"Oh, of course."

Cecil casually reached into his pocket. Levine made sure to press the barrel of the gun harder against his head, reminding the small man not to try anything unless he wanted his head blown off. Without incident, Cecil passed his car keys back to Levine who then tossed them to Chad.

"Of course, he drives a Lexus," Chad scoffed.

"Whatever you think you're going to do, just know that you're already dead. The First Patriots have been around longer than you know and our reach is farther than you think," Cecil warned.

"We'll take our chances," Levine said.

"For the queer? Really? I thought you called yourself a

Conservative."

Levine instantly became enraged at the accusation, "I'm not sure where you got the idea that being Conservative means you kill and eat gay people but I think we have a different idea of what our principles are."

"Clearly. We believe in the country. You believe in something else. It's not your fault, you probably have sympathy for that whore sister of yours and the bitch of a boyfriend this fag had."

"Okay, I've heard enough!"

Chad took the handgun from Levine's belt waist. Before the radio host could object Chad had smashed Cecil over the head with the handle of the weapon. It didn't knock him out immediately, so Chad hit him again. The second shot did it. Cecil collapsed in a heap at the bottom of the steps.

"I thought —" Levine started.

"I'm not going to kill him. I should, but that's not me."

"It's not me either."

"Hell has frozen over. You and I finally agree on something."

Between the time Levine had entered the basement until now, the mansion had settled into an eerie quiet. The staff had gone home, the lights were turned off, the kitchen shut down, and the dining room area stripped of its finery. Levine and Chad emerged from the basement, keenly aware of their surroundings as they cautiously walked through the various rooms towards the front doors. Given how sadistic the First Patriots were, it wasn't beyond reason to think they were setting them up. Turn the lights down, make them think no one was awake, and then ambush them right before they reach the front door. In fact, Levine assumed that was what would happen and as they crept closer and closer to the double doors.

He began to sweat profusely. He felt his body shaking from anxiety, the thought that at any moment a bullet could come out of nowhere or he'd open the door to see an army standing between them and the cars.

No such thing happened.

Chad opened the front door and the only person there was the butler who was gazing at the night sky. The old man had no idea they were there and was genuinely shocked when he saw the bloodied prisoner and his armed escort sneaking their way to the fleet of vehicles parked to the right of the mansion. *Say nothing*, he thought. *They'd kill you. The one's got a shotgun, and the other looks feral.*

"Eight of these fuckers had to have a Lexus, didn't they?" Chad complained as he kept trying keys in any car matching that model.

Levine was keeping watch, "I want you to know I was never a part of any of this. These people called me about some business proposition. I didn't ask them to do any of this."

"I know you didn't," Chad answered, another car door failing to open as he did. "I have to admit, for the last twenty-four hours I thought you had. Why did you break me out of there anyway? You could have just left, and they wouldn't have known any better."

"I was going to," Levine admitted, ashamed now as the words came out of his mouth. "If Cecil hadn't brought me down there I honestly would have left you here."

"Heh, good to know."

"We're not friends. I did it because it was the right thing to do. That's what people like me do."

"Sure it is," Chad mocked Levine's attempted rationalization. "You're not like them, but you're not far from them. It's people like this who take the things you say and actually act on them."

"They were like this way before they ever heard me on the

radio."

"Yes, but you validate this shit. You speak the same language they do."

This was not the time for this conversation and Levine was starting to get angry, "No, I don't. What I talk about on the show is about preserving things that people like you want to convince the world is outdated simply because you want it to be."

"No, I'm standing up for people like myself who have had to live in the shadows too long. Who can't express themselves in public like you and these shitheads can? Who have to hide who we are unless we're mocked or ridiculed or held prisoner, if you hadn't noticed."

"You're conflating me with them," Levine replied. "I don't want you locked up. I certainly didn't want you murdered or your partner to be murdered. That's not what I'm about. I want people who are like me to not feel like we're somehow oppressing you for simply existing."

Chad laughed at the claim as he tried another car door, "Are you fucking serious? You are the majority, Mr. White Christian Man! You are the oppressor. I've just been oppressed by your kind —"

"You keep acting as if we're the same."

"— and in the government, the same thing happens just in different ways through the courts and law enforcement and corporations. If you really think it's not all lumped together with this place, then you are as delusional as I thought you were."

The key fit, the lock turned, and the car door opened.

Chad knew he had to end this debate now if they were going to survive, "I'm not trying to start an argument, but you have to see how this is all connected. What you say matters. What I say matters. If this insanity hasn't shown you that, then you might as well have left me in that cell."

As much as Levine wanted to continue his stance against Chad's indictment of his role in this whole mess, he realized his line of thinking had changed. He wanted to hold onto his old beliefs and felt anything this man said to him would collapse the whole thing like a house of cards. Have to defend them, no matter what Chad said or what sense he made, if he gave in that would mean his enemy was right. Then what? He wasn't about to march in a gay pride parade or look the other way if someone broke the law. But something, some kernel of truth, had been planted in Levine's head that perhaps—just perhaps—the way he presented his case was the issue and not so much that he thought differently than the Chad Ortiz's of the world did.

Levine looked over his shoulder and saw the lights of the mansion flickering on, one room after the other. The troops were gathering as it was obvious now that their escape was no longer a secret. Time to speed this up.

"I'm driving, you still look a little out of it," Levine said as he took over the driver's seat.

Chad had no objections. The mansion was emptying of its occupants who were now gathering in the courtyard nearby. They hadn't spotted the car thieves yet, but it was only a matter of time.

"No matter what I say, and I know I say a lot," Chad said as Levine started the car, "thank you for saving me. You're not like them. It was wrong of me to say that, but I do hope you see what I was getting at."

With a grunt, Levine put the car in reverse, bit his lip, and in a rare moment of humility he responded to Chad, "You may have a point. But we need to be alive for me to think about it. Put your seatbelt on."

Surprise would be their best chance. Levine pushed down the gas pedal, and the car lurched backward. The mob was alerted. Several shouts of "there they are" rang out from the courtyard. It was no matter, they were too far away now to be stopped. Levine spun the car around as they neared the dirt road leading to the plantation, shifted the car into drive, and began down the long driveway.

"I thought they'd have guns. Why aren't they shooting at us?" Chad asked.

"Yeah, this seemed too easy didn't it. Let's not look a gift horse in the mouth though," Levine added.

"You were going to tell me earlier about what happened to Devon."

Levine squirmed in his seat. Not this, not now. How in the hell was he going to explain that he had eaten part of Chad's boyfriend in a way that wouldn't make either one of them vomit?

"It's a long story. Let's get to the police first. Here, check to see if there's service out here now."

Chad took Levine's phone, "So, that's why you haven't called the cops. I was wondering." The screen lit up, but the bars were still low. "Nothing. No service at all."

"Keep an eye on it. The further we get away from the place I'm sure we'll pick up something."

"I will. But don't dodge the question, Shawn. I know you know what they did with his body. Tell me."

He wasn't going to let this go, was he? Levine did not want to talk about this now. Too much was going through his mind: how to get to the police, how would they get back home, would he be safe from this day on knowing they'd be after both of them? But, if it meant Chad would settle down and not keep asking for the next hour, it would be worth it.

"I'm not sure how to tell you that —"

The windshield of the car shattered instantly, glass showering both passengers. Levine hit the breaks, and the car spun to a halt, just missing a large oak tree that was on the side of the road. He checked himself for harm then looked over at Chad who was in a state of shock. What had hit them? A bullet perhaps?

"Levine!" Chad said alarmingly.

Ahead of them was The Executioner in full sprint towards the car. Levine hadn't realized how massive this man was—if it was, in fact, a man at all. Nearly as wide as the car and as tall as a bear, the giant stormed towards the driver's side, punched through the window, and dragged Levine into the road.

The series of events happened so fast that Levine barely knew what was going on when the rain of fists came down on his body. He was a tall man himself, but there was no matching the size and strength of this monster. Whatever he did to defend himself it wasn't enough. The blows were finding their mark, again and again, with such violent force Levine thought his lungs would explode and his skull would crack.

Chad did his best to stop the assault, but his skinny body that was already weakened was nothing more than an annoyance. The Executioner swatted him away and continued to beat on Levine.

The brute smelled horrid, like a wild animal fresh from the field, stinking of rot and sweat. He grunted and howled, savoring every punch, bloodying his victim's face and his knuckles in the process.

Levine's thoughts went dark as the corners of his vision turned black and he felt his body going numb. I'm going to die here on the side of the road. They're going to serve me for breakfast; my heart, my liver, my thighs. Lord knows what part of my body that viper Cheryl would want to keep for whatever pleasure she desired. No! Must get to the guns.

The shotgun was too far away, but the handgun was still under his belt. The Executioner caught what he was trying to do, and before Levine could aim the weapon, it was taken from him and thrown against the side of the car. That was it then. He just hoped the pain would be over soon.

Chad had not given up, and the giant's dismissal of him as a threat was his only advantage. He saw a flash of silver shoot from the two men in the dark and rest against the rear wheel of the car. The gun! He scampered towards it while Levine continued to be pummeled.

"Fuck!" Chad yelled as he picked up the weapon.

How does this work again? Right, cock the weapon, aim through the sites, pull the trigger. Pull the trigger! It wasn't working. Fuck, the safety, that's right. Now he was ready. Aim. Fire!

The shot rang out across the empty road. It was a hit. The bullet passed through the shoulder of The Executioner, and Chad whooped. His celebration was short lived. The wound didn't seem to do anything but infuriate his target. Within seconds the Executioner was bearing down on Chad who struggled to get off another shot. Too late. The giant had him by the throat with one hand, raising him in the air. His massive, rough hands felt like a vice around Chad's neck, squeezing tighter with every gasping breath he took.

Chad looked at the twisted face of this man as he was held high above. The scars on his face, the flat nose, the abnormally large and ape-like forehead, the rotten teeth. Abused, certainly, but there was no empathy in this mindless abomination. Behind the grotesquery of The Executioner's face came a flash in the road. It was from the shotgun. Levine had recovered.

Once again the warmth of blood and tissue sprayed against Chad's body. The irony didn't escape him as his neck was released and he fell to the ground. The Executioner howled like a wounded dog, clutching at the gaping hole in its side. Normally, Chad would have compassion for such a sound, but this was different. This was the piece of shit who dismembered Devon in front of him. This man, this thing, deserved neither sympathy or life.

"Fuck you! Fuck you!" Chad screamed over and over as he stood over the wounded man firing shot after shot into its deformed skull.

Levine struggled to get to his feet but watched as Chad exploded his revenge all over The Executioner's face in a stream of bullets. He emptied the entire clip, turning the giant's skull into a pile of hamburger and bone. He kept pulling the trigger regardless, the action so fulfilling that he didn't want to stop. A thousand bullets wouldn't be enough to satiate him or stop the stream of tears that were rolling down his face.

"It's done," Levine managed to say through a mouth that was bloodied and missing a few teeth. "Get in the car."

Chad was shaking. He couldn't believe what he had done, but it was what he wanted to do. The cathartic release of revenge, the adrenaline rush of the control he had in taking out not only his hatred of the man who murdered his lover but on the culture that created this thing, surged through him still and he didn't know if he could stop shaking. It took Levine to grab the gun from him for him to stop. We need to go, he thought. They'd be after us.

It was then that he felt the same pain. A shot came from the courtyard. The bullet sliced through Chad's left shoulder and out the other side. Levine could only watch as he crumpled to his knees, reaching out for him but failing.

"Chad!" he yelled.

Chad was still alive somehow, but there was enough blood splattered against the car to suggest he wouldn't be for long. Levine pushed him into the backseat of the car and then ducked as a shower of bullets ricocheted around them. The mob was getting closer, and while their aim wasn't great, they'd eventually hit them. In a panic, he started the vehicle again. Another shower of bullets came, one of them piercing the side of the door and striking him in the leg. Levine howled as he grabbed his thigh.

"Shit! Come on, get it together," he said to himself, trying to will himself past the pain to the task of getting the car moving.

The wheels spun. Were they stuck? God no, not now. More bullets came, hitting the oak tree, the road, the car, nearly everything around them was being ripped to shreds. With one last attempt, Levine put the car in reverse and spun the wheel. Yes, that worked. Now, back onto the road. He shifted the car to drive and floored it. The car sped off in a cloud of dust despite another round of shots coming from the mob. After he passed the first few turns, Levine knew he was out of range, and they had escaped.

Luke watched the car's red tail lights dim and eventually disappear behind the forest of trees on the edge of his property. From the balcony of his bedroom, he could see everything, and it was here that he lamented involving the First Patriots with such people. He had taken care of one of them though. Casually, he lowered his rifle, with which he had only taken one shot. There was a choice between the two, and he'd certainly feel more at ease with killing the gay than the traitor. They'd deal with Levine eventually. He couldn't hide from them forever, but now there were more pressing matters.

"A shame really," Cheryl said as she sipped on a glass of bourbon. "I thought he'd come around."

"Don't blame yourself, Cheryl. We've all picked bad ones before. None this bad, mind you, but it's happened. You know what to do. Get the house cleaned out, get all the guests transportation out of the state and back to their homes, and have the staff bleach and burn that basement. Everything in the bedrooms needs to be sanitized as well. We've got maybe two hours," Luke instructed.

"So, we're just going to let him tell the police about us?"

"Our people in the department know what to do. But they will come and investigate this place, so we have to clean it." Luke sighed as he took Cheryl's glass and swallowed a mouthful of her drink. "A shame though. I liked this place. Nothing lasts forever."

"I'll get everyone moving. I guess we'll meet in Germany in a month then after this all cools down?"

"Yes, the German's have the safest house these days. I'm sure you'll find their dinner parties a bit old-fashioned, but that comes with its own charm. Until then, my love."

Cheryl said no more and left Luke to himself. With a few moments to savor the view from his room, the First Patriot breathed in the fresh southern night air and then packed his belongings, ready to disappear once again from the world.

"You alright back there?" Levine asked.

Chad pulled himself upright in the back seat, his blood gushing from both sides of his body. Minutes, he thought. Minutes left to live. Minutes left to think, to feel, to be. Most of his body had gone cold and what wasn't had gone numb. A haze came over his vision, blurring everything he saw to where the only thing he could make out was the black silhouettes of trees outside the car and the outline of Levine's head.

"Change it," he said quietly.

Levine darted his eyes back and forth between the road ahead and the rear-view mirror. The cell phone was damaged when The Executioner attacked. Even if there was a signal, they couldn't call anyone with it. He had to focus on finding their way back to civilization, a hospital, a police station, anything where they could get help. He knew Chad wasn't going to make it, but he was going to drive as fast as he could while he still drew breath.

"Change what?" Levine asked.

Chad was calm, his arms crossed over his midsection while he slumped down in the backseat of the car. His blood had pooled underneath him, and all he could think about was what a mess he was making of this car's upholstery. Good! Fuck Cecil and his fucking expensive Lexus. One last shot to those bastards.

"Change what you present to the world. I ... I ... know you ... can do better. You know you can ... too ..."

He started to slip away as his eyelids fluttered. Levine saw this and started talking louder, not wanting to accept what was inevitable.

"Stay awake back there!" he yelled. "There's got to be a hospital nearby or something. Just hang on."

Chad laughed, "Heh, I guess ... I guess people can change after all. Shawn Levine cares about a ... a gay man."

"I care about Chad Ortiz living past tonight."

"Then, you're caring about the wrong thing," this one sentence not hindered by his failing health. "Care then ... care about ... what people will do with what you say. Care ... change ... do something. You hear me, Levine? Do ... something ..."

Levine waited for more, but nothing came. He looked back in the mirror and saw Chad's eyes had closed, his mouth had shut, his arms had uncrossed.

"Come on, Chad! Wake up. Chad, wake up! You can't let me have the last word! Come on!" Levine started screaming.

He knew it was no use, but the words numbed the pain for a moment. It wasn't enough. It was then that the weight of everything that had happened—more importantly, that in a way he had a hand in causing it—crashed in on Levine. The tears came, and he did his best to wipe them from his eyes, smearing them across his face with the dried blood and dirt. He couldn't stand it. He let loose the loudest and longest scream of his life, so forceful that he felt his throat swell and strain from the effort. He stopped the car and shook himself in his seat, beating the palm of his hand against the steering wheel, each time howling louder and louder.

Levine's head was awash in a swirl of revelations, contradictions, and evaluations. He went back and forth between wanting to stay true to his convictions, which he still believed in and held close to his heart, and the reality of what he had seen. The reality of what people like his sister and Chad and Devon had experienced. The tragic way in which their lives ended. The inhuman way in which people who shared his beliefs could treat others. But at the same time, he couldn't throw himself on the other side of the fence and forget everything he had known true throughout his life. Not to mention how would he explain this dead body in the car and the bullet holes? Would the police even believe him? Where they on the First Patriots' payroll?

Too many thoughts. Too much to process. Just scream. Yell at God. Yell at humanity. Yell at the world. Yell at himself. It was all mixed together in this quagmire of death, lies, hate, and viciousness.

"Change it," he finally said, his voice cracking from the strain of his outburst. "Change it, Levine."

He started the engine back up and proceeded down the road. In a few hours the sun would come out, and he'd have weeks of investigations, interviews, explanations, and apologies to endure.

He wasn't without friends in power, and he'd need them now more than ever for his own protection and to help expose who and what the First Patriots were. It would put his life in jeopardy for the rest of his living days, but he'd be at peace with that. There was a better way, there had to be. If this was the road that he helped to build, it was time for him to start making a detour. He had the ear of tens of thousands of people. Some would reject him, others would embrace him, but they all would hear him.

The world would hear him.

Postmortem II

"A tie?" The angel smirked as she gathered her cards.

"How was that a tie? I get nothing out of that," the demon grunted in response.

"I get the couple—they both lived well and did well. You get the girl they killed. She wasn't innocent by a long shot and has done far worse than those people even knew."

"Right."

"And the giant."

"I don't get the giant."

"Why not?"

The demon took a puff of his cigar and coughed violently. He sounded like a sickly old man who knew what was killing him but still enjoyed the exhilaration of a good smoke. He spat down into a funnel that, until this point, Omar hadn't realized was tied to a tube. His eyes followed the tube down past the edge of the table, around the back of the demon, and to its unexpected destination. Behind a pile of trash and boxes was a small man whose body was squished together as if he had been molded in a box and didn't how to stretch out his limbs. In his mouth was the other end of the tube. The demon's bile flowed down and into the mouth of the slave, who choked on it, the excess spurting from his nose.

"The giant has no fucking soul!" the demon screamed as the two card players continued to argue over the outcome. "I want a trade!"

"You can't trade now," the angel answered.

"I want to trade the girl for the radio host."

"You know you can't do that. He redeemed himself after that, and his life won't be up for another hand in this game. It's too far out to make a trade."

The demon slammed his fist against the table, took another puff of his cigar, and then regurgitated another wad of black phlegm into the funnel. Omar would have vomited if he was still capable of doing so.

"Fine," the demon growled. "You win this hand, then. But we will do another media game, and I will shuffle the cards this time. You had the deck stacked in your favor anyway on that hand. Prisoners who had no chance of escape unless someone saved them, really? If there was a more stacked deck towards spirits going to your pile, I've never seen one!"

The angel smiled, her glitter-covered pale cheeks blushing now. "I don't make the scenarios. I just got lucky with that hand."

"Yeah, the hand you dealt. I'm keeping my eye on you from now on, *God bitch*. Play fair, or you know what happens to this one," the demon nodded towards Omar.

"Do you think it was fair?" the angel asked him.

"I think that ..." Omar stopped short of answering as the demon's wild reptile eyes peered at him. It wouldn't be wise not to provoke him. "I don't know what I think."

"Hah! See that? He's useless. I don't know why we're letting him stay here."

"You know why he's not answering. He's scared of you. Let's just start the next hand. You're using the same deck for this one?"

The demon grinned slyly. "Yes, the same deck. We'll do media again, but this one will be slightly different. And we're using conjuring in this one, so if anyone is killed by a summoned demon, I get their souls, not you."

"The same goes in reverse. If a demon is extinguished by a human, that human's soul is ours whenever it passes on."

"Understood."

After watching two hands, Omar was starting to get the hang of the game. The players would pull cards from various decks that held circumstances in which people would be involved. It could be anything from natural disasters to supernatural monsters to an attempt to save a life. Basically, anything that could be life or death was fodder for this game.

This conjuring rule was something new. While the demon shuffled the cards, the angel explained to Omar that the first game had been based on spirits—in that case, *Se'irim*—that had already been conjured. Using conjuring in a hand meant that demons or angels were not inherent to the situation and could be invoked at any time by either player. So the demon could play a conjuring card to have a human summon a curse while the angel could play a conjuring card to enact a divine object or summon a human's guardian angel.

It was complicated, but the game was starting to fascinate Omar. He wanted to see more. He wanted to learn more. He'd give his full attention to the next game.

The demon stopped shuffling the cards and licked his thumb with its forked tongue. The deal began, the card faces were displayed, and Omar could immediately tell this game was going to be quite different in tone than the two before it.

CLIVE REZNOR

That Bad Interview with the Movie Director

Tens of thousands of people watch the YouTube live feed *Film Talk* every single weekday religiously. The movie review show, hosted by an array of the best and brightest of the online movie review community, became a small sensation over the last few years with diehard movie nerds around the world for their strong opinions and banter between each other.

Although the crew of freaks and geeks would at times disagree on what they liked and didn't like about the week's films, they seemed to universally hate the big budget, special effects, hyped productions of one movie director in particular:

Mitchell Gray.

Known for excessive explosions, loose narratives, one-dimensional stereotypical characters, and his tendency to sacrifice substance for spectacle, Gray had nonetheless made himself and the movie studios he worked for unbelievably rich. While the critics and fans panned his films, the audiences would show up constantly for them, with two of his films even being listed in the top ten highest grossing films of all time.

What would a man with so much power, influence, and box office draw have to worry about from a ragtag group of twenty and thirty-somethings on a YouTube movie channel?

At first, nothing. He was high above them. He made more money in a month than the entire staff did in two years. However, his recent film, which was an adaptation of yet another 80s cartoon (he had done two previously with great success financially) bombed at the box office. The scuttlebutt around Hollywood was that it had a lot to do with the cumulative effect of years of negative reviews. Things got heated when an article in the *New York Times* quoted two of the reviewers from Film Talk:

> *I'd rather have a turtle bite the tip of my penis off, pour salt on it, and fry it in battery acid before I'd watch another film from this money-hungry hack.*

Dre Schnapps, the most seasoned and opinionated of the entire crew, gave that verbal jewel to the newspaper while another member of the staff had a more to the point comment:

> *It's pure garbage. It nearly ruined my childhood.*

Sarah, known on the show by her moniker Gamer Girl 86, took personal exception to Mitchell Gray even making an adaptation of one of her favorite TV shows from the 1980s. She later stated that calling it "pure garbage" was her trying to be nice.

As with most things, when something fails it is often human nature to place the blame elsewhere. For Mitchell Gray, the blame was to go on this one show out of Burbank and its staff of "geek leeches" as he called them.

On his social media accounts, he called out the *Film Talk* team in a passing comment, stating that he would be more than happy to go on their show, get them views, just for the opportunity to debate with them the merits of not only his latest movie but the history of harsh criticism they've given his entire career.

Fans of the *Film Talk* show immediately took to social media, giving their opinions and encouragement for the interview to actually happen. Many thought Gray did not intend to actually be on the show and was just venting his anger towards his critics while others certainly felt that the *Film Talk* crew should call him on his bluff.

Two weeks later, after trying to ignore it as best they could, the boss at *Film Talk*—an experienced reviewer himself named Burton Camp—addressed their audience and Mitchell Gray specifically by extending an invitation for the director to appear on their show. Within fifteen minutes, the invitation was accepted.

"If he's actually showing up today, I'm telling you right now, I'll be surprised," Burton Camp said as the team prepared for their show.

The set was much like any other talk show on television with an array of cameras, wires, lights, and sound equipment circling a stage with a large desk where the hosts sat. Behind each host was an animated screen featuring the trailers of upcoming and current movies playing on a loop with the words "Film Talk" carved out in a large beveled sign above it all. Camp sat in the middle seat while the rest of the hosts flanked him on either side.

They rotated hosts on different days of the week but today

in particular Camp chose the panel to fit their guest. He wanted those who were highly outspoken about Mitchell Gray's movies on the show as the viewers would absolutely want to see a showdown between them and the director.

"Burton, Mitchell Gray is a man of conviction and flashy entrances. He'll be fashionably late, and we'll all be in awe because of it," sarcastically quipped Jeremy Ferris, the most light-hearted of the panel who moonlighted as a stand-up comic.

Sitting beside him was his co-host on their own internet show, *The Bros Know*, Chris Chartoff. "I think I'm going to take a step back on this when he gets here. I mean, I don't care for his movies either way and he's really got a bone to pick with you two," he said, pointing to the opposite end of the table.

There sat Dre Schnapps and Gamer Girl 86, the two whose quotes had started this whole thing.

Dre was a tall, thickly built black man approaching middle age with a wild thinning afro, patches of grey in his goatee, and a vintage T-shirt from a cult classic horror movie out of the 70s. Having made a few movies of his own, Dre knew how the movie process worked. Add to that his undying love for all things retro, his unique laugh, and several catchphrases he had developed on the show over the years, Dre was a favorite among the *Film Talk* audience.

Gamer Girl 86 was just as informal and just as *nerd chic* with her dyed pink hair tied atop her head and held together by a pair of chopsticks, a loose-fitting tank top featuring her favorite comic book heroine, and her arms colorfully decorated in a mosaic of tattoos. Even though she was very much a tomboy, her features were decidedly feminine, which she had been annoyingly reminded of day after day since she was a teenager. *You should be a model* was a phrase she heard over and over again, but her complete abhorrence for that industry and anything that looked to objectify women for their looks allowed her to not fall into that trap. Instead, she carved her way out on the internet with her own series of podcasts, articles, and videos that had established her as a credible voice in pop culture punditry and a shining example for women in an industry that was dominated by male voices.

"As long as he's respectful, I'll be respectful," Dre said to the panel as they kept their eyes on the door to the studio. "But I'm not pulling punches. If we talk about his sucky movies and he asks why I think they're sucky, I'm straight up telling him why they're sucky. For real, son."

"Same here," Gamer Girl added. "I mean, we're here to be honest, right? There's no reason to be fake. That would disappoint our fans who are watching this. Just because he's some millionaire director doesn't mean we have to act like we respect his work and be all fake."

"Straight up, sister," Dre laughed as he fist-bumped his fellow critic. "If he's man enough to show up, he's man enough to take us being honest with him."

"Oh boy," Camp grinned to himself as he reviewed the show notes, "what have I done? What have I done?"

One of the interns for the show came running in from the production area waving his arms around. "He's here! He's here!" the boy said, his voice cracking as he caught his breath.

"All right, calm down, Cody," Camp said.

"But he says he wants to go on the air raw, without meeting you first. So, I guess we start the show as normal and bring him in, right?"

Burton Camp found this a bit suspicious, but he agreed to it. They were five minutes out from their live broadcast anyway and had planned on going on air with or without him. Whatever games Gray was trying to play with showing up at the last minute didn't matter. Their views were about to skyrocket. It was worth the annoyance.

"We'll do it live!" Ferris jokingly said, making a mocking reference to a famous, and often angry, cable news show host.

Camp couldn't stop laughing but nodded to Cody. "Okay, okay. Just bring him in after we do the day's news."

Five minutes later the show started as normal. Burton Camp welcomed the viewers to the show and helped guide the show along, giving his opinions on various topics from box office receipts to creative choices in casting on upcoming films. Chartoff and Ferris brought the back-and-forth banter from their *Bros Know* show with Ferris providing humorous observations of whatever was brought up and Chartoff guiding a more focused and nuanced analysis. Gamer Girl, who wasn't a regular on the show as she had various other gigs of her own, added a different spin on the news, often chiding studios for their excessive capitalistic tendencies over the creative side of filmmaking. These thoughts were echoed by Schnapps who had harsh words for most of the big-budget adaptations of franchises he loved as a kid.

Camp felt that Schnapps and Gamer Girl were gearing up for a verbal fight. Their commentary on big budget movies and "sucking the soul out of anything creative" basically indicated that they were not going to pull punches with Gray.

As they wrapped up the last news story, it was time to start the interview. Camp smiled to the camera, took in a deep breath, and started his prepared introduction.

"As many of you who follow this show know, we have been at the center of some recent stories regarding famed director Mitchell Gray. Some of the criticism we have all given his movies over the years has shown up all over the press and social media, which is nothing new. However, recently Gray had his own, let's say, critical responses towards some of us on the panel here and proceeded to invite himself onto the show to discuss it in person and we have accepted.

"Now, this is not going to be some pissing match here. We

don't expect that from Mr. Gray nor should he expect that from us here. We are all professionals."

"Well, you guys might be. I'm just here for comic relief," Ferris added.

"That you are, Jeremy," Camp laughed. "But, as you can see here, this is going to be a fun interview. So, without further ado, let's welcome the director of multi-million-dollar box office hits like *The GoFormers* and *Gang Girls 1&2*, Mr. Mitchell Gray to *Film Talk*!"

Cody was rushing to the main door of the set as Camp delivered his monologue. With perfect timing, the young intern brought Mitchell Gray onto set and immediately the room grew silent. None of the camera operators, the producer of the show who was watching backstage on his monitors, or the other hosts who weren't on air today but had shown up to watch this anyway, made a sound. Instead, they all watched as the tall and lanky director made his way towards the set.

This was a man of great wealth, and from his appearance, it was clear he enjoyed it. The suit he wore was worth more than the wardrobe of the entire group of hosts combined, tailored to fit him without a crease out of place. Gamer Girl noticed his cologne as he passed by her to get to the center seat at the table. At first thinking the scent was pleasant but then immediately retracting that feeling as she knew it was some expensive concoction that only a greedy bastard like Mitchell Gray could afford.

Showing that he was here to be a professional, Gray shook the hand of everyone at the table before taking his seat. In an attempt at levity, he complimented the set design and noted the only person at the table that was close to his height was Dre Schnapps who reluctantly nodded in agreement.

"Wow! I'm here!" Gray said as he adjusted his seat to accommodate for his height. "And no one died."

"Yes, and no one died," Camp repeated. "How was your

flight here?"

"Well, it was without incident. I tell you what, coming here from Miami is not the same as it used to be. The fuel costs alone were nearly double what they were last year, but there was no way I was missing this show."

"That's not even a First World Problem," Ferris giggled. "That's like a one percent of the First World Problem. A good problem to have, mind you. But I have trouble just filling up my Prius on the way to the studio here so I can't imagine how insane it is for you on your private jet."

"Private jet," Gamer Girl mumbled under her breath, trying to make it sound as lighthearted as she could, but the undertone of disgust clearly came through.

Camp wanted to move past her comment as quickly as he could. "We are happy that you made it to the studio and took the time out to have this sit down with us."

"Yeah, it should be entertaining."

"We've made our positions very clear on this show from time to time about what many of us think about your movies. Our fans are well aware of our thoughts, but we want to give you this time to address some of the things you've heard. Do you think these are fair criticisms or do you take issue with critics like us who, quite frankly, find what you produce to not be our ..." Camp looked up to the ceiling as he tried to find the right words. "... our cup of tea, let's say?"

Gray smirked at the roundabout question. The situation Burton Camp was in didn't go unappreciated by Mitchell Gray. Here was a guy who had carved out a piece of the internet and was doing quite well with what he had done reviewing movies and amassing a staff of talented and colorful characters on his show. How awkward it must be to sit in a position where you want to maintain credibility but not completely shit all over the A-list guest who is increasing your viewership at the same time.

"Any criticism is fair. That's part of the game now, isn't it? I am a creator, and the style of movie I make isn't going to be to everyone's taste. No director, writer, actor, or any creative person is going to please everyone. So, I take the criticism well when it's warranted and fair."

"Would you consider our criticism of your films fair?" asked Camp.

"For the most part," Gray answered with an incredibly smug grin.

Body language was saying more than the words at this point. Schnapps and Gamer Girl were on the left side of the table. The way Mitchell Gray had positioned himself was such that his back was turned to them, almost as if on purpose. Gamesmanship was at play here. Why talk to them when he could save face by discussing his career in a cavalier way with the less hostile members of the panel?

Not wanting to be left out of the conversation, Schnapps spoke up. "Your new movie that just came out last month is what this really is about, isn't it?"

"Yes, I guess we should get to that. I think you were the one who said it ruined your childhood, am I correct?" Mitchell answered.

"No, that was her," Schnapps nodded towards Gamer Girl. "I'm the one who said I'd rather a turtle bite off the tip of my penis."

"Oh yes, the turtle and the penis. Now I remember."

An awkward silence followed.

"I don't think he liked the movie, Mitch," Ferris chimed in, trying to break the tension in the room with a joke.

"That's quite alright," laughed Mitchell. "If you can't take a little criticism you shouldn't be in this business. Now, it's true I wasn't entirely happy with the production of the film and many things went wrong."

"There are videos online that pretty much show that,"

Schnapps confirmed. "You seemed pretty upset yelling at all those production people. So, is it safe to say some of the problems with the film were in the execution by the staff?"

"I wouldn't say that. I also don't think that's what you took issue with."

"So, what do you think was wrong with the movie?"

"I'd rather you elaborate about the turtle and the penis."

A few chuckles could be heard from behind the cameras. The production manager, Chris Chen, kept tabs on the viewership of the video which started to spike during Mitchell Gray's appearance. The "likes" on the video skyrocketed as well with the exchange between Schnapps and Gray.

"Look, I'm just saying that it's not my cup of tea. I know there are plenty of people who like your films ..." Schnapps said.

"Millions," Gray interjected.

"... well, yeah, even millions. But just because millions of people see something doesn't mean it's quality. There are several cases of movies that have made a lot of money that were terrible experiences while other films were fantastic but didn't make a fraction of one of your films. It's really about marketing."

"You see, I disagree with that. And I resent that notion somewhat," Gray shot back. "If millions of people go and see a film, buy it on Blu-ray or download it at home, I don't see how you can say it's terrible. Clearly, a large majority of the moviegoing audience liked what was produced."

"I think what Schnapps is saying," Chartoff interjected, "is that money doesn't always equal quality. There are plenty of people who eat fast food, but I think most sane people would say that there are much better choices for meals out there."

"Well, let's not get too far off base here. We're talking about my films that many people on this show have trashed over the years. I came here really to answer those criticisms and to find out just what it is that you don't like about them. So far all I've heard is that you don't like that they make a lot of money."

Gamer Girl, visibly fuming and itching to get a word in, balled her hands into fists as she fidgeted in her chair. Oh, the things she had to say to him! Before today, she just assumed he didn't care about the numerous reasons he was a blight not only on the movie industry but popular culture in general. Now that she was sitting here next to him and heard him speak in person, this man not only knew what he was putting out there in the public was trash but saw nothing wrong with it. This overpaid hack with his sweeping surfer hairstyle—that would have been better suited for a much younger man in another decade—and his suave suit and wafting cologne, no matter how damn good it smelled, created a churning rage inside her that she hadn't felt in years. She had to speak. She *must* speak and let her thoughts be known to the millions of people who were now watching this broadcast.

"It's not the money, and I think it's really simplistic to try and say we're just suffering from class envy. The problems I have with your films, beyond the excessive use of explosions and loud noise to shock people into thinking they're seeing something great, or the simplistic way in which you represent minorities, is the objectification of women," she argued.

The expression on Gray's face hinted he was surprised by her statement. Whether or not this was a genuine response or feigned indignation was unclear. It didn't matter. Gamer Girl had just gotten started.

"Every female lead in every single movie you have made is a throwback. Damsels in distress, half-naked models with flawless faces bending over muscle cars, vapid dialogue, the nerdy girl who is really hot because she was never really nerdy in the first place. All of it! It's just terrible, and I'm frankly offended by just about every movie you've ever made."

"I think you're exaggerating," Gray protested.

"Am I?" Gamer Girl's eyes were wide with fury. "Go ahead and name me one, just one female character who wasn't any of those stereotypes in any movie you've made. I'd love to hear this."

She was a handful, Gray thought. She's one of those pumped up feminist who found fault in boys enjoying the sight of a sexy girl. As if it doesn't happen the other way around, but clearly she wasn't going to see it that way. On the other hand, she was extremely attractive herself underneath the tattoos and hair dye and piercings and all other manner of dress she used to make herself look as unconventionally beautiful as she could. But there was no hiding it. She was attractive.

"I can see you're upset," he started, taking great care not to look confrontational. "And I get where you're coming from. But you yourself use your looks to your advantage, do you not?"

That was the wrong thing to say, "Are you freakin' serious?"

"I've seen your shows, Gamer Girl 86. You mean to tell me that you think you'd have anywhere near the following you do if you were 200 pounds with double chins or if your face wasn't so luxuriously well-defined? Of course not. Like it or not, looks play a part in what people like to watch ... what people *pay* to watch ... and there's nothing wrong with admiring the female form. You benefit from it just as much as I do."

Aghast that he'd even say such a thing, Gamer Girl raised her finger and started her rebuttal, but she was so enraged that her words did not come out and she started stumbling over herself in response. After a few ums and uhs, Burton Camp chimed in to steer the conversation in another direction.

"Clearly, there are differences in opinions here. And without a doubt, you are a much-celebrated director who has a fanbase. As I always say, all film is subjective, so while many of us may not like what you put out, there are people who would agree with your point. To be fair to my colleague though, Gamer Girl did not get where she is because of her looks. She is extremely talented," said Camp.

Gray smirked, "And you don't think her looks have anything to do with her popularity?"

"I didn't say that; I said she's talented and that's what elevates her beyond just another pretty face," answered Camp.

He was now growing frustrated with the director. In fact, the entire table had sour looks on their face as Gamer Girl started to become more and more annoyed with the situation. It wasn't fair to pick on her and what Gray had said, whether his points had merit or not, was not something you'd say to a woman with the background she had. To try and reduce her accomplishments down to sex appeal, as Mitchell Gray was implying, was tasteless.

Dre Schnapps wasn't going to let it go. "You can say whatever you want and try to spin this story with a bunch of B.S., but you're actually proving what we've been saying."

"Exactly," Chartoff added.

Schnapps wasn't done with him yet, "You came on here and made yourself look like a jackass just now by essentially trying to slut shame one of the best female talents on the internet. Quite honestly, I'm offended. Deeply. How dare you."

The staff behind the camera was growing uneasy. They had seen Schnapps angry before and knew it could end badly for everyone on the set. Even though he was measured and controlled in the way he admonished Gray the two tall men were staying in their chairs. How long that would last was another story.

"Don't point your finger at me. I know who you are too. Some failed movie writer who was lucky to get gigs on C-list indie movie projects and D-list cartoon shows. You have no idea how to do what I do," Gray was pulling the status card here, trying to diminish Schnapps as best he could.

"You're right, I don't know what it is to do what you do and I don't want to know! I thought today I'd give you a fair shake, son, but I can honestly say this," Schnapps said, taking a moment to breathe before continuing his point. "You are in fact ten times worse of a person than I thought you were as a director. If this is how you conduct yourself on here, I can only imagine that all those rumors about you losing your cool and treating your cast and crew like garbage are true."

"You know nothing about my cast and crew. I—"

"You should be ashamed of yourself."

Chartoff couldn't help but add to this. "I can't disagree with Schnapps. I mean look what you did. You tried to belittle Gamer Girl. You tried to belittle Schnapps' career. And this is you being nice?"

Mitchell Gray could see that he had lost this public affairs fight. Unwittingly, he had given them all the ammunition they needed to come out the better of this exchange. He knew he was taking a risk even coming here. What director would sit in between five of his biggest critics? But he thought it would make him come off as tough fighting against five other people. It was just the opposite. No matter what he said or did now, he'd be seen as the bully and the small, ragtag group of internet movie reviewers would be seen as the heroes.

"Thank you for your time," Gray said, turning to Camp and extending his hand.

Camp, surprised at what had just happened, reluctantly shook Gray's hand as the director removed himself from the set. The two lackeys he had brought with him were quick to attend to him with a bottle of water as he rushed out of the studio, his head held high as the cameras followed him out the door.

Still shocked, Camp did the only thing he could do, with a smile, "And I guess that's it for this episode of *Film Talk!*"

♥

After the show wrapped up, the entire crew gathered in the common room. Completely baffled by what had just happened, everyone took a seat around the meeting table to decompress from the worst and best interview they had ever done.

"Well, I can say this," started Chris Chen who had managed the show behind the scenes, "we got nearly a million and a half views on that just from the live show overall. The comment section has exploded. So, from that perspective it's a big win."

"Am I the only one who thought that was the weirdest thing we've ever done on this show?" asked Jeremy of the team. "I've never in my life seen someone make such an ass of himself on camera and I do it for a living."

Dre Schnapps was less jovial about the situation, "The guy was a total asshole. And I'm sorry if I ruined the show, Burton, but I could not sit there and let him run with the garbage he was spewing from his lips." He then broke off into a high pitched nerdy voice to mock Mitchell Gray, "I'm a creator! I'm on a totally different level than you! You don't understand." Then back to his normal voice, "Fuck off you hack."

"No, I don't have any problems with what you said out there, Schnapps," Camp confirmed, although he was clearly concerned about what the response would be and what the show's standing in the movie industry would be afterwards. "Time will tell whether or not this is going to hurt us or help us, but we'll survive."

"But are you okay Sarah?" Chartoff asked Gamer Girl 86, turning the attention away from the show to the person who was the most affected by what had happened.

With her face still flush with blood and biting her lower lip,

Gamer Girl just sat at the desk with her arms crossed.

"I thank you guys for having my back out there. I'm just disappointed in myself that I let that jackass rattle me like that. I couldn't even speak."

"Don't even worry about it. You know, if anything people will respect that you didn't just sit there and take it from him," Schnapps said to her as he started munching away at a hot dog.

"Yeah, we'll just reassess this tomorrow. We've got a lot of work to do for the rest of the day. Bros, you guys have to get set up for your show," Camp said.

Chartoff and Ferris were scheduled to do their own *Bros Know* show live in two hours and had done little prep for it. In fact, the entire team had a mountain of work to do before the next show went on the air so they couldn't spend too much time in this post-production meeting.

After they reviewed what needed to be done for the rest of the day, Burton Camp took off to a meeting at another studio while everyone else went about their usual routine. This meant the production team prepped for the next show while most of the hosts started writing and reading stories on the internet in between practical jokes, video game sessions (which Gamer Girl sorely needed in order to calm her nerves), and responding to social media which was on fire after the interview.

Everyone involved with the staff received hundreds of messages, tweets, likes, comments, and more on their own individual accounts. Most were supportive of the team sticking together and not bowing to the fame and fortune of Mitchell Gray. There were a few, of course, who were not so kind and had nasty things to say, from calling Gamer Girl a whore to claiming the whole thing was a setup and there was some conspiracy around the interview so Mitchell Gray could get publicity for his terrible movie.

As savvy media people, the *Film Talk* team was used to negative comments on the internet by outraged people, *trolls* as they were often called, trying to make a stink on the web. Between grammatical errors, sexism, and racism, most of these comments were pointless to look at.

An hour had passed and the comments and phone calls were still coming in. There was more pressing work to do as the two hosts of the *Bros Know Show* were finishing their pre-show meeting. It was then that the lights in the studio went out, the cameras powered down, and the *Film Talk* team sat in complete darkness.

"Who didn't pay the electric bill?" Jeremy joked.

"That's weird. Maybe that's a hint that Hollywood is shutting down our show for good," said Chartoff.

The emergency lights came on within seconds, casting a blood red light throughout the facility. An old building, the *Film Talk* studios had been upgraded in most aspects except this one. What was usually a bright and vibrant workspace now looked like a lost level of hell with deep shadows in every corner and crimson bulbs illuminating the hallways.

"Yeah, that's not creepy at all," Jeremy commented. "Can someone find out what's going on? Chris!"

Chris Chen entered the meeting room in as much confusion as everyone else. When things went wrong, he was the one they usually looked to for a solution. It was clear he had none for this.

"Just sit tight. I'm going to go outside and find out what's going on. It might just be the circuit breaker," Chen suggested. "We can still do the show though; the cameras and laptops are on batteries so if we need to we can do it that way."

A loud crash could be heard from the studio space. This had gone from an inconvenience into slight worry as everyone was now standing and on alert.

Chen went towards the sound and was followed by the

remaining staff who wanted to know what was going on. Did a camera fall over? Was there some sort of electrical fire? If it was something serious, they wanted to know so they could get out of there as soon as a possible. There were few fire exits in the building. Having fifteen or so people panic and try to escape through one opening was not ideal.

The problem wasn't hard to find once the crew entered the studio. The main doors were wide open and standing there, bathed in the bright light of the California sun, was Mitchell Gray. His silhouette was unmistakable. It was a scene straight out of one of his blockbuster films, an entrance for a star. Casually, his silhouette sauntered towards the crew as the giant doors behind him closed, chopping off the rays of sunlight.

"What the hell is going on?" Dre Schnapps yelled.

"Did you cut off the power to our studio?" asked Chen.

Gray wasn't answering any questions this time. He simply paced back and forth, the soles of his shoes clicking against the concrete floor of the studio and echoing throughout the space. He stopped, turned on his heel, and walked back in the other direction. Behind him, his assistants were dragging a large case. It was hard to see in the dark, but it looked heavy as the two men struggled to place it on the ground behind Gray.

"This has gotten way too weird," Chartoff said to his co-host.

Ferris agreed, "I think he's lost his mind if I'm not mistaken. This is out of some horror movie."

"Now, that you mention it, where is Sheri anyway?"

"Sheri Shimmeroff? She's over there, hiding behind the desk."

Shimmeroff indeed was cowering behind the table on the set. Her cup of tea was horror films, and even though she loved them and knew everything about them, in real life she wasn't so brave. As easy as it was to make her laugh in the office, it was just as easy to scare the living shit out of her with a well laid prank at Halloween.

"You don't have to hide, Sheri. He's not going to do anything to us," Ferris called out to her.

The short redhead stood up from behind the desk, looked around at the situation, and forced herself to join the rest of the staff who were in a visual standoff with Mitchell Gray.

"I didn't know what was going on," she said. "All I heard was a loud bang, so I ducked for cover. I thought we were getting shot at."

"That's pretty crude," Mitchell Gray said, overhearing Sheri's comment. "I am known for explosions and gunfire in my films, but that's not my style. I wouldn't blow you up."

"So, this was you," Schnapps said. "We're calling the police. This is ridiculous. Get the hell out of here."

"You can try, but it will be a waste of time," Gray laughed as he placed his hand on the strange black container that his henchmen had brought in.

Several of the staff went to their phones, but it was no use. Every screen read "no signal available." They all checked with one another out of disbelief but it was true, there was no communication with the outside world and the studio itself didn't have a landline. They were cut off.

"How did he do that?" Chartoff asked.

"I have no idea, but nothing is working," Intern Cody said. "Nothing is working anywhere in the building. Not even the air conditioning."

Schnapps and Chen broke off from the group and approached the film director. While Chen wanted to talk, Schnapps wanted to fight. He had seen and heard enough from Mitchell Gray for one day and whatever stunt he was pulling to try and scare them was not going to work. He was a big guy and not afraid to put a few bruises on the over-tanned face of this millionaire prick. In fact, he relished the idea.

"Turn the lights back on!" Chen yelled.

"Seriously, this is fucking stupid. You've got two minutes to get the lights and everything turned back on before you get a foot up your ass, son!" added Schnapps.

Gray pushed his hair away from his face with a laugh. He turned his back on the two men and strolled towards the container behind him, putting it between him and his aggressors. As cocky as he had been before on this show, this little display sealed the deal of him being an obnoxious jackass.

Tapping his fingers against the top of the container, he stood tall behind it like a speaker at a podium about to deliver a commencement speech. Schnapps was counting down to the makeshift colonoscopy he had promised Gray while Chen examined the strange container.

Gray noticed, "I see that you're the smart one. You're trying to figure out what this is. I don't know how much movie lore you're familiar with, but I'm sure someone here knows what this is."

Schnapps and Chen looked at each other and each shrugged their shoulders. It was a box, wasn't it? Maybe it was filled with weapons or some sort of weird toxic gas. Why did it matter?

"Come on," Gray called out to the rest of the staff. "Does anyone here, among you fucking egotistical movie nerds, have an idea as to what this is?"

No answers came. Mitchell was a bit disappointed that none of them knew what he had brought to the studio. These were supposed to be the biggest of movie geeks on the internet, and they had no idea. It took a bit of the fun away from his grand plan here, but he'd have to go on with it.

"Wait, wait, wait," a voice came from the back of the crowd. "I know what that is. But, it can't be what it is. That's not real."

"Yodi, what the hell are you talking about?" Chartoff asked.

"You're sounding as crazy as he is right now."

Yodi O'Reilly didn't have a show of his own but was a contributor from time to time on air and a writer for their website. He was also the biggest movie trivia geek of the entire crew. If anyone would know what that container was, it would have been him.

"It's an Eternity Box," he said.

"A what?" laughed Ferris. "You mean that thing from the Revengers movies?"

"No, it's not," Schnapps said.

"Yeah, it is. Or at least he thinks it is. Look at the front of it. The six symbols on it. That's the sign of the Eternity Box from the comics."

"No, it's from the movies. The comics it was different in design," Schnapps corrected him.

"Who gives a shit? What the hell is this about, Gray?" Chen asked.

Gray shined his award-winning smile at them and pointed a finger in their direction as if they had just correctly answered a question on a gameshow.

"The little short guy is right," he said. "This is an Eternity Box. It's really the only one that I know of. I bought it at considerable cost, and it's helped me throughout my career. Never thought I'd have to use it against people like you, but you all have earned it, believe me."

Ferris, who hadn't paid too much attention to the lore behind the movies he watched, quietly asked Yodi what the box did. After giving Ferris some flak for not knowing, he explained that, according to the movies, the box allowed the user to control six aspects of reality. Theoretically, Mitchell Gray could control finance, energy, communication, perception, attraction, and influence.

"That sounds stupid," Ferris replied. "No wonder I hate those Revengers movies."

"Yeah, but it kind of makes sense when you think about it," Yodi said. He put his finger to his patchy beard as he puzzled over the thought of an Eternity Box actually existing. "It'd explain how his shitty movies keep getting green lit and make all that money."

"Fair point," conceded Ferris.

Gray continued his speech to the *Film Talk* team. He prattled on about how he had used the box to achieve great heights in the movie industry. It had brought him fame, success, wealth, and adoration. However, it could not control the minds of those who dared to look deeper. The illusion it created on the screen was only temporary, and if anyone examined what the Box had conjured they would find the flaws in what he had produced.

The problem today was that he had been exposed as a person. The interview earlier had weakened the Eternity Box's powers and he noticed that his influence—a key component that the Box let him control over the masses—had diminished almost instantly. His only recourse now was to eliminate the ones who had started it and hopefully, with time and effort, he could restore the public's perception of his creations through the Box.

"I don't know what it is you're smoking but seriously, your time is up. Get the hell out of here and take your monkey box or jack-in-the-box or whatever that stupid thing is with you," Schnapps said.

"Where's the girl?" Gray continued, ignoring the threat. "I really want her to see this. Gamer Girl! Where are you? It's dark honey, I can't see you."

Gamer Girl 86 emerged from the crowd and took her place beside Chen and Schnapps. Had she the ability to melt people with her looks, Mitchell Gray would have been a puddle on the floor right now. He was the one however with supernatural powers it seemed, and while she was brave enough to step forward, she did fear for what he would do to her.

"I have good news and bad news for you. Which do you want to hear first?" Gray asked her.

As disinterested as she could possibly look, Gamer Girl responded, "Whatever."

"So enthusiastic as always. Well, the good news is that I can guarantee right now that you are the one who is going to walk out of this studio today alive. The bad news, you won't quite be yourself."

"What in the hell does that mean?"

"Just hold on a second." Gray placed his hand back on the Eternity Box and tapped twice on one of the symbols. "I think you'll find your opinions of my films and me as a person to be quite improved."

Where his posture had been relaxed and defiant, it now became erect and accommodating. Her frown was replaced by a gleeful smile, scarily so, as her eyes still retained a hint of the anger she felt for this man.

What had he done to her? A sensation ran through her body like a river of ice water crawling just under her skin. It called to her muscles, her blood, her tendons, forcing her body to walk towards Gray and stand at his side, her smile like that of a demented clown and her body as stiff as a mannequin.

"Are you okay?" Chen asked her.

"That's it!" Schnapps went to strike at Gray, but Gamer Girl stepped between the two, her smile quivering as she protected her master.

"This is some voodoo shit, son!" Schnapps said as he lowered his fist.

"No, it's just willpower," Gray corrected. "I can do pretty much whatever I want with this. And now, what I want the most is for this show to be off the air permanently. But let's have a little fun, shall we? I know your worst fears here, and I can't think of any better way to shut this down than to use them."

"What is he talking about?" Chartoff whispered to Ferris.

Gray tapped again on the Eternity Box, this time in an intricate and deliberate pattern around two of the symbols. A hint of light pulsed from them in shades of red and yellow, leaving particles of energy trailing through the air.

Another loud crash came from the left of the stage where it was the darkest. A breeze of rotten air flowed through the studio, a stench so rank that several of the staff were on the verge of vomiting. It was then from the blackness that several pairs of white slits appeared, blinking on and off as they grew in size.

Gray continued tapping on the Box, and another symbol flashed. With it came the voices, one voice to match each pair of eyes, rising in volume with each passing second.

The first creature stepped into the harsh red light of the studio, its feet oversized and hairy. Then came its legs, boney a bowlegged, up to its torso, which was hidden in a stained shirt that barely covered the enormous gut that burst forward as if the creature was pregnant. Lastly, the head came into view. Its forehead was flat with deep furrows above two sets of beady eyes, tufts of hair randomly forming a beard, and a long nose oozing mucus from its abnormally large nostrils.

And the chatter it started as its brethren followed into the light, what a sound. Some of the voices were high pitched, some monotone, but all recognizably human and not monstrous. What they were saying at first couldn't be made out, but after a few moments, the words and phrases became clear.

"Tell me those aren't what I think they are," Chartoff muttered to Ferris.

With his usual deadpan sarcasm, Ferris confirmed his friend's fear. "Yes, Chris," he said, "those my friend, are *trolls*."

More and more trolls were emerging from the darkness of

the studio to the point where it was impossible to count them. At least thirty could be seen, but there were likely more coming. While disgusting, these creatures weren't very tall, the largest one being just under five feet tall, which made them threatening but not necessarily terrifying.

"Let the *Grayhem* begin!" shouted Mitchell.

On cue, the legion of trolls advanced towards the *Film Talk* staff. Cody was not impressed with the mob and decided to take a stand here and now. The skinny boy who was no more than twenty-years-old himself didn't have any fear. In fact, he was more annoyed than anything else that his production schedule was being screwed up by this invading group of monsters.

"Do you have any idea how much this equipment costs?" Cody hollered at the creatures, causing them all to stop in mid stride. "You can't just go around destroying things. Look at the mess you've already made! The floor is covered in filth. It's going to take me hours to clean that up! Take your little costumes and go back to whatever casting agency for midgets Gray found you."

Shimmeroff tugged on Yodi's shirt, "Does he not think they're real?"

"I don't think so," Yodi said. "But they did stop. Maybe he's ..."

Before Yodi could finish his sentence, one of the larger trolls silenced the intern with a thrust of its claws into his neck. The strike happened so quick that Cody was still trying to chastise the little creatures before he knew what had happened to him. With three deep puncture wounds in his throat and the flesh hanging like jagged ribbons of meat from each, he gargled on his own blood before collapsing to the floor of the studio, staining what he was so concerned about having to clean.

"... and maybe not," Yodi finished.

The shock of their intern's death was enough to send the remaining members of the show running in all directions. The trolls gave chase, cackling as they waddled throughout the darkened studio in pursuit of whoever they could find.

"This is insane," Schnapps said as about five of the little monsters rushed towards him.

Their teeth were sharp, their claws gleaming in the crimson light, and their beady eyes darting back and forth as they sized their largest target. Each one continued to grumble nonsensical rantings. Some were calling him wrong for condemning Gray's movies, others made fun of his hair, some insulted his mother, all together in this symphony of irritating insults.

"Relax! Relax!" Schnapps told them. "You little creepy *sweaties* need to chill out. I order you to cease any and all supernatural activity and return forthwith to your place of origin or to the nearest, convenient parallel dimension."

A pause. The trolls looked puzzled as they milled over Schnapp's statements. It was then that one mumbled the words "not Gozer" and the other trolls repeated the phrase. Seeing his attempt fail, Schnapps did the only thing left available and balled his fists.

"I ain't afraid of you little monsters. Bring it!"

The trolls agreed. They all rushed him at one time, tackling him to the ground as he tried in vain to fight them off. Outmatched by the numbers, Schnapps disappeared under a pile of angry trolls.

Chen used this as a distraction to get to his desk where the control booth was. It was here that he published their show to YouTube daily and the settings were already configured to air the *Bros Know Show*.

No one would believe any of this. There'd be some coverup, and the entire *Film Talk* crew would disappear under some mysterious circumstance. As ridiculous as it would be for anyone to believe they had been murdered by an army of trolls conjured by Mitchell Gray, Chen knew if he put it live on the air, people would know the truth.

"At least everyone will see this," Chen said as he hit the button to make the show live.

Sure enough, the battery operated handheld cameras began broadcasting. The laptop was fully charged so at least a full hour of this would wind up streaming on the internet. The only problem he saw is that people might think this was a publicity stunt and not call the police, so he typed a message in the video for viewers to see.

Not a part of the show. This is real. Call the police.

Three of the trolls had caught onto him and began to circle around his desk. Chen was scrappy and wasn't going down without a fight. He picked up one of the awards from the trophy stand behind his desk and swung wildly at the monsters. He managed to hit one, but the blow sent a shock through his hand that made him drop his weapon. It was easy then for the trolls to overwhelm him, hurling insults at him as they tackled him to the ground.

"What in the hell is going on?" Yodi screamed as he ran through the narrow hallways between the studio and the meeting rooms.

"I don't want to know," Shimmeroff said, trying to keep pace with him. "Just keep going. I don't want those things getting a hold of me."

"They're everywhere," Chartoff warned as they neared the end of the hallway only to find three trolls waiting there for them.

One of the taller ones charged them, splitting the group into two. Chartoff and Ferris ducked into one of the smaller meeting rooms, which drew the attention of more trolls who followed. Shimmeroff and Yodi weren't as lucky. Their only recourse, and God did Shimmeroff hate this, was to hide in the men's bathroom, a place that carried its own horror stories beyond conjured trolls and homicidal movie directors.

"I don't think they saw us. No one is trying to get in here," Yodi told Sheri as he kept his back against the door, listening for any signs of forced entry from the other side.

"Jesus, is there any wonder why? This place smells like a locker room and farts!"

Shimmeroff's disgust wasn't unfounded. She pinched her nose to keep the odor from overwhelming her, but it was pointless. The bathroom was a single stall, single urinal, overused space that eighteen men shared on a daily basis, and none of them seemed to be too keen on personal hygiene. There were stains on the floor that made Sheri glad the lights were off. What smelled like raw sewage was coming from the sink in droplets, which wasn't nearly as bad as the stench that emanated from the actual toilet. What a disgusting display!

"You have to pee in here?" she asked Yodi.

"We don't have much of a choice, Sheri. Don't act like the women's bathroom is spotless."

"It's not, but I can tell you honestly that it doesn't smell like an ogre took a dump and drenched it in sulfur. What the hell do you guys do in here?"

"Keep quiet!" Yodi warned her. He pressed his ear against the door, hoping that what he heard was the trolls passing by. "They're right outside the door."

"What are they doing?" whispered Shimmeroff.

"They're muttering something," Yodi answered. "I can't ... I don't know what ... it sounds like they're complaining about something."

Yodi could go off topic sometimes, so Sheri was immediately confused as to what he was talking about. She joined him at the door and pressed her ear against it to hear what was going on outside. No, he was right. These little monsters were, in fact, complaining to each other, or so it seemed.

They were making random critiques of the *Film Talk* crew. Everything from how their set was designed to their views on certain movies to some members of the staff not knowing the backstory of certain films before giving a review, and so on and so forth. Mitchell Gray's private joke wasn't lost on them: these were trolls in both the physical and metaphorical sense of the word.

"My head doesn't look like an egg!" Shimmeroff muttered under hear breath in response to one of the troll's comments.

"I am not an insufferable know-it-all!" Yodi grumbled. "I'm telling you right now, if it weren't for the fact that I'm scared out of my mind I'd knock that little bastard on his ass!"

"We need to get out of here," Sheri began looking for another exit from the bathroom. "There has to be a trap door or something."

"They thankfully just put in an exhaust system in the ceiling. Yeah, up there! We might be able to get out that way."

Yodi pointed up to a newly installed vent that was large enough for both of them to get through. The men's bathroom had notoriously been without one for years until the stench got so bad that Burton Camp took part of the budget to have one put in. Sheri looked at the vent, then back to Yodi, then back to the vent, and shook her head.

"We're the horror movie reviewers, right?" she said.

Yodi didn't know where she was going with this, "Yes?"

"You know that's the worst cliché of any horror movie, right? Go climbing in the ventilation system to escape monsters? Are you trying to get us killed?"

"Do you see another way out of here?"

He was actually right. There was no other way out of this room. It was either that or go back into the hallway where who knows what was waiting for them outside. All the times she had slammed low budget horror movies for using this troupe over and over again had come back to bite her.

With a frustrated grunt, she nodded to Yodi, and then asked him to help her get up to the vent. The ceilings of the building were pretty low, so it wouldn't take much for him to get her up there. How he would follow was another case entirely. Yodi wasn't a large man, but he was too heavy for the rather demure Sheri Shimmeroff to pull up into the vent.

"I'll figure it out. Maybe ... maybe I can stand on the trash bin?"

As he went to grab the trash can, the door of the bathroom burst open and a half dozen trolls flooded in. Sheri screamed as she watched them overtake Yodi who, to his credit, smacked one of them in the head before being completely overtaken.

"Just go! Just go! My god, I've turned into a horror martyr! Go!" Yodi yelled before he was hauled away by the little nightmares.

Almost in tears, Sheri leaped into the vent and pushed her tiny body through the ducts. They got Yodi, of all people in the office, he deserved it the least. She was going to make it; she had to. Watching horror movies since she was a young girl in soccer camp who preferred Freddy over Barbie, this should be easy for her. She knew the traps, she knew the do's and don'ts, if anyone was going to get out of the studio alive it would be her.

There was one problem. She had already gotten herself into a cliché. Crawling through a ventilation shaft not only seemed more idiotic now than when Yodi had proposed the idea, but it was nothing like the movies had represented. This place was disgusting, filled with spiderwebs, dead bugs, and so much dust that she couldn't help but sneeze every few seconds. The flimsy metal walls of the shaft were closing in on her, getting tighter and tighter the further she crawled.

Don't panic. Keep your eyes forward and keep moving your arms. Shit, there's a dead mouse! There's nowhere to push it off to the side, and the shaft was way too tight to avoid it, so the only solution was to push it along. Disgusting!

"This ... really ... was ... a dumb ... idea Yodi. Rest in peace," Sheri grumbled, letting loose a tiny eek every time she had to touch the wretched rodent corpse.

She stopped suddenly as a scratching could be heard from the darkness ahead. Hoping it would stop if she stopped, Sheri kept quiet and waited. If it was another mouse, or even worse, she'd lose her mind. The scratching continued and was getting closer. No way she wanted whatever this was to come crawling towards her face. It might just be better to back up and head back to the bathroom. The trolls were probably gone by now.

"You've got to be kidding me!" she moaned as the back of her shirt was caught against a rivet in the air duct.

The more she tried to force herself backwards, the more she heard ripping. Good, rip the shirt she thought, just get out of here before this thing catches up with her.

The scratcher revealed itself slowly, pushing its form from the dark shadows ahead into the small shaft of light that was coming from one of the vent openings. Sheri could now see that it wasn't a rodent, but one of the smallest of trolls that had made its way into the shaft. Its little face was covered in pimples, its hair looked like a bird's nest. Its long nose pushed up against the dead mouse, causing the rodent corpse to spill its contents. It stopped, sniffed the mouse, then snatched it up with its claw-like hands, biting off the head and chewing it ravenously.

Sheri was going to puke. The troll mocked her, saying that the other girls were prettier on the show, and then spit chewed pieces of mouse at her face. She screamed, she gagged, and then she became furious. Using as much force as she could, she pushed with her legs to get away from the troll. It was strong enough to rip her shirt even more but this unfortunately also ripped open her back. In tears, she cried out just before the bottom section of the ventilation shaft was wrenched open beneath her. The larger trolls had found her and tore apart the shaft to get at her. Her cries echoed as she fell, leaving the miniature troll to watch as it finished eating.

Chartoff and Ferris were hunkered down in the main meeting room, hidden behind a sofa and a few overturned tables. They had seen a few of their co-workers carried out by the trolls. Clothes had been ripped, blood had been spilled, and they knew that they were high on the list of targets for these revolting creatures.

"Okay, so there are trolls. They are dragging everyone away somewhere," Ferris started.

"I know what's going on, Jeremy," Chartoff snapped at his friend. "What are you, running commentary?"

"I'm just trying to wrap my head around the fact that freakin' Mitchell Gray came here, opened up his Magic Box of Death, and conjured up a horde of trolls to attack us. Yes, Chris, I need to say that out loud to process it in my mind."

"Well, keep your voice down," Chartoff said as he peered over the top of the sofa to see where the trolls were. "There's two of them over there sniffing around just outside the door."

The two trolls continued their search. Chartoff listened intently as he overheard both of them mumbling to themselves, spilling out random phrases and insults.

Ferris joined his friend to take a look. If the trolls had better awareness, they would have easily spotted the two men peeking out over the top of the sofa, but they were so focused on their own commentary to notice what was right in front of them. After a few moments, they moved on through the hallway, searching and sniffing and snickering as they went.

"We need to get out of here," Chartoff said as he lowered himself back behind the sofa.

"They're standing guard at the front door," Ferris explained. "I don't see how we're going to get out that way."

It was now that Ferris' natural cowardly instincts kicked in. He was figuring out how he would survive and was starting to understand he might have to leave his fellow co-host behind. Chris was the taller and larger of the two, and certainly the more aggressive. If it came down to it, Chartoff would fight and prove to be a bigger target for these nasty monsters than he would. Yeah, that's it! Use the big lummox as a shield. So what if he had kids at home? Ferris couldn't stand kids and could rationalize how much better off the world would be with him in it instead of Chartoff breeding more patrons for awful kids movies.

None of this was going through Chartoff's mind. His focus was more on how to fight his way out of the studio and what he should do next. More than anyone else on the staff, Chartoff was a fan of science fiction films, in particular, *Star Wars*, so his mind was running through every scenario he had seen in a *Star Wars* film to try and equate it to his current situation. The best he came up with was Ewoks, and that was a losing situation all the way around. No, these little trolls weren't Ewoks. Maybe they were more like Jawas. Those, Chartoff could handle. They were all much smaller than him and as long as they weren't in great numbers, they shouldn't pose a threat.

"I think you should go out there, distract them, and I'll make a run for the door," Ferris said.

"And what happens to me?" Chartoff asked.

"I'll come back for you." The response was met with a questionable glare. "Seriously, would I leave you behind? What kind of a coward would I be to just run off and leave everyone else for dead? I'm surprised you would think that of me, Chris."

"I don't know why you'd be surprised because that's exactly what you would do, ballbag."

"I thought we agreed never to use that word again."

"Well, when it applies ..."

"Alright, alright. Aside from me making a break for it and saving everyone by going to the cops, what would you suggest we do?"

For this, Chartoff didn't really have an answer ready. He was still working out scenarios in his head. From what he could tell, they were the only two left that hadn't been abducted by the trolls and carried off to God-knows-where. He couldn't see the studio area from where they were, but he knew the layout of the building like the back of his hand.

On the opposite side of the building were two exit doors that were unguarded. If they could make it there, they'd be home free. It wasn't as if they were in some far-off place in the middle of nowhere. A number of businesses, dealerships, and of course the local movie theater were within a few blocks. At that point, he'd just have to hope everyone else could hold out until the cops arrived.

But how to get to that door?

"Okay, this is what we'll do," he whispered to Ferris. "You go over there and throw something. Make a noise, a distraction. I'll try to get to the door on the other side of the building and get help."

Ferris did a double take as he realized what his co-host was saying. "What?" he replied in a high-pitched whisper. "How is that any different than what I said?"

"It's not the same thing you said."

"Yes, it is."

"Are you going to argue with me or help?"

"I'm totally up for helping you out when it doesn't involve

me being ripped to shreds by evil movie trolls."

"Shhh, here comes another one."

This particular troll was built like a fireplug, short and wide. Its thighs were massive, like two tubes of cookie dough spilling over themselves. It surveyed the meeting room with yellow eyes, sniffing with a wide flat nose at the ground. Then, it caught a sent. With each snort, the troll's excitement grew. Head down to the ground, it continued to follow whatever it had picked up. Could the thing smell them? If not, they could certainly smell it; a pungent mixture of feces, sweat, and moldy fruit.

"What the hell is it doing?" Ferris asked.

Stinky troll became excited and darted across the room to a table far away from Chartoff and Ferris. Relieved he hadn't found them, they peeked over the sofa again to see what it was that had drawn this troll's attention.

As it flung pieces of equipment across the room, Chartoff noticed the T-shirt the monster was wearing. When the troll lifted one of the handheld cameras into the air and cackled with glee, he started to fear what this meant. The shirt had a familiar symbol on it: a stick figure made from a horizontal line and two other lines which formed and "X" beneath it and one final line extending from the center of the X upwards and through the horizontal line. The monster turned the camera's light on and then started searching the room again, this time picking up on an entirely different scent.

"You have got to be kidding me," Chartoff moaned.

The troll had found their scent and was waddling as fast as its chubby legs would allow towards their hiding spot. Ferris and Chartoff started to run as it closed in on them, fleeing the meeting room while the troll gave chase, using the viewfinder of the camera to see.

"Great! Now we're in a freakin' first person horror film," bemoaned Ferris as he ran.

"Forget it. Just get to the other side of the studio!" Chartoff said.

In all truth, the little troll was in no shape to catch up with them in a foot race. However, the hallway was blocked by a legion of trolls, which cut off any escape route Chartoff and Ferris could use. The confused pair looked around for any other possible exit when Ferris tugged at Chartoff's shirt. He pointed excitedly at a ladder at the far end of the hallway that led to the roof.

"That's a bad idea!" Chartoff muttered.

"Do you have a better one? Come on!" Ferris said, grabbing his friend's shirt and leading him towards the ladder.

Stinky camera troll had finally caught up with them. Chartoff started climbing up towards the hatch in the ceiling that would lead to the roof, but his co-host had stopped at the base of the ladder.

"What are you doing?" Chartoff yelled down to him.

"I ... uh ... I forgot that I'm afraid of heights."

"Are you serious?"

"I ... well ..." Ferris turned back to see the stinky camera troll stop to call his fellow trolls to follow. "That's not good."

The hallway was filling with trolls of all shapes and sizes, muttering to themselves as they closed in on Ferris who was still of two minds between his fear of heights and his fear of being dismembered. By the time he made up his mind, it was too late. He let loose a screech before trying to ascend the ladder, getting five rungs up before the clawed hands of angry trolls seized him by his ankle and ripped him violently from the ladder.

Chartoff watched as Ferris screamed for his life before disappearing in the mass of trolls, his screams muffled until there was nothing left to see or hear. It wasn't time to feel sad for his friend. He had a daughter and a wife who he needed to think about now. Earlier in the morning, he had actually lost his temper with his daughter because she had made a mess in the kitchen. Even though he had apologized, he could see she was still visibly upset with him when he dropped her off at school. That was not going to be the last memory she had of her father. He had to get out of here alive!

Down below, the trolls had started to climb up the ladder themselves, or at least, made an attempt to. The first three monsters didn't have the physical ability to make such climb, each one becoming instantly exhausted from the effort and falling back down into the masses below. Chartoff used this time to further the distance between him and the creatures, rung by rung ascending towards the small door in the ceiling. If he could just get there and get out of the building, this nightmare would end.

The trolls, seeing that none of them could make the climb, began cat-calling Chartoff. They criticized his hair, his love of science fiction movies, brought up every single time he had gotten something wrong on a show or misquoted someone, and worst of all, mocked him being invited to premieres of movies.

"I hate trolls," he said.

He was only fifteen rungs away from the roof. Inspired by his growing annoyance with the constant barrage of insults coming from below, he sped up his climb, straining his muscles to pull his body to the top. It seemed the higher he climbed, the harder it was to move—as if gravity was playing a trick against him, pulling at his legs every time they took a step.

The ladder started to shift. What was this? He looked at the wall in front of him and saw the bolts that kept the ladder attached were starting to come loose.

"Stop it!" he yelled.

The trolls were pulling violently at the ladder, shaking it with all of their might. If they couldn't climb up as high as he had, they would certainly rip the ladder from the wall and bring him down to them. The insults grew louder, the pulling continued, and with a few cracks and pops, Chartoff saw the ladder start to break free from the wall.

Only a few more to go, he said to himself. They couldn't stop him. The fact that they were trying to shake the ladder loose confirmed that he was on the right path to getting out of here. Just five more to go. Four. Three.

As he looked up at the trap door to the roof, it suddenly flung open. The brightness of the day nearly blinded him after being in the darkness of the powerless studio for so long. That wasn't the worst of it. A troll was already there on the other side staring down at Chartoff with a giant, bloodshot eyeball that swiveled back and forth in its socket. The sight shocked Chartoff so much that he recoiled, forgetting his hold on the ladder. Immediately realizing his mistake, he plummeted towards the floor. The trolls watched him fall and in one smooth motion moved out of the way. The only saving grace was that there was a table nearby, which he fell through, exploding the table into a shower of splinters as his broken body crumpled beneath the wreckage.

Mitchell Gray watched with a pleased look on his face, his arms crossed and his chest puffed out, while the last few members of the *Film Talk* crew were dragged into a pile before him. Still alive, each member wore the scars of the chase. Foreheads were cut, arms were broken, legs punctured, and each one of them had a miserable look on their face. Gray had never seen a larger, or more satisfying, collection of broken bodies and spirits before.

To his left, knelt down on the ground in a slave girl outfit was Gamer Girl 86. Still defiant to the end, she wore this costume (which no one quite knew how she got into it in the first place) with an incredulous smile, forced on her by whatever power Gray had conjured from the Eternity Box.

"Is this not easier?" he asked as he walked paced the floor between him and the *Film Talk* staff. "Isn't this your natural state? Beneath me!"

"You stole that from a movie," a voice cried out from the crew.

Still smartasses to the end, he saw.

"What exactly did you expect to happen at the end of this?" Yodi asked, his face a mask of bruises and blood. "I mean, what the hell was the point of this whole thing? You want to make us say your shit movies aren't shit?"

"Nothing so simplistic," Gray laughed. "You should be happy little man. I just gave your audience the best show you've ever done."

Gray pointed to the cameras in the studio, the handhelds a few trolls had picked up, and the monitors on the nearby tech station. This entire ordeal had been broadcast on their YouTube channel since the beginning. Despite his agonizing pain, the massive amount of live views displayed on the monitors made Chris Chen smile through his broken teeth.

"But, every story has to have an ending. I'm afraid, for my first real horror movie, that it won't be a happy one," Gray proclaimed as he walked back to the Eternity Box.

Shimmeroff and Chartoff were sitting next to each other near the back of the crew. Their arms, like those of their co-workers, were bound behind them, but they could still talk to one another. Chartoff had a punctured lung, a broken collarbone, a broken arm, and one of his teeth had pressed up through the soft pallet of his mouth and was now hanging out of his nose.

"He's going to kill us," he said to Shimmeroff.

The woman had no more tears to shed. She had been frightened, tortured, and beaten for so long that she could barely keep her eyes open. However, her ears worked just fine. She listened to the rants of Mitchell Gray, but behind them was another sound, one she had heard the entire time. The trolls were still hurling insults at the *Film Talk* crew. It was continuous, illogical, and petty. A never-ending stream of sophomoric comments and irrational exaggerations.

It was then that she had a flash of brilliance.

"They're trolls, right?" Shimmeroff said.

Chartoff didn't get why she was asking this, "Yeah, Sheri. They're trolls. We know they're trolls. What's your point?"

"What's the best way to upset trolls?"

A light bulb went off in Chartoff's head. Years of arguing with anonymous people on the internet had taught him how to deal with trolls and, more importantly, how to upset them. If these were Mitchell's manifestation of that unfortunate side of the internet, common sense would suggest he could deal with these trolls in the same way.

"Hey!" he yelled to one of the trolls with a handheld camera. "You, the ugly one with the stupid T-shirt. Yeah, you, shit-troll."

The little monster moved over to Chartoff, the camera still filming and focusing on his beaten face. What a mindless creature it was, consumed with filming people in distress while being easily summoned like a dog.

"You want to shoot first person movies? Right? Well, they all suck. Especially those stupid horror movies. How many shaky cam shitfests can we actually watch?"

The troll recoiled in anger, babbling incoherently in response.

"I'm even a horror fan and I have to say, whatever this is you're filming is probably worse than *Blair Witch 2: Book of Shadows*!" Shimmeroff added.

The troll dropped the camera and started crying. Shimmeroff felt bad for a split second but quickly continued her insults along with Chartoff. A few of the other trolls were beginning to wilt as well, all reacting to the words as if they were witches caught in a rain shower.

Ferris quickly saw what his friends were doing and added to the cause. "You know what, *The Exorcist* is overrated."

Now the groans were coming from more and more of the trolls. One of them screamed out in agony, some threw their hands up in the air and stomped the ground beneath their feet, all in a furious temper tantrum that rivaled any child's on a playground.

By this point, the rest of the *Film Talk* crew caught on and were coming up with every shocking statement they could. Anything they could think of that would ruin the collective group-think of these trolls was fodder for the fight, each statement crippling their captors into crumbling heaps of sweat and tears.

"*The Lord of the Rings* is boring!"

"I've never seen *Scarface*!"

"Kirk is a better captain than Picard!"

"I got to see *Star Wars* a month before you did!"

"You need to stop ignoring Tyler Perry's box office appeal!"

"DC movies are better than Marvel's!"

The tables had turned. After throwing out nearly three dozen phrases that the trolls couldn't stand to hear, the *Film Talk* crew had managed to reduce the mass of nightmares into whimpering crybabies. Not only were they in an uncontrollable fit of rage mixed with confusion, their sense of entitlement to be here, in the studio running the show, was fading away. So much that the trolls were retreating back into the darkness from where they emerged.

All it would take was one final, devastating blow to completely destroy the army. One sentence that would break the spirit of every single troll in that mob and end this invasion once and for all.

Yodi knew just what to say, and he did so in a loud, brave voice.

"The *Star Wars* prequels aren't as bad as you think they are!"

That did it! The volume of outrage, crying, complaining, and literal screaming that erupted from the army of trolls shook the walls of the studio. But it worked. They were leaving in droves. They couldn't stand to hear it any longer. Many covered their ears as they fled back into the shadows while some spontaneously combusted where they stood, leaving a smoking pile of hairy feet behind.

While all this was going on, Shimmeroff had managed to free herself from her bindings and went about the task of untying her friends. Schnapps was the worse for wear, his body tattooed with cuts and bites, but he'd live. They'd all live.

"Now, let Gamer Girl go and get the hell out of here!" Chen demanded as he approached Gray and his two bodyguards.

"It's not over!" Gray yelled as he rushed to the Eternity Box.

"There's a bunch of us, and there's three of you," Schnapps pointed out. "Even though we're beat up, we'll still kick your ass, son! Believe that!"

Gray turned to his bodyguards for protection, but they didn't seem too confident in their odds. Even worse, they had shown up unarmed. Both looked at each other through their slick sunglasses, adjusted their ties briefly, and made a mad dash for the exit.

Left alone, Gray knew he had one last card to play. He wouldn't be able to use the Eternity Box; his enemies would easily overtake him before he could complete any kind of spell. But, he did still have Gamer Girl under his control.

"Stay where you are," he yelled as he pulled her to her feet.

The poor girl looked like she was drugged. Her eyes were

rolling around in her head, her mouth was open, and she swayed from side to side. Gray then put his hand on the Eternity Box and waited to see what the *Film Talk* crew would do.

"If you take another step closer, I use this box and she's a vegetable," Gray bluffed.

In truth, he didn't have that power, but they didn't know that. His threat worked as the vengeance he saw in the eyes of Chartoff, Schnapps, and Chen dissolved into acquiescence. Once again, they'd have to do things his way, which Gray liked. Even though they figured out the trolls, they couldn't stop him.

"Stop being a pussy and let the girl go," Yodi said.

"No, that would be stupid. Why would I do that?" Gray answered.

"He does kind of have a point, Yodi," Ferris said, his wit returning to him now that the wasn't in any immediate danger.

Gray was turning his hand on the Eternity Box while he distracted the team with his arguments. He used any villainous line he could think of from his own movies, phrases and speeches that had been regurgitated over and over again for the last few decades in cinema. The longer they argued, the more time he had to work this spell without them knowing.

"Perhaps I made a mistake using trolls," he finally conceded. "But, this time, I'm going to use something much worse. Meet your—"

Before he could finish his monologue, the large doors to the studio opened up behind him. He turned in that direction and watched as the afternoon poured into the dark studio once again, flooding everyone in its luminance.

Silhouetted in the sun's rays was a lone figure, standing with his hands on his hips and his chin jutted forward like a superhero from a comic book.

"Camp?" said Gray.

It indeed was Burton Camp. He had watched the entire

fiasco take place on his way back from his meeting, and his face showed a fury that only the most disposable of interns on the *Film Talk* staff had ever seen.

"I was trying really, really hard to be nice to you today. But you know, I have to honestly say, for me personally ... you are without a doubt the single biggest asshole I have ever seen in this industry. Hands down!"

Earning a few laughs from his co-workers, Camp didn't get any such reaction from Mitchell Gray. Despite Camp's grand entrance, there was nothing he could do to stop Gray. The spell was almost finished. There'd just be another victim to add to the list, the king of all the movie nerds himself. What a coup this would be after all!

"It's going to take more than you to save them, Camp," said Gray.

Camp nodded in agreement, "Oh, you're absolutely right, which is why I brought back up."

From the left side of the doorway came a slender woman, long red hair, thick rimmed glasses, and the best resting bitch face anyone had ever seen. Claire Fox was the greatest mind in horror films of the entire staff. If anyone would know how to handle whatever nightmares Mitchell Gray would manifest from the Eternity Box, it would be Fox.

She wasn't the only backup. From the right side of the doorway came another figure, much taller, thicker, and intimidating than Fox. He walked with the swagger of a gunslinger from an old western movie, complete with a cowboy hat and the stern grimace of a grizzled fighter.

"Steve Bocha? He brought Bocha?" a puzzled Chartoff asked, seemingly not as confident in Burton Camp's backup as he'd like to be.

"Great," Yodi moaned. "I don't know who is worse: Bocha or Gray."

"I heard that, Yodi!" Steve Bocha yelled, his voice overly

aggressive. "But I'm not here for you this time. I'm here for this scumbag right here!"

Bocha pointed at Gray who didn't quite know what to make of this giant of a man who was more caricature than character. The rant that would follow came off more as a pro wrestler talking to a camera than someone who legitimately wanted to fight.

"Yeah, you can talk all you want about *Film Talk*. You can make your little jokes and put Gamer Girl in some lame cosplay outfit. You can even summon an army of little wannabe trolls to terrorize everyone. But listen to me! I'm coming for you and that stupid shit-box you have with you! There's no escape! None at all! In fact, I think ..."

Camp tried to calm down Bocha, "Okay, okay Steve."

But he kept going, "... you are so scared of the power that's in these hands ..."

"We get it, Steve," Ferris added.

"... that you needed to come here with two wimpy guards. Where are they now?"

"God, I knew this was a bad idea," Yodi said.

"They ran out on you just like I'm going to run all over your face right now! And another thing—"

"Who the hell is this?" Mitchell Gray asked.

"Nevermind," Camp answered. "The point is, you need to get out of here right now, let Gamer Girl go, and take this ..."

"Shit-box," interjected Bocha.

"Yes, shit-box with you."

Gray scratched his chin. He was clearly outnumbered and surrounded on all sides. It still didn't matter. The spell was almost finished.

"I don't think so."

With a twist of his hand, the spell was initiated. The Eternity Box began to hum as motes of energy spilled out from its sides. Everyone backed away from it out of fear. They had seen what this box could do and weren't interested in another round of whatever terrors Gray was about to unleash from it.

Everyone except Bocha.

In what looked like a fit of anger, he clumsily stormed towards Gray, unaware of what danger was about to come. The two men struggled as Bocha barked in Gray's face. One disadvantage to this was that Bocha wasn't nearly as rough and tumble as his persona would suggest. He wound up stumbling into Gray, knocking the director backwards into the Eternity Box.

"What did you do?" Gray yelled.

Bocha stood up and put his cowboy hat back on, but the damage had been done. The box started spinning out of control, pieces of it flying in all directions. The first consequence of this was the release of Gamer Girl 86 who awoke from her spell and immediately gasped once she realized what she was wearing. *What a fucking pig*, she thought, and began slapping Mitchell Gray repeatedly.

He ignored the blows as his main concern was the box. The gems on the front of the box began to disappear, and with them other changes came about. Mitchell's clothes changed from dapper to dirty, his pressed suit replaced with a ratty T-shirt. His expensive watch morphed into a cheap knockoff Rolex. His perfectly crafted hair withered into a receding hairline. It seemed that whatever disruption Bocha had caused was reversing everything Mitchell Gray had gained from the Eternity Box to the point where he was nothing more than an average looking schmoe who no one would look twice at.

"What have you done? What the hell have you done? I'm ruined!" Gray cried out as he knelt down in the wreck of the Eternity Box.

The energies of the gems began to disappear until they flickered one last time before going completely dormant. Right before his eyes, the famed director of countless of million-dollar films saw his entire career go up in flames. The damage wasn't limited to his appearance either. Unbeknownst to him, his bank account went from millions to one with ten dollars and an impending overdraft fee. His home was in foreclosure, and his contract with the movie studio was terminated. History had been rewritten, and all the success he had attained was now replaced by a story about a director with one failed attempt at an action movie that critics hated and general audiences remembered as being garbage.

The legacy of Mitchell Gray was over.

Over the next twenty-four hours, the *Film Talk* crew did their best to return their beloved studio to normal. Most of the crew went to the hospital to have their wounds tended to while some even sought psychological counseling.

Burton Camp came up with the idea to explain the entire scenario that their audience had seen as an experimental film that went wrong. The public wondered why they'd waste their time with a struggling movie director to do such a thing but overall the reviews were positive. Some called it the best piece of meta-entertainment ever put on YouTube while a few (correctly) suspected the entire thing was real. *The Mitchell Gray Incident*, as it came to be known, would be part of every *Weird and Strange Facts About YouTube* top ten video for years.

As for the staff itself, they each handled the aftermath in their own way. Gamer Girl 86 went back to her own show but seemingly developed an affinity for cosplay. Dre Schnapps became inspired by the incident and made a documentary film about other failed directors and movies in Hollywood history. Ferris and Chartoff grew closer as friends, but their banter between each other on the show didn't change much. Poor Cody however was not resurrected from the dead.

On the anniversary of the incident, the now famous *Film Talk* crew was drawing in millions of viewers every day for its show. Every so often they'd reference the incident, but on this day, they would do a retrospective show.

"It's hard to believe that all actually happened here," Dre Schnapps said as he walked into the studio. "I'm so glad that asshole is where he is now."

"A psyche ward?" Sheri Shimmeroff asked as they both settled into their seats on the set.

"What better place for him? I always said it's insane how his movies fooled so many people into watching them. Thank God we're the only ones who remember that actually happened."

"Well, Schnapps, it takes a certain amount of talent to be able to rewrite history. And who better to benefit from it than us?" Jeremy Ferris added.

"The only thing is ... well, poor Cody," Shimmeroff said with a hint of sadness in her voice. "That poor kid, I feel so bad for him."

Schnapps, Chartoff, and Ferris sat at the table with blank stares on their faces. They looked at each other, trying to get consensus on mourning of the intern who was the only casualty of the Mitchell Gray Incident. Collectively, they shrugged their shoulders.

"That's so mean!" Shimmeroff said.

Ferris didn't feel the same, "Eh, he was an intern. That's what they're here for, to take the crap that we don't want to."

"Does anyone know where Camp is? We need to start the show in five minutes?" asked Chartoff.

"He's back there with Bocha," Schnapps answered. "So, he might be a while."

In the meeting room, Burton Camp was finishing writing his notes for the show while Bocha was on his daily rant about how everyone owed him for saving their asses the year before. He was upset that he wasn't scheduled to be on the show, but Claire Fox had to remind him that if he did let the world know, the spell would be broken and things would go back to the way they were.

"You don't want that do you?" she asked Bocha, trying to appeal to his reason.

"I know Fox but ..." Bocha's ego was fighting with his common sense. "It just doesn't seem right that people don't know. I'm the one who did it. Me!"

"Yes, yes, we know Bocha," Camp conceded. "Isn't that all that really matters? We all know."

"And if we ever forget, you'll certainly remind us, won't you?" Fox said, shooting an insincere smile to the hyped-up cowboy.

Even though Bocha wanted recognition, he knew better than to cross Claire Fox. She knew more about the dark side of movie magic than anyone else and for several reasons, he had to listen.

"Well, I think it'd just be cool to do something, you know? Think about it, guys."

Bocha had said his piece and then left the room. Burton and Fox waited for him to leave before bursting out in laughter. As much as they did acknowledge Bocha being the reason they all were even alive today, he didn't do so with bravery, he did it by accident. His outbursts every few months were a minor price to pay in the long run.

"Okay, I'm heading out to do the show," Camp said to Fox.

"Are you going to be okay with what you need to do here?"

"Same as I am every day," Fox answered.

"Okay then, let's get to it."

Camp left the room to join the rest of the crew on set. Claire Fox was left alone in the meeting room. She casually walked to the storage closet, which was installed after the attack a year ago, and carefully opened it.

A cold blue light flowed from the inside as she knelt down and placed her hand on its source: the Eternity Box refurbished. With a grin, she pushed back her glasses, placed her hand on the box, and softly spoke to it.

"What's in the box?"

Postmortem III

Omar sat at the table, befuddled at the scene he had just witnessed. The demon had been feverishly at work during the last hand, throwing just about everything he could at it. Even with all he attempted, all he tried, he managed to come away with only one soul, and even that he'd have to wait years for.

The angel made out much better, saving five souls and claiming one, the poor intern, as an extra bonus. She sat cheekily as she counted her cards, adding to her pile of and shuffling them, excessively so, in front of her opponent.

Still unaware of how this really worked, Omar was privy to everything the card players saw. There were manifestations of scenes that appeared above the game area, whispers of actions carried in a hazy mist that floated above the table. At times, he could even hear voices, smell odors, and on some occasions, feel the happiness or fear of a particular soul as it was bargained and bandied for.

"There's no way that was real," Omar said as the deck was being shuffled for the next hand. "Little trolls attacking people from some magic box a movie director had? You're fucking with me, right?"

The angel sighed in annoyance. "You do understand what those trolls were."

"Yeah, I get it. I've used the internet before and know what trolls are. The cleverness around what happened isn't lost on me, but shit. What the hell? That made zero sense."

"Not everything has to make sense. Not everything does make sense. You're here, aren't you? And I haven't sent you off to heaven—whatever you think that is—and he hasn't eaten you yet."

The demon licked its lips at the prospect. "And don't think it's out of my kindhearted nature I haven't, either."

Omar squirmed in his chair. He wished the angel wouldn't tempt the demon so. He didn't know what manner of rule or law kept the demon from eating him or worse, but he didn't get the sense that there would be much the angel could do to stop him if he wanted to.

"Well, it's a shame, really. I liked Mitchell Gray's movies," Omar admitted.

The angel and the demon looked at him and then slyly rolled their eyes towards one another and laughed. Omar didn't see what was so funny. So what if he liked simple, popcorn movies? Fuck them. If he didn't fear the repercussions of telling them that, he'd do so right this instant.

"Are you sure he's smart enough to sit here?" the demon asked. "We may be wasting our time with this one. What little time he has left."

"Oh, it's all relative," the angel countered. "He has eternity, and then again, he may not."

The subject needed to change.

Omar rubbed his nose and scooted closer to the table. He still feared them both but was more comfortable now. At the very least, they'd be playing another hand, and even with the insane nature of the last one, he was greatly curious about what incomprehensible situation would come next.

The angel shuffled the deck confidently and then plucked the next topic. Her expression as she read the card was indeterminate; a hint of worry was in her eyes while the corner of her mouth twitched in an awkward smile.

She laid the card on the table and began to pick her hand. The demon leaned forward, extended its forked tongue down at the card, and then eased back in his chair. Much like the angel, his reaction didn't indicate much to Omar what he felt about the card on the table. What he could tell was that this hand wouldn't hold the same dark humor as the previous one.

The One and Lonely

G aiste Communications had emerged during the last decade as a premier corporation for creating advanced tech gear for home use. Everything from automated ways to watch television to implants that alerted a user to their health status to enhanced hearing devices had been produced and marketed through the company. To earn a job, a certain amount of skill was required that wasn't common in modern society which meant those who were employed by the company needed to have the ability to keep their mouths shut and live solitary lives. In fact, Gaiste went out of its way to find candidates in every aspect of their workforce who met certain psychological and social criteria.

One of their employees was Garrett Canigula.

While having much of the traits that Gaiste looked for, Garrett's personality went a bit further than the common introvert. The majority of the staff had social lives, some had families, many spent time together both in and outside of the workplace. Garrett, in contrast, didn't have a family, had only one friend in the office, and his extended family members were either deceased or lived far away (he never told anyone much about them). Mostly, his co-workers accepted his lone wolf attitude. It never was a problem for any of them. He communicated when needed and was cordial when spoken to. When given a choice to socialize though, he often declined, choosing to eat alone than in a group, go home instead of to happy hour, call out on a sick day if there was ever a group event.

The one friend he did have at the office, Maggie Strowman, didn't share the same lifestyle. She was by no means a socialite, but she had a normal social life: dates, friends, family, holiday get-togethers. Her friendship with Garrett was never romantic – he was an okay looking guy but not her type, she preferred more masculine men, he preferred thinner women – but it was one of trust and a few commonalities. Movies, coding practices, and taste in exotic food.

Every so often she'd try to encourage him to come to lunch with her and their coworkers but never pushed. If he didn't want to go, he wouldn't, and it was pointless to nag. The last month he did open himself up to having lunch with her, just her. She soon found out why. He had been dating a young lady for some time and was seeking the advice of a female on how to best propose to her. Maggie felt genuinely honored he had come to her and for a few weeks they'd discuss the best way for him to pop the question, what clothes he should wear, where he should do it, in public or alone at home, and a dozen other options he had considered.

Last week, he declined to have lunch with her and the next day didn't show up for work at all. Maggie was concerned but also knew Garrett was prone to disappear from the social radar when he wanted alone time. It was nothing new. When he did return to the office after two sick days, he still declined lunch with her. The rest of their coworkers continued to ask her questions about him. Was he okay? Did he seem suicidal? Who was this girl he was dating and had he run off to elope and not tell the team?

Today would be the day, though. She had grown tired of not knowing what was going on with him, not out of concern for his well-being but out of her own curiosity. Something was going on, she knew it, and she needed to know what exactly it was.

"Hey," Maggie said as she approached Garrett's work area. "You know what I'm going to ask."

"Yeah," Garrett answered coldly, still typing away on his keyboard and observing three monitors filled with nothing but code.

She waited for him to say more but he didn't. This was going to be awkward. "Well, do you have an answer or do you just want me to stand here and look stupid?"

"I'm just finishing this last bit up," he answered.

That was his way of saying I'm going to keep working until you go away. Maggie rolled her eyes and took a seat in a chair next to him. Their workspaces were open and mobile, each employee could choose a workstation anywhere in the office where they could dock their laptops and spend the day. Some didn't like the arrangement as it prohibited personal space. You couldn't leave pictures or paperwork or art at your desk because tomorrow it wouldn't be your desk. Garrett found it refreshing as he never brought anything personal into the office in the first place.

"Look, Taichi is making Pho down the street at that

restaurant that just opened up. You know, the one that waitress at Mama Lucille's told us about because we asked her where they had Pho in this area?" His typing slowed. "It's a tough place to get reservations, but I did manage to snag a table for this afternoon's lunch shift." He stopped typing altogether. "Of course I'm paying."

Finally, he looked at her.

"Do I even want to know how you pulled that off," Garrett asked with an accusatory tone.

"I have my ways," Maggie answered, the smirk she gave confirming Garrett's suspicions.

"I don't even want to know."

While Maggie was a larger sized woman, her excess was in all the right places. She was big-boned, as the expression goes, with enormous breasts, wide hips, a perfectly round ass, and the face of a woman much thinner. She wasn't big on fashion but knew how to dress to make herself look attractive in an understated way. Even though she didn't look the part, she was a promiscuous woman who used her appetite for sex as a way to get favors around the city. Only a few people (aside from her male suitors) knew about her sexual exploits and no one at work, except for Garrett, had a clue she was such a predatory creature behind closed doors.

"Well, do you want to go or not?" she asked.

Garrett closed down his monitors and stood up from the desk. "Of course! It's Pho," he responded. "But no interrogations, please. It's been a rough week."

"We'll only talk about what you want to talk about."

Saigon Pho was indeed a hot spot for lunch. The restaurant could hold 300 people, and every table was taken with a line of hopeful patrons stretching around the corner. Maggie and Garrett sat at their table, ordered lunch, and waited for their food to be served. This gave Garrett time to do one thing he always liked to do the few times he'd go out in public: people watching.

Look at these sheep. All of them outside trying to cram their way into the front doors just because someone else told them to be here. Every hipster and overpaid middle management suit had formed the line outside, and just as many were crowded at the bar and tables within. He felt a bit like a hypocrite just for being here. What made him special to get a seat where these other people couldn't get one? It was what disgusted him about consumer culture and one of the many reasons he rarely went out to bars or restaurants. The faux status games surrounding places like this truly made him ill.

"What's wrong?" Maggie asked.

"Nothing. I'm just thinking. So, what's new with you?"

"No, no, no, that's not why I asked you to lunch. I want to know what's new with you. Where have you been the last few days?"

Garrett bit his lower lip, "I said no interrogations."

"This is a conversation, not an interrogation. That would require a bright spotlight and handcuffs."

"Both of which I'm sure you have in your bedroom."

"Fair point," Maggie laughed. "But seriously, are you okay? That's the only reason I asked. Is everything good with Lauren?"

Garrett eased back in his chair and took a sip of his water. It was the question he didn't want to answer, but somewhere deep inside he knew he took this lunch because he wanted to talk about it. Might as well get it over with.

"We broke up," he said flatly.

Garrett watched for Maggie's expression. Her face went immediately from playful to disappointed. That was not what she expected. Gently, she took hold of his hand, but he pulled away from her instantly.

"I'm sorry, Garrett. If you don't mind me asking, what happened?"

"It's nothing too complicated, we just grew apart."

Maggie wasn't buying it. "You grew apart overnight? Garrett, last week you were picking out wedding bands. Seriously, what happened?"

The waiter arrived with their food. The young boy tried his best to be cordial and strike up a small conversation with his customers, but it was clear this table didn't want to be bothered at the moment. He set their dishes in front of them, asked if they wanted anything else, and when they answered with silence, he simply left to attend his other tables.

"I'm just not good at communicating, you know. Neither is she. I told her I didn't feel like I was ready for someone to be in my life that much, at least not right now, and she took it that I wanted to break up."

"I would have too," Maggie said.

"You see, that's just it. I didn't want to break up with her. She jumped to conclusions and hung up on me before I could say anything else."

"When did this all happen?"

"A week ago."

"And you haven't talked to her since? She hasn't taken any of your calls or text messages?"

"I haven't sent any."

"Garrett! Why the hell not?"

He was about to answer, but something in the back of his mind told him not to speak. Instead, he took a bite of his food and chewed as slowly as he could while thinking about what to say next. It wasn't any use though, Maggie could see right through him, and he knew it.

"You do this a lot you know," Maggie started in on him. Here it comes. "You take anti-social to a whole new level. Come to think of it, I don't think I've actually met any of your friends outside of work if you have any. And I'm you're only friend at work. I've never seen or heard of any family either."

Garrett swallowed hard, he needed to answer this.

"I have plenty of friends," he protested.

"Random people you curse at while playing video games online do not constitute friends, Garrett."

"Whatever. I don't have to explain myself to you."

"No, you don't. And I'd rather not get into an argument at lunch. I'll just say Lauren was the best thing I've seen happen to you in the four years we've known each other. Don't let your pride, or your sense that everyone else in the world is stupid except you, get in the way of finding happiness with someone."

What she said made sense. Of course it did. Garrett knew he could be extreme in his pushing away of people. It was a well-earned personality quirk, forged after years and years of being mistreated and disappointed by people he put his faith in. All of them let him down. Parents, cousins, former co-workers, ex-girlfriends, ex-best friends, every single one of them had chewed up his loyalty and spit it out. The slightest sign it might happen again was enough for him to shut down. He knew he was doing it now with Lauren, and so did Maggie.

"Let's talk about something else, okay?" he said before continuing with his lunch.

Back at the office, Garrett stashed the leftovers from lunch in the refrigerator everyone else in the office shared. The plastic container that he kept his food in didn't close all the way, and the latch kept opening. He tried to close it one last time before going back to his workstation, but the latch popped open, mockingly, which frustrated him to the point he slammed the refrigerator shut.

Its fine, he thought. No one would dare mess with his food. What kind of asshole would touch another person's food? On second thought, that's exactly what he had come to expect from people. Some jackass (most likely Jared in Content Development) would do something. Well, he didn't have time to worry about it. Five minutes until the team was required on a conference call. Against his better judgment, Garrett left the container open in the fridge and went on about the rest of his day.

Garrett's evenings after work were pretty routine. Most nights he'd order food (once a week he'd attempt to cook) and eat his meal at the dining room table in front of his laptop. Even though he didn't watch much television, he was an avid fan of internet shows. Anything from countdowns of the *Top 10 Prom Fails* to interviews of celebrities to full TV shows on a streaming service, he relished this time of the day where he could just relax and not think for a few hours.

One of his favorite shows was *Film Talk,* and after they had a brief period off air, he was eager to see their first episode back after their most recent publicity stunt.

The leftovers from lunch were calling to him so he went to the refrigerator and pulled out the plastic container of Pho. The lid still was temperamental, but it didn't matter. He poured the contents onto a plate and heated up his meal in the microwave. This was his evening, and a fine one at that, he thought. Indulging in his favorite shows online while eating his favorite food with no distractions, no interruptions, no outside world to invade his space. Just him and his laptop.

Halfway through the show, he noticed a rumbling in his stomach. At first, he thought it was just indigestion; perhaps he had too much soda. He had tried to swear off the sugar water for a long time but again tonight was one for indulgence.

"What the fuck?" he muttered as he clutched his side, a crippling spasm causing him to arch forward in his chair.

He sucked in a few deep breaths, hoping the pain would subside in time and the breathing would help minimize his anguish. It seemed to work. After a few seconds, it was over.

Returning to his laptop, he thought to open another window while letting the *Film Talk* show play in the background. Social media: a pleasure and a pain to him. While he enjoyed talking to his friends and seeing the milestones they shared, he also cringed at every nonsensical political debate, self-serving meme, and badly constructed joke that littered the timeline.

But there was a post from Lauren, sandwiched between the latest tirade against the President and another video of a cop assaulting a minority. Damn, she was beautiful, he thought.

The post itself wasn't anything revealing or intriguing, just a comment on her workout and how tired it had made her. Why wasn't she talking about him? Why was there no sadness here? Did she care at all or was she just moving on with life as if he didn't really matter?

"Damn," Garrett muttered as he moved the mouse over the messaging icon, his finger stopping just short of clicking it.

Why not send a message? It'd be rare, for sure, that he'd send anything online. She was quite familiar with his lack of communicating in this medium. He was still a phone person, even in this new era of online social interaction and despite his career being in the technology field. Human interaction was still paramount to him. Hearing another person's voice, the inflections, the sighs and gasps, the coughs, and grunts, it made it real. Emails and instant messaging were a construct of that, and hid so much of what the author was really saying.

The spasm in his stomach shot back again, doubling him

over the dining room table to the point he nearly smashed his head into his laptop. The pain shot through his thigh, down to his knee, and stopped in his right foot. It felt as if a spike was in the ball of his foot, expanding and contracting in rhythm, ripping at the insides of his tendons and muscles with a reckless hunger.

Garrett sucked in a few breaths, trying desperately to regain any sense of composure. Panic began to set in as he realized whatever ailment he had contracted was much more than a stomach ache. Was it the food? Did this new Pho place poison him? If so, did they poison everyone else who ate there today?

"It'll pass. It'll pass," he kept repeating to himself.

After a few seconds, the pain did subside into a dullness; a quieted throbbing in his foot, still present but not crippling.

Reaching up to his forehead, Garrett wiped away a thick film of sweat and continued to gasp for breath. He needed to get out of the house and get himself to the hospital. At this time of night, he only had the emergency room to rely on. The last time he had done so was six years ago when he had a scary bout with pleurisy that nearly killed him. The staff didn't seem concerned about his pleas and cries at that time, he had no reason to believe they'd be any different this time. But what else could he do?

The cliché of a macho man who toughed out the pain was not part of his identity. If something needed professional help, he'd seek it out. No sleeping it off, no walking it off, he was getting in the car and getting as many drugs as they could pump into his system to keep from feeling that kind of agony ever again.

"Okay, okay ..." he muttered to himself, bracing his hands against the top of the dining room table before attempting to stand. "It's okay. Just need to get to the hospital. Shit, I'm never eating there again!"

Garrett tightened his abdomen in an attempt to minimize

the pain. Gently, he pushed himself up from the table to stand. To his satisfaction, there was no sharp pain. A relief! Taking a step proved to be an entirely different story.

The wrenching twisted every fiber of muscle and every cell of fat in his leg, to the point he thought it was broken. He howled in pain, clutching at his thigh. Whatever had invaded his body had taken root, and literally rooted him to the floor. He peered down at his throbbing foot through salty tears and realized he couldn't move it. A strange tingle spread across the soles of his feet and then back up through his calf. Garrett began to cry out again, realizing the infection had complete control of his leg, like a steel mesh of filaments pushing into the floor beneath while simultaneously crawling up his leg.

His socks prevented him from seeing what damage had been done. He had to know, he had to see. Using the fork he had eaten dinner with, Garrett tore at his sock, and after a few attempts, the seriousness of his predicament became frighteningly clear.

The skin of his foot was discolored, green and black, with open sores about the size of a pinhead in a honeycomb pattern, each one with a strand of bloody flesh glistening in the open air. Exposing the wounds to more oxygen only intensified the pain and increased their growth. He couldn't see the bottom of his foot but felt the nasty roots of this disease digging into the porcelain tiles, stretching beneath the surface, and anchoring him to that very spot, a place he had known as a sanctuary, now made a prison.

His phone was his only salvation now. There was no way for him to get out of the house and to a hospital. He'd need to call for help. His unreliable neighbors, who had made a reputation in the neighborhood for being busy-bodies, constantly spying on everyone else from the windows of their home, were on vacation. What a time for them to not be listening in to his activities through the wall (a practice he knew they certainly did with regularity). No one could hear him scream for help, even though the thought had crossed his mind. No, it was the phone or nothing.

Taking a minute to draw in a few breaths, Garrett reached back up towards the table top and grabbed his phone. He hadn't realized until now that his whole body was shaking, right down to his fingertips. It made the grip on the phone loose, and he dropped it. For a brief moment, a bolt of terror rushed through him, fearing he had damaged the device, but it was intact. Thank God for him buying the more expensive model and not the cheap one he had originally looked at.

"Emergency services. 9-1-1," he said while fumbling with the touchscreen.

It was ringing. Just need to get them to come out to the house.

Garrett waited as patiently as he could for the operator to pick up the line. Each ring was met with another stabbing pain throughout his abdomen and leg. All he needed to do was suck it up for a few more moments, and he'd at least know help would be coming. What was taking so long? Pick up the phone already!

"9-1-1, how can I help you?" came the soulless female voice.

"I need help! I need help now. There's something wrong with my leg—"

"Please state your emergency."

"I said, there's something wrong with my leg."

"Sir, we'll need to know what exactly is going on. Are you being attacked right now?"

"Attacked?" What a silly question to ask, Garrett thought. "No, I'm in pain on the floor of my kitchen."

"Sir, please state your emergency."

"I need help. Please! There's something wrong with my leg. It's some kind of ... well, I don't know what it is."

"Please hold for a second."

"No, wait!"

Garrett was treated to the most dispassionate form of elevator music he had ever heard in his life. The audacity of this woman to put him on hold when he had told her three times he was in pain! He wasn't even able to give out his address. Now, he'd have to wait for who knows how long until this bitch picked up the line again.

He kept telling himself to be patient. With every wave of excruciating pain that traveled up and down his leg, it became harder and harder to wait. Then, his intestines shifted, and he felt the troubling sensation of something else ripping away from his abdomen down his other leg. The damn thing was spreading and now threatening to take over his entire lower body.

"Come the fuck on!" he yelled at the phone.

The screen flashed briefly and then went completely black. An emptiness swelled inside Garrett has he quickly realized what was happening. He hadn't charged his phone since this afternoon, and it was shutting down, its battery depleted and with it his hopes for a quick rescue. He cursed himself for letting this happen. Hours ago, he had told himself to put the phone on the charger but brushed it off, waiting for later in the evening to do it after he watched his show. Always, after the show. It was one of those moments where if he could have kicked himself for his procrastination he would have. He knew, he just knew, it would come back to bite him, he just had no idea it would be something this insane.

What made it worse was the charger was a good distance from him on the other side of the room. The smooth, white plug was already in the wall socket with the long charger cord dangling from it, mockingly within a two-second walk from the table, but here on the floor without the use of his legs, it might as well have been in China.

The infection was not going to be upstaged by an uncharged

phone and sent a series of stabbing pulses up from Garrett's feet, through his thighs and groin, and into his lower intestines. The sensation was so sudden and so violent he couldn't control himself and his recently eaten dinner came rushing up through his esophagus, burning the inner linings of his throat, and spilling onto the kitchen floor in a sloppy stream of brown liquid and irregularly shaped chunks. The stench caused another reaction. Pho was not the best smelling food coming back up after being half dissolved, and the odor was so profound it made Garrett involuntarily cut off airflow through his nose, which with the vomiting, shut off any air intake to his system. Once he realized this, he tried to breathe again through his nose, but the confluence of actions was so extreme he couldn't, nor could he stop throwing up, and he feared he would suffocate before his stomach was emptied.

Pinpricks of light started to develop around the corners of his vision, his head felt as if someone was grinding their knuckles on his temples, and his eyes welled with tears. He coughed up the last bits of food and fluid onto the floor and took in a desperate gulp of air. A few more breaths, shorter but just as needed, finally calmed his system. Casually, he wiped off a few chunks of food and strands of saliva from under his chin as he surveyed the mess before him. He hadn't realized he had eaten so much, or better yet, that so much food had yet to digest in his system. The puddle of puke was still slowly expanding across his polished floor as Garrett took a perverse fascination with his own discharge.

It was one of those things he was sure other people did: look at their vomit. Try to decipher what chunks were made up of what food he had eaten today. Yes, it was gross, but it took his mind off the pain in his lower half for a few moments.

As much as he wanted to charge the phone, it would take way too long the way this growth was progressing through his body. There needed to be another option and there was. His laptop was still open on the table above him so he mustered as much strength as he could to push himself off of the floor and back into the chair. He regretted now not working out more, his upper body strength was barely enough to get his overweight body from floor to seat. But, he did it. Sweating profusely now, Garrett opened a new window in his web browser and connected to his social media account.

Twenty of his friends were online. A red dot signaled as such next to the small thumbnail of photos beside each of their names in his list of contacts. He hated using this website and rarely posted, but if it was good for anything now would be the time to be useful.

As if the growth knew what he was up to, it crawled further up his body from his lower intestines now throughout his digestive system, filling the space he had emptied onto the floor earlier. The pain was so intense he could barely type with his left hand, and eventually let it fall to his side, opting to type with the right. He managed to get out one single message on his timeline: help!

It was done. Now, he just needed to wait for a response. Someone would see it. Someone would respond. They had to.

"I don't give a fuck about what the President did today," he muttered in anguish as he scrolled through what his active friends were posting about online.

Everyone had become a political pundit now. Their thoughts and attention were targeted to commentary on Washington D.C. and the current occupant of the White House. It was trivial nonsense, Garrett thought. None of these people knew a lick about what was happening behind the scenes and were just regurgitating what they had heard from paid pundits whose main goal was to get people agitated, so they continue to watch, listen, and repeat.

Hopefully, one of them would veer away from making grand proclamations online about equality, liberty, fairness, and rights to see something they could actually help with. Five minutes had passed now, and the fact that no one had responded – not one like, comment, or instant message – started to anger him.

What the fuck? Was he invisible? Did they even see this post? They're all online, the little red dot says so. They were just ignoring him, that's what it was. No one gave a shit about actual grief, just that which is so removed from them that they actually don't have to do anything about it.

"This is a waste of time," he said.

Another option presented itself. He had never used an online phone service before, but this would be the time to do so. If he could contact the police or the hospital he could get them here just as if he used 9-1-1.

Unfortunately, the options online were buried under so many procedures of sign-ups and credit card information that getting a phone service would take way too long. The growth was numbing his right leg now, and the sensation was spreading rapidly. He needed help immediately.

Forget the phone service, he thought. Just go to the website of the nearest hospital. Typing with one hand was becoming tedious now, and he struggled to hit the right keys. Then, a mistake in his search. He had spelled the name of the hospital wrong and instead was receiving search results for Madison Country Golf Course instead of Madison County General Hospital. For God's sake, why was this so difficult? As a programmer himself he started to curse the developers of this search engine and how over-intuitive they made it. He retyped his search request and hit the Enter key.

Finally, the correct results were on screen. He clicked on the first listing and entered the website for Madison County General Hospital. What a terrible design he thought, it was about a decade outdated and had a navigation system that would confuse anyone. Just click on the phone number. Where the hell was it?

"I'm going to die sitting here at this table. Come the fuck on!" he yelled.

At the bottom of the page were the words "contact us". He eagerly clicked on it and waited for the next page to load. Another shot of pain surged through his leg, doubling him over again in anguish as his vision blurred. Garrett blinked twice before being able to see straight again. The website had played yet another trick on him. There was no contact number here, just a litany of paragraphs describing the service the hospital provided, where it was located, and various departments in a long list. If he didn't need his laptop, he would have thrown it against the wall.

Garrett turned his attention back to his foot which was black in color now from the bruising, internal bleeding, and the throbbing network of webs the Growth had formed under his skin. He could only imagine the sight under his pants and shirt. No, to look at it now would make him panic. He didn't need to panic. He needed to get the hell out of this house.

At this point, even though the pain he suffered was debilitating he had been able to manage it to where he could function and move without collapsing. Or so he hoped. The only problem was the Growth had weaved itself into the floor beneath his foot and he'd have the same problem as before. He couldn't go anywhere unless he broke the connection. He'd have to pull his foot as hard as he could to rip the fleshy web free.

Now, Garrett wasn't an idiot. He knew full well that doing such a thing would cause him more pain than he could ever imagine, but it would subside over time, and he'd be free to leave and get help. There was no choice. He couldn't wait for his friends to step out of their social media bubble to realize he actually needed help nor could he spend another hour trying to figure out the convoluted workings of the hospital's website to contact anyone. No, it was this, or he'd certainly die at his dining room table over the stench of his own vomit. Not at all how he imagined going out.

Let's start with the heel. Garrett gently lifted his Achilles and then the back bulb of his right foot. A bit of a strain but his foot was mostly numb. He dared to push a bit further, arching up on the balls of his foot. The sickening squish of moist flesh and diseased strands of the Growth made him cringe, the same sound he knew from slowly opening his mouth just a thousand times more disturbing. At least he wasn't in pain anymore. He could do this.

"Keys, where are my keys?" he asked himself.

Over on the coffee table in the other room, he spotted his car keys. It was a straight shot from here to the coffee table and the front door. He visualized himself doing it, making the escape, hobbling perhaps but getting himself to relief. How he'd manage to drive with two numb feet was a question for later. Right now, he needed to move.

With one deep breath, he pushed himself to stand. A slight pain pulsed in his stomach but it wasn't too bad. Okay, he thought, here we go. Just go slow and easy, then when he felt the tension, rip his foot free. Lift the back of the foot, press down on the balls of his feet and arch up on his toes. The process was working so far. Now, lift the foot. He had glued himself when he was a kid to a wood block with super glue in school. He couldn't help but remember that now as he continued to feel the resistance the Growth was giving him. It was now or never. Garrett flexed his thigh muscles and with one single motion lifted his foot violently from the floor.

Oh, how he immediately regretted this decision.

The webbing of the Growth in his internal body was so extensive that his attempt to free himself sent an indescribable shock wave of anguish through every fiber of his leg, intestines, and groin. It was as if he had been sliced along the inside and outside of his leg with a razor blade, kicked in the balls by a mule repeatedly, and stabbed with a rusty nail multiple times in the stomach. And the pain was not stopping. The Growth was going to make him pay for attempting to escape.

Garrett's foot slammed back into the floor upon his defeat which accompanied a deafening crack. His bones shattered from ankle to kneecap. The last thing he saw was a spinning blur of his kitchen as he crumbled to the floor, succumbing to the pain and the blissful nothingness of unconsciousness.

When Garrett regained consciousness, it took him a few moments to orient himself. Perhaps that was all just a dream, a terrible dream that felt entirely too real. There was no pain he could feel right now. Beside his face was his cell phone which he grabbed immediately. The screen was still black, and in its reflection, he saw the grim reality returned to him. His face was bruised from the fall, his cheek swollen and his eyes bloodshot.

So, it wasn't a dream. Garrett looked down at his lower body disappointedly and saw the results of time on the Growth. It had taken over his entire body. His right foot, still anchored to the kitchen floor through filaments of rotten flesh and decay, didn't resemble anything human anymore. It was a pus riddled mess of tissue, like an open tumor, throbbing as the Growth continued to work itself beneath the surface. He opened his shirt to expose his chest and confirmed his fears that whatever it was had entered his lungs, liver, and rib cage. His heart still pumped and appeared to not be affected. Was it possible this alien invader knew better than to stop what kept its host alive?

As disturbing as these new wrinkles in his imprisonment were, it wasn't the only activity that had transpired while he slept. A trail of liquid extended from the pool of vomit towards the living room as if something had crawled from it and pulled its loathsome carcass from its afterbirth into the rest of the house. Garrett's eyes followed the green-black trail but could see no further than the couch. Whatever it was had made it to the door, fumbled with trying to escape, and then took a detour behind the couch. Where it was now, he had no idea.

"Hello?" he called out, a mixture of hope and apprehension that there'd be a response. "Is someone there? Hello?"

Nothing.

"I have to do something," he cried, the tears welling as he realized this nightmare was not going to have a happy ending unless he found a way out.

Any attempt to use the laptop to call for help was thwarted as he saw what remained of it smashed into pieces on the floor. Either he knocked it over when he fell earlier, or whatever monstrosity that had emerged from the pool of vomit had done so. No trails leading that way, so it was likely Garrett himself. Back to the phone charger, he thought.

Ten feet at this point in time was an unbearable distance. In order to get to his phone charger, he would have to crawl along the floor and then pull himself up to the countertop where it was. Not to mention he still needed to find a way to move that far without causing the insane amount of pain he felt before by trying to rip his diseased leg from his Growth-created moorings.

He took a minute to think about his next move. As soon as there was a strain on that leg, he knew the pain would increase tenfold. He couldn't handle that again. But that was the only way, and even with all the effort he put in before, the Growth showed no signs of being damaged. It was as connected to the floor as ever, and in what Garrett could only assume had been hours since he blacked out, it was likely the diseased roots had gone deeper and taken a stronger hold of the subfloor.

It was then that the kitchen knife had caught his eye. It was the only thing besides the laptop he had that could be used. No, he couldn't do it. If he chopped his foot off, he'd bleed to death, and God only knew what kind of reaction that would trigger from the Growth.

Once again, Garrett confronted the fact that there were no other options, no deus ex machina to save him. It was the only thing he could do to ensure he'd be able to move. He was betting (or hoping) that the phone would charge just enough for him to make a phone call before he bled out, and this time not to be held online by 9-1-1.

As if it read his mind, and by this point, Garrett wouldn't be surprised if it could, the Growth crawled up his back, extending its poisoned web into his shoulders and the base of his skull. The pain of a hundred migraines shot from the back of his head to the front of his forehead, a shock so violent Garrett thought his eyes would pop from their sockets.

That was it. The foot had to go.

Fighting through the anguish, Garrett pulled himself along the floor with his arms – his legs now nothing more than dead weight – and reached up to grab the knife from the kitchen table. He looked it over, again his beaten reflection staring back at him from the cold tempered steel. The sweat of his palms made his grip loose on the tool, but he readjusted twice, making sure his hold on it was firm.

He raised his arm above his head, his breathing becoming more intense with each inch the blade was lifted. The time for second thoughts was now. Maybe he should stop, maybe there was something else he could do? No. Fuck this. It was now or never.

With a panicked scream, Garrett lowered the blade into the fleshy part of his right leg, just above the ankle. He felt the slightest of twinges in his leg, but there was little pain to speak of. That was somewhat of a relief, although the image of his diseased flesh oozing liquids the colors of which he didn't have words for proved far more distressing.

Again, he hacked away at the meat. The knife dug in deep this time and got stuck, hitting bone, and not wanting to let go of it. Garrett wrenched the tool free and watched the results. There was a wilting to the Growth there. The webbed network of the invader withered and dried as it released a sickening perfume of rot.

Further encouraged by this reaction, Garrett screamed again as he repeatedly struck at his leg with a viciousness he never knew he possessed. With every strike, he gained more confidence, his wild-eyed expression exaggerating with every hack until there was little bone left to cut through. A few more blows and that'd do it.

He could feel the Growth moving through the rest of his body, now abandoning the leg entirely and opting to take up new residence in his scrotum. A sudden tug there caused him to stop momentarily. Garrett didn't care, the pain here made his eyes water again, but he had come too far now. Just a few more strikes and he'd be free.

It took four, and on the last swipe he broke through the bone of his leg and felt a sudden shock up from his balls through his spine and to the back of his head. He dropped the stained knife in the muck of vomit and collapsed. He spread out across the floor on his back, wet with sweat.

"Can't ... stop ... here," he said, looking up now at the phone charger that was now reachable.

A rush of blood and fluid started to pour from the wound in his leg. The jagged cut was being invaded by the Growth. Knowing now that the attack was over, it was attempting to re-establish an anchor in the ground. The pulpy filaments of the virus found nothing but air, twisting and twitching from the fresh wound.

Garrett inched closer and closer to the charger. As he got within arm's length, he began to laugh uncontrollably.

"I beat you! I beat you!" he started screaming.

Gripping the phone between his teeth, Garrett forced his way up to the countertop and rested on his arms once he had. Blood was draining from his body, and the effects were starting to show. His lips started to quiver, a chill was surging through his body, and worst of all his hands were shaking. He'd need to steady them to plug the phone in.

It took a few attempts, but Garrett managed to insert the charging cord into his phone. At last! He then relaxed as much as he could against the countertop and waited for the gadget to work its recharging magic. One-minute tops.

From here he could see the rest of the kitchen that he couldn't before. In particular, the clock on the microwave oven. It was two in the morning. It had been four hours since he collapsed.

The white light of the cell phone illuminated his bruised face, and excitedly he picked it up. Surely, in four hours someone had seen his message and tried to contact him. He'd just have to wait for the message system to boot up and then call back.

There was nothing. No messages on his phone, no instant messages on his social media account, not a single response to his posting, nothing at all. Garrett's heart sank as he closed and reopened the apps on his phone, hoping each time that something had gone wrong and he just needed to wait for them to refresh. Still, there was nothing.

Most of the same friends who were listed as online before were still there, and many had posted since he had put out his message. Not a single one mentioned him. Not a single one showed concerned over whatever his message of help was. With over two thousand people he was connected to through this social platform, his howl for assistance had gone totally ignored, and he had never felt lonelier in his entire life.

His first instinct was to call 9-1-1 again and get an operator on the phone. He dialed away and this time got an answer immediately. Before he could give out his information, his speech began to slur. The trembling in his hands forced him to drop the phone. As it clattered to the floor of the kitchen, he followed suit, letting all of his muscles relax so he could just plop down in a heap, watching the minutes of the call tick by on the phone's screen as the operator continued to ask how she could assist him. He wanted to speak, and tried to form a few words, but all he could manage were a few mumbled pleas for help. Deep down inside though, he didn't really want help.

The loneliness had taken hold of his rational mind, which was already under siege from blood loss and hours of torturous pain. He had fought and fought but for what? He sent a call out to the expansive and endless world wide web, and it was heeded by no one. What was the point? The part of him that just wanted to slip into a quiet sleep took over, and his eyes began to flutter as the 9-1-1 operator finally gave up on the call and disconnected.

"Why not ... why bother ..." he mumbled as the chill he had felt earlier turned into freezing cold. "No one cares. No one fucking ... cares."

A crash came from the living room, but Garrett was too drained of life to turn his head to see what had caused it. Certainly, it was the vomit creature, now come to make a meal of him. Again, what did it matter? At least he'd make the news when the stench of his body became too much in a few days for his neighbors or mailman to take. He had dabbled with the concept of his own death a few times before this; wondering who would be affected, what they would say at his funeral, what secrets they would confess to his prone body as it lay in a coffin at the wake. It seems he'd find out.

Just as his eyes closed, for what he thought would be the last time, the phone vibrated against the floor. It took what little strength he had left to open his eyelids but force them open he did. There on the phone was the number and picture of his beloved, Lauren, her avatar his favorite photo of her. She smiled at him, her gentle face a mix of affection and understanding. Damn, she was beautiful.

He had to talk to her. His arms had to move, his fingers needed to touch the screen and answer. There was too much he had to tell her. He was going to die but he wanted to hear her voice, and he wanted her to hear his apology before the Reaper claimed him. As he reached out to touch the screen and answer her call, the Growth sent another spasm up his spine and through his brain. His arm wrenched backward behind him, his body contorting in such a way that he was now facing the living room.

The phone stopped vibrating. The picture of Lauren faded from the screen.

Before Garrett's eyes shut for the last time, he saw what had emerged from his spewage. The creature was grotesque, but its form was familiar. In fact, he knew exactly what it was. A shriveled humanoid bearing his face with every bit of sadness and regret etched in perpetuity, glaring back at him as if to bid him farewell. He laughed, one tiny chuckle, before his eyes rolled into the back of his head and he expelled his last breath.

Postmortem IV

Neither the angel nor the demon knew which one of them could claim the card. The soul sat on the table between the two of them, exhausted and depleted, small motes of dark energy lifting from its surface and disappearing in clusters of light above the table.

In some respects, the soul could be seen as redeemed, having confronted his personal failures and understanding the mistakes he had made in life that ultimately lead to his death. In another sense, it could be said that Garrett gave up and allowed his life to end, which would be tantamount to suicide.

Both were a stretch, which made it hard for either the demon or the angel to rightfully claim the soul. They debated the topic for some time before continuing the game.

"At this point," the angel said, "I'd be more than happy to let this one go to purgatory and chalk it up as a tie."

"You would?" the demon grunted in response, puffing away

on a newly lit cigar.

"As hard as I tried, we both know that he was not going to call his friends. He relied on the internet to connect with people instead of doing it directly."

"You're assuming his friends would have answered. Believe me, I saw to it that they wouldn't have."

The angel tossed her golden hair back over her shoulder. The glittering stones embedded in her cheeks reflected the harsh light of the lamp that hung overhead. To Omar, it could have been any kind of light from the sun to the moon. The angel was an exquisite design of feminine beauty, her eyes sparkling as she negotiated her position to the demon.

"So you've basically sabotaged this entire hand," she stated, her lips pursed as she realized that there was really nothing she could do to win this hand outright. "I can't let you claim it either."

"Why the fuck not?" the demon shot back.

"You know the rules of this game. The humans have to be able to choose their way out of the situation. If you eliminate the choice, then it's not up to them, it's up to you."

"They wouldn't have answered anyway. Those people are so self-consumed, especially that poor bastard's friends—if you can call them that. He would have deteriorated on that floor for weeks, and none of them would have cared except when he didn't show up for work for a week."

"The girl cared."

"We're arguing in circles," the demon broke the stalemate. "I agree. Chalk it up as a tie and throw his ass in limbo."

What a harsh way to handle someone's eternal soul. Omar felt like speaking up but still knew his place at the table. But it still enraged him; discarding someone into the abyss of nothingness as if they were some defective toy that neither of these creatures wanted to play with anymore. The angel agreeing to this was especially disturbing to Omar. For all her beauty, the elegance of her wings and the flawless texture of her skin, there was no heart there that he could see. No championing of the human species or their plight on the earth. Only the game—that's all that mattered to her.

"Next hand?" she asked politely, taking the game cards from the previous hand and flinging them off the table.

Setting his smoking cigar aside, the demon took the fresh pile of cards and shuffled them extensively. The monster peered through squinted eyes towards Omar. What the hell was he thinking now? With every hand, the monster appeared increasingly agitated by Omar's mere presence. Trying his best not meet eyes with the demon, Omar slumped in his chair and lowered his head to the ground.

With a smirk and a huff, the demon released the human from his intense gaze. The cards had been shuffled enough. Time to see what this next hand unveiled. The demon placed seven cards down in the middle of the table (Omar was still unclear as to why the number of cards displayed changed each hand, but he wasn't about to ask).

Both of the eternal spirits observed what had been dealt. The players shrugged at the upturned cards, each seemingly okay with what they were playing for. Even though Omar didn't know the details, he could tell by two of the seven cards played—one a ghastly piece of art featuring a lone human soul, and the other with the image of a brain encircled in the symbol of an atom—that this next hand would mesh opposites. How ironic for a game for souls to be played around the man-made construct of science.

The Hitchcock Algorithm

The winding road that lead up into the mountains of Bogata didn't do anything to calm Rebecca's fear of heights. The railings along the side of the narrow two-way street were flimsy and she feared the slightest miscalculation would send the car over the cliff and her to a dramatic death, something she wasn't too keen on no matter how beautiful the Bogota River was.

This was exactly why Keisha was driving. Unlike Rebecca (known as Bex to her friends) this wasn't the first time Keisha had been to Colombia and not her first attempt to navigate a roadway high in the cliffs. She quite enjoyed the experience, being part daredevil and part pragmatist, both sides resigned to the notion that if she were to die in some freak accident, it was meant to be and there wasn't really anything she could do to stop it.

No matter how many times Keisha told Bex to look at the scenery, her passenger curled up in a ball and looked in the opposite direction, caring not for the breathtaking view of the forest-covered mountainside or the heavy mist that clung to the basin below. She was scared. The sooner they reached their destination the better. After a few failed attempts, Keisha thought it best to distract her passenger with reportage over reverence.

"So, I have a new case when we get back home," Keisha informed her friend. "It's one of the craziest things I've ever heard of."

"Do tell," Bex responded, happy for anything to distract her from the road.

"It sounded like a typical worker's comp case. Some big corporation our firm has under retainer had an issue with one of its employees who was hurt. Standard stuff, right? Well, not so much. The guy was a programmer who got sick from something he ate."

"How is that their fault?"

"His friend claimed that it was something in the refrigerator at the office that leaked into his lunch—some leftovers from a restaurant. The guy took it home, ate the leftovers, and then got violently ill. They tried to pin it on the restaurant but they threw that shit right back in their face, claiming no other patrons had gotten sick ever from their food. It didn't help that the guy's friend took a picture of the refrigerator the same day, showing how there was some funky sludge inside it. She did it to complain about how disgusting the frig was, later it turned out to be evidence. The container that leaked the sludge was part of some product they were testing."

"How's the guy doing?" Bex asked, her interest now piqued. "I bet he's suing for all he can."

"Not really. He's dead."

"Shit."

"Yeah. The family is trying to get millions. Needless to say, my hands are going to be full when I get back home."

Bex milled over the situation in her head while fiddling with the radio. She had a soft side for victims. In fact, many of her friends had tagged her with the SJW (Social Justice Warrior) label because she would always take the side of anyone who claimed mistreatment from a corporation or any group that was in power. She was a teacher though; far away from the legal battles and court drama that Keisha's job was wrapped up in. The two were at odds often about Keisha's work. Bex wanted a bit more compassion but Keisha, being the pragmatist, thought it better to get paid defending those who would win court cases than be poor defending those that would lose.

It wasn't the only thing they had in common. This trip was based on a much deeper connection the two women had, one that stretched back before they even knew each other.

"So, what do you think she wants?" Bex asked, still trying to find a station on the radio.

"It could be anything. The woman's a nut, you know that right? I never really understood what he saw in her. Maybe she was a freak in bed, who the hell knows."

"Oh, we're not going to compare sex stories are we? That's kind of creepy."

Keisha laughed at the thought, "No, I'm not that crass. At least not without a few drinks in me. Besides, I don't think either of you could compare."

Bex turned her eyes to Keisha in astonishment. She couldn't believe she had implied something so unladylike. Keisha held a straight face for as long as she could before laughing which was enough to draw the same reaction out of Bex. Both covered their mouths—a tick they both had when laughing hysterically—yet another thing they had in common.

"Seriously, why do you think Serenity asked us out here?" Bex asked, now feeling a bit more comfortable.

"Honestly, I couldn't tell you, Bex. I mean, we can pretty much assume it has something to do with Oscar."

Ah, the other thing they all had in common.

"I know," Bex mused, her mind now off into the realm of memories.

Keisha noticed her friend's distraction and patted her on the knee to bring her back out of her melancholy. "Don't get all sad on me. Look, we all dated Oscar, his passing was unexpected so I'm sure she just wants some company. For her, it's all very fresh, you know. I dated him four years ago. And you it was, what, six years or so?"

"Yeah, six years."

"Right. They were together when he passed. At least I think they were. I mean, the girl is weird, no doubt. We've all seen what she was like last summer; ranting and raving about all that nerd science shit her and Oscar were into."

"Well, at least they bonded on that level," Bex countered. "I never understood half the stuff he was talking about. It sounded interesting but it also sounded very complicated and, I don't know, it just wasn't for me."

"Me neither!" Keisha said with conviction. "I make no bones about it. Oscar was a dork but he was a hot dork, and there was just something about him that was appealing. You know what I'm talking about. But in the end, we are all friends, even though we shared the same dick."

Bex cringed at the bluntness of Keisha's analysis.

"You don't like the word *dick*?" the driver asked.

"I don't have a problem with it. It's just—"

"Too soon?"

"No."

"Too much?"

"No, I—"

"Come on, Bex. You know that's how I am. I mean, what did you call it? His cock?"

"Keisha!"

"Weiner? Wee wee? His pump stick?"

Bex couldn't help but laugh at the last one.

"No, none of those," she said.

The car went quiet while Keisha waited for Bex to tell her. The answer wasn't coming and Bex clearly didn't want to continue. That wouldn't do. Keisha wanted an answer, and an honest one.

"Bex. What was it? Come on, tell me," Keisha said, smiling gleefully.

"Rawhead," Bex answered, in almost a whisper.

"Rawhead!" Keisha repeated with such an outburst of shock and humor that she almost choked. "Was it because he wasn't circumcised?"

"Well, that and ... he liked this book. God, I've never told anyone this before! It was from some author he thought was a genius. The name kind of stuck one night when he made me watch the movie version of it. Terrible film. But, I read the book and it kind of fit his personality."

"What kind of book?"

"Horror. Real visceral kind of stuff."

"You read something like that?" Keisha asked. "I wouldn't take you for a horror fan. But, the movie was terrible?"

"Rubbish."

"A shame. I would have watched the movie. I sure as fuck ain't reading the book."

As they approached the address given to them, the road

made one last turn to reveal a lonely building sitting just off to the left, peering out over the edge of a cliff. The rushing waters of the Bogota River could be heard splashing against the rocks far below. On the other side of this great chasm was a roaring waterfall, the hints of a rainbow appearing and disappearing between it and the hotel.

Keisha noticed the empty parking lot. Not one single car, truck, or van to be seen, just the decayed concrete and weather worn painted yellow lines by hands that had long since forgotten their work here. She parked the car and both women carefully exited, embracing their surroundings. *Such a warm day* she thought as the sun's heat gently touched her face.

Bex was less enamored by the scenery, still fearful of how close they were to the edge of the cliff with no protection from a fatal fall except her own willingness to stay far away from any such possibility.

The exterior of the hotel, called *Cascada de Tequendama*, was a mixture of stone architecture from centuries past with a heavy dose of modernism injected. What had once been a hotel and a museum now sat as a private building owned by a think tank of unknown donors. At least, this was as much as Keisha was able to find out about the place from her law firm. How Serenity wound up being the sole occupant here was the first of many mysteries she wanted answered.

"It's a bit creepy," Bex stated as they passed under the arches of the front door. "It's like a hipster took over a castle."

The interior confirmed Bex's assessment. While the outside looked weathered and elegant, the interior was sleek and sterile. It was obvious that heavy renovations had been made here; the lighting was recessed in the ceiling behind sleek metal panels, the walls were solid sheets of white marble dotted every few feet with the same recessed lighting behind vertical panels, the furniture here all was organic in shape and while beautiful to the eye seemed like they'd be uncomfortable to actually use. The floor itself was wood with circular panels of light cut into it, making a pathway from the front door to other rooms within the building.

"Well, someone spent a lot of money on this," Keisha mused. "How in the world did she manage to set this all up?"

"Such an odd contrast," Bex added as she walked to one of the few paintings that hung on the wall between the black panels. It was Wassily Kandinsky's *Composition VI*. A remarkable reproduction that she felt compelled to touch, wanting to place her hands on the canvas to feel the texture of each brush stroke and the thickness of the lines. As she got closer to the painting she realized it wasn't a reproduction but in fact an original.

"Don't touch that," a calm but stern female voice came from the other end of the hall.

It was Serenity. The woman was as Keisha and Bex had remembered her from their last meeting over a year ago. Her red hair was tied back in a ponytail exposing the shaved sides of her skull and the detailed tattoos that wrapped around from temple to temple. As expected, she was dressed down in jeans that had seen better days and a black t-shirt of some obscure punk band that neither of them knew.

"It's Kandinsky," Serenity informed Bex.

"Yeah, I know who it is. It's the original?"

Serenity smiled in acknowledgment, seemingly proud of the painting as if she had created it herself.

"I didn't take you for a classical art fan," Keisha said, still standing by the entrance with bags in hand.

"Expressionist art actually. Yes, I'm not just some weird nerd, Keisha." There was a hint of condescension there but Keisha would let it slide. "But don't stand there, come on in. I was about to have lunch, are you two hungry? You should be hungry. It's a long drive from the airport."

"I could go for some food actually," Keisha confessed.

"Ah, but first ... come here ..."

Serenity extended her arms to both girls and brought them in for the most awkward of hugs. She was strong and her embrace nearly squeezed the breath out of both women. Bex and Keisha were a bit surprised by this but responded in kind.

♦

Serenity guided them through a brief tour of the former museum. The updated interior design extended throughout, every room bathed in the modern with a hint of the old dropped here and there in the form of paintings, sculptures, and the arched windows of the outer rooms. The dining room was the last stop on this quick tour of the main floor and the three women sat down for a bite to eat. Roasted chicken and rice were on the menu, the aroma of the bird and the accompanying scent of rosemary and thyme elevated Bex's appetite from slightly interested to mouthwatering.

"So, what's this all about Serenity?" Keisha asked, being less concerned with the meal and more with business. "You asked us here all the way from the States. Something about Oscar's last wishes?"

"Something like that," Serenity grinned as she popped a grape into her mouth.

Such a peculiar woman.

"Are you going to tell us or are we supposed to guess?" Keisha asked.

"Well, before we get to all that, I want to know that you're comfortable with this. And when I say *this* I mean talking about Oscar. You see, this building is where we've been working the last year before he died and what we do here is pretty damn confidential. I'm actually taking a big risk for even allowing you to be here."

"The rest of the staff will get upset?" Bex asked.

"There is no staff. It's basically just me. Every few days the groundskeeper comes by and there's Mariana who delivers food here every week, but besides that it was just Oscar and I here doing our work."

"What work?" asked Keisha.

"Ah ah!" Serenity waved her finger. "First things first. You know you can't discuss any of this. It's a condition of his will. If you do, anything left to you will be forfeit, agreed?"

Now, Keisha was well aware of the legal parameters around a Last Will and Testament so she was comfortable with keeping secrets. She was a lawyer after all and that was par for the course. Bex didn't quite understand what she was agreeing to here, or if she was going to agree to anything at all. This was already too cryptic for her tastes.

"I don't like this," she said. "And to be honest, I don't really need money or whatever it is Oscar left."

"Really?" Serenity said. "I know your finances, Rebecca. A teacher ... scratch that, a substitute teacher, living in a one bedroom apartment where you've been late on rent four of the last six months? Keisha had to pay your airfare here, right?"

Bex and Keisha threw each other concerned looks.

"How did you know that?" Bex asked.

"I have to. It's one of the perks for working for my bosses. And since we're being so honest with one another let me reassure you that this isn't some trap or game. We can't involve any outside people for this because of our research. Oscar made it clear that I could talk to you two, and only you two, about this in person. Not even his mother knows about any of this. So, I'm telling you both once again, you cannot speak of this to anyone, ever. If you can't do that, then I suggest you walk out now and I'll handle his last wishes in some other way."

What else could they possibly say? Yes, Serenity had the personality of a rattlesnake but this wasn't about her. It was about Oscar, who despite their differences they all loved in one way or another. Not to mention that Serenity had piqued their interest in this secret project she had been working on with Oscar for over a year. It was a piece of his life that he had hidden from them for so long, and even though they really didn't ever push the issue, they felt that there was this closed part of his life Serenity was allowed inside of but they were not. This was their chance to climb over the wall; pass beyond the veil and see what was on the other side. Ultimately, the value of that access outweighed whatever privacy issues they'd have to agree to.

"Sure, if you have some disclosure agreement or something for me to sign ..." Keisha answered.

"No need for that. You've already agreed on camera," Serenity said, nodding up and beyond Keisha and Bex at the far corner of the room.

The two guests turned to look in that direction and saw a tiny circular device just above the crown molding of the far wall. In fact, every corner of the room had one. It was a camera they surmised, the reflection of its lens just barely visible.

"How about you?" Serenity asked Bex who looked put-off by the realization she was being recorded. "Do you agree or should we find a way for you to get back to the airport?"

A tough question to answer. While her distrust of Serenity and her displeasure with mysteries in general made part of her mind want to leave, Bex's curiosity and attachment to Oscar made the decision for her. Sure, she was in a foreign country with no means of getting back to the airport on her own—no way was she driving a car on the winding road—but if Oscar wanted her here and had something to leave her, it was worth the inconvenience for a few days.

"I'm in," she said.

"Well, it's settled then. You two enjoy lunch, I have some things I need to attend to and we'll be able to get started. Your rooms are upstairs. Just leave the kitchen and take the first stairwell on your left or the elevator. Pick any room you want. Meet me down here in about an hour," Serenity instructed.

She stood from the table, took a moment to draw in a deep breath, and then left the room. Keisha and Bex stayed behind with their plates still full of food but neither of them felt like eating now. Neither felt like talking either, although there was plenty to say. Right now, they'd take Serenity up on her offer and move their luggage into the guest rooms upstairs.

In the hour that passed both Keisha and Bex had spent their time unpacking and trying to work through the mystery of this entire trip. What had been anticipated as a time to remember their fallen friend—an ex-boyfriend they had all shared and loved deeply—was now turning into a strange journey into the unknown part of Oscar's world that neither of them had been privy to before. And Serenity, what a piece of work this woman was.

Bex didn't mind Serenity's exotic taste in dress or the quirkiness of her character, but there was just a hint of madness to the redhead. It sat behind the eyes. They were a strange shade of blue, like forged steel catching the reflection of the sky.

Safety was Keisha's main concern. She spent her time checking the bedroom for listening devices, hidden cameras (outside the one that was in the top corner of her room in plain sight, she'd have to protest that later on), and any other devices that violated her privacy. Then again, she just agreed to have any rights to privacy, real or imagined, waived in order to stay here. How stupid, she thought. She was a lawyer after all. It was her job to know better than to agree to something like this. But it was done, and hell, this was for Oscar.

Serenity was waiting for them downstairs. Night had fallen

outside and the numerous geometric light panels that adorned the ceiling, walls, and floors of this building gave the interior of the former museum a warm feeling in contrast to the darkness outside. The tall windows of the dining area let in beams of silver light from the waxing crescent moon.

"Follow me, if you will. I'm excited for both of you to see," said their host, her smile now pleasant and less condescending.

Keisha immediately knew why as a pungent aroma caught her senses. An earthy musk clung to the air like a trail behind Serenity as she left the dining room, an odor she was well familiar with.

"You've been getting high while we were upstairs?" Keisha commented.

"She's what?" Bex said, apparently her senses were not as familiar with the scent.

"You can't smell that?" asked Keisha.

Bex shrugged. How innocent Keisha thought, little Bex had never smoked weed before. It actually fit her personality. Never one to drink excessively or curse without purpose, Bex had always been somewhat of a wallflower that only occasionally let a wild streak show. It was suspected that in her private moments with Oscar that wild streak did more than shine.

"So, you've been smoking weed this whole time? That's what you needed to attend to earlier?" Bex questioned the host.

"I've been smoking since before you two arrived. Don't worry, I smoke all the time. It calms my nerves and for the record, Ms. Lawyer," her gaze went directly to Keisha, "I have permission to do so by the law and my employers. It helps me focus."

Keisha's expression didn't show she was convinced.

"Whatever," Serenity said, now pulling out a joint from her

shirt pocket and lighting up freely in the house. "If it bothers you too much just let me know, but you won't be around me when we get down there."

Bex waved a cloud of smoke from her face, "Down where?"

"The lab."

"Okay, enough of the secrecy. What is this all about? What are we going to see down there?" Keisha asked.

Serenity stopped in the middle of the small corridor beyond, turned her head slightly while taking another puff of her joint. Inhaling deeply and exhaling with a measured confidence, she proudly answered, "Oscar's work."

♦

What Serenity had referred to as a lab looked more like a bedroom. To be more specific, it looked like Oscar's bedroom. Not one for material things, Oscar had lived simply and rarely changed the decor. Both Keisha and Bex recognized everything in here from the low-to-the-ground double bed from Ikea, to the small shelf that held his collection of books, to the painting on the wall, once again a Kandinsky, *Composition VIII*. The lighting in here was low, matching what they had known of him. Accent lights providing small blooms of yellow-white light above the headboard, over the nightstand, along the walls, and an odd piece of art that doubled as a lamp. Three plaster birds, carved with intricate detail, formed the base of the lamp with their open beaks upturned to a waiting egg that doubled as the light bulb.

Their host was not in the room with them. She said what was in there was for their eyes only, and in fact, her presence would ruin what Oscar had intended. More mysteries. Keisha was already apprehensive about the whole thing and being in Oscar's room just seemed inappropriate. The man had died and they all cared for him, but keeping this shrine of sorts went beyond boundaries of good taste.

Of course, cameras were in the room, nestled in the darkened corners with their little eyes focused on every movement the two women made.

"This is kind of sick, right? I mean, why the hell are we in this room that looks like Oscar's," asked Bex. "Is that door locked?"

Keisha went back to the entrance and checked. Although it was closed the door was not locked. She turned the knob and heard some sort of mechanism working in the walls. Within a few seconds, the door opened just an inch and let the cool air from outside in.

"No, we're not locked in here. I can't believe we're doing this."

"She said we'd know what we're looking for when we see it. I don't see anything. It's just Oscar's old stuff."

"He left something behind that only we would know. Just look around I guess. The sooner we're out of here the better."

Something caught Bex's attention at that moment. Out of the corner of her eye she saw movement, a flicker of something just off behind the bed. Once she turned completely in that direction, whatever it was had gone. She put her hand to her eyes and rubbed them. Perhaps it was the toll of the trip or all the questions swimming in her head but she had become lightheaded. *Get it together*, she told herself.

Keisha tugged at her sleeve, drawing Bex's attention back to the bed. It wasn't a figment of her imagination, there was something there. At first it was an outline, flecks of some shape dimming in and out of the low lights in the room. Then, a line, and another shape. The shapes then connected, creating an outline of something similar, familiar, human. They witnessed the beginnings of a skull, then fingers, and a torso. As the face took shape, it confirmed what Keisha and Bex had suspicions: it was Oscar.

The shape didn't hold together well as some lines were enhanced and others barely visible. Was this Oscar's ghost? Had it been in this room all along? It didn't look like what they had expected from a spirit. No wisp of white light, no shadow staggering through three-dimensional space, this was a solid form and looked every bit of a man standing in the room with them, naked and strong. In life, Oscar had worn glasses, but this representation of him did not, nor did he have the long hair they had known him for. Instead, the apparition was nearly bald, about an inch of hair covering a cranium that continued to phase in and out of reality. His whole body followed suit, parts of him appearing as solid mass, muscle, skin, tissue while others disappeared in thin air as if he was a projection clinging to clouds of smoke to make himself visible.

"You're not afraid are you?" he asked as he approached the two women.

They both backed away. Keisha took a more defensive posture while Bex was stiffly shuffling her feet to move away from the spirit. How in the world could this thing ask if they were afraid or not? Of course they were! Here was the spirit, or some sort of facsimile, of their beloved ex-boyfriend walking towards them as if he was still flesh and blood.

"What the hell is this?" Keisha shouted, more for Serenity's ears than for Bex or this ghost.

"I understand you're startled," the ghost was trying it's best to calm her without advancing any further. "But you're in no danger here. Keisha, you know I'd never do anything to harm you."

"How the hell do you know my name?" Keisha snapped back. Her lower lip was quivering uncontrollably as she tried to muster up an image of strength yet failing to do so. "You're not Oscar. Oscar is dead."

"Well, you're half right. In a very true sense, I am dead from your perspective. But you are wrong that it is not me. At least,

I think I'd know if I was me or not."

"This is really sick!" Keisha was not going to be swayed by whatever illusion this was. "I'm not playing your fucking game, Serenity. I don't care what this is or how you did it, I'm leaving."

"Please don't ... my *Lady Boss*."

The phrase caught her mid stride as she was turning to the exit, but it was enough to keep Keisha from leaving. *Lady Boss*, it had said. She hadn't heard that term since the last night she spent with Oscar, years ago, in a luxury suite in New Orleans. The phrase—that term of endearment—and the subsequent memories that now flooded her mind, brought on paralysis in her system faster than any toxin could. After a few moments she managed to turn her head and look back at the spirit.

It smiled at her, half of its Oscar-like face translucent, but still showing the charming grin that she had known him for. Could it be possible? Was this really happening?

"How? Just ... how?" is all Bex could say.

Oscar turned to his other ex and started towards her, cautiously but assertive. The transitions of his body from solid to almost invisible came with such a grace and fluidity that it was a marvel just to watch him move. When his arms swayed they'd vanish in the light one second and reappear the next. When he stopped moving, the shifts in his visibility continued to flow around his body. Cloudy streaks seemed to pass through him, phasing in and out of sight as they connected and separated over and over in an endless hurricane of the solid meeting the ethereal.

"It's a long story," he spoke casually, as if none of this was strange. That was certainly an Oscar trait if there ever was one. "But I just want you two to know that this isn't some plot by Serenity. This was my work. This was our work, to be more accurate. I did pass on and now, through what we managed to uncover here over the last year or so, I can communicate with you."

"So, you're not really here? Is this some sort of computer program or AI or something like that?" Bex asked.

"No machines made me. It's ... well ... it's complicated. I know I say that a lot", another Oscar-ism, "but it would take too long to explain and I don't think this is the right time for you both to hear it. Just know that the whole point of you being here is to confirm that our research worked."

"Why us?" Keisha asked, now warming to the idea just a little. "Why do you need Bex and I to confirm that you're ... doing whatever it is you're doing? We aren't scientists, if you can even call this science."

"I don't understand any of this," Bex added.

Oscar darted his eyes back and forth at both women. He cocked his head to the side and took a few steps back himself.

"I can see it's going to take some time to convince you. But, that's the test now isn't it? You are both here because of all those who knew me, you two knew me best. You would know if this really was me. It's what I asked of Serenity before I left there and came here. My last wish, my last thoughts, my last request. I can only ask that you help her prove what I had worked half my life to realize."

Keisha was now more curious than outraged and wanted to know more. "And what is it that you want to realize?"

"Whether or not we managed to break the code of consciousness."

◆

After leaving the lab—or bedroom as it would now be more appropriately called by them—Bex and Keisha tried to find Serenity who had not told them exactly where she'd be observing the encounter from. It wasn't too hard to follow the trail of ganja smoke through the hallways to a balcony on the other end of the complex.

Serenity was leaning over the railing looking down at the pooling water of the nearby waterfall below. It was hard to see at night, especially one without a bright moon, but the sound of the falls crashing against the rocks below, the smell of the water in the air, the nocturnal animals and insects of the overgrowth in the cliffs forming all sorts of exotic calls in the night, all of it provided the most unique setting for a pot smoker to indulge in a late night puff.

"Tell me that's some sort of virtual reality projection or some shit like that," Keisha said.

Serenity turned around nonchalantly and grinned, "It's far more complicated than that."

"No games, Serenity. I want to know what that was."

"You know what it was."

"It can't be."

"It is."

"Stop! There's no fucking way that's Oscar's soul down there."

"Well," Serenity stopped to think about the question, looking up to the night sky as she took another puff of her joint. "Technically, you could be right and wrong. I can't quantify souls but I can quantify consciousness."

"Bullshit!"

Keisha turned away from Serenity in a huff, covering her face with her hands as she sought some relief on the other side of the balcony. Bex was less hotheaded but not without questions of her own.

"How did you do it?" she asked Serenity as inoffensively as she could.

Serenity scoffed at the question, turning away to look at the moon while taking another puff. This was theatrics. She wanted to tell them if for no other reason than to boast about her accomplishment. It was on her face, half turned upwards to the sky wearing a grin that showed that very pride.

"It would take me a month to catch you up to what all of this is based on and that's if you're able to follow it. I'm not trying to sound like a bitch here but seriously, it's extremely complicated and deals with science, and things others wouldn't consider science, to be able to do what Oscar and I were able to."

Bex called her bluff, "Well, explain it to me like I'd explain calculus to my fifth graders. They can't comprehend that level of math at their age but I can give them an idea on how equations work."

It was a reasonable request, mixed with some humility. She knew that would stroke Serenity's ego just enough: painting herself as a fifth grader and Serenity as the all-knowing expert.

"Perhaps some other time. Let us enjoy the night. It's beautiful out here," Serenity answered.

She wasn't wrong. The brilliant darkness of the night, with the sound of water crashing against the rock far below them and the silver of the crescent moon glittering off the waterfall across the giant chasm beyond provided the perfect backdrop for a night that had unveiled possibilities. The possibilities of life, the possibilities of the afterlife, and most of all, the possibilities of reconciliation.

"Give me that," Keisha muttered as she snagged the joint from Serenity's hand. She took a deep inhale and blew out a cloud of wispy grey-green smoke. Relaxed now, she quietly made peace with Serenity. She had much to ask of the strange scientist and being adversaries wouldn't answer any of her questions.

♦

The morning brought a clear sky, intense humidity, and a shift in perception for Keisha. Part of that was due to her and Serenity spending the prior evening getting stoned (Bex did not partake). Her raised curiosity over what she wanted to say to Oscar, given now that she believed slightly that this creation in the lab was indeed Oscar, drove the rest of her confusion. What did she really want to say to him? What would it take to prove that this was in fact his consciousness manifested and not some computer simulation?

Sleepily, Keisha made her way into the kitchen to get some juice and fruit for breakfast. Nothing solid, she didn't think her system could take it right now. Outside the giant windows she could see the groundskeeper tending to the weeds around her car. Too much equipment on him she thought. But what did she know about lawn care? The last plant she tried to grow died within two days. She would make a note to Serenity to keep the man away from her car. For some reason it didn't set right with her.

"He's not going to be here long," Serenity's voice came from behind the refrigerator, startling Keisha whose mind was on the groundskeeper.

"No," she stuttered. "It doesn't bother me. Well, yes it does. Does he have to be so near my car?"

"He's not going to steal it, Keisha."

"That's not what I was getting at. It's just ... well, you know it's a rental and all that equipment he has on him ..."

"He won't dent the car. He's a professional. But let's talk about more important things." For someone who smoked so much weed, Serenity was unusually sharp this morning. "Did you think about what you wanted to ask him today?"

"Well, I did give it some thought this morning when I woke up. I mean, in the courtroom there are ways to get people to reveal who they are, what they really mean, what they really feel. But, I'm not so sure you want me to approach this like Oscar's on trial."

"Why not?"

The question surprised Keisha. "I just think that would be too confrontational. This isn't a cross examination, this is just a way to see if he knows what Oscar knew."

"Have you never cross examined Oscar when you two were together? I'm sure you had an argument or a disagreement where you used your skills as a lawyer to get to the answers you wanted."

"But is that going to prove it's him?" Keisha's question was valid. How would her treating him like a suspect to a crime get anything but defensiveness? "Unless, of course, that will expose this whole thing for being a farce."

Serenity rolled her eyes. "It's not a farce," she said, annoyed at the topic being brought up again. "Look, last night you had a genuine reaction to this whole thing. Disbelief at first but then an understanding that this wasn't some sort of game. What I need—what Oscar needs—is for you to treat him the way you normally would. To see if he is who you knew him to be in life. Don't overthink it. Don't try to figure out how this is all working. Just have a conversation with the man we both loved."

◆

"So, we have a bit of a problem then," Oscar said well into his conversation with Keisha.

He sat at the edge of the bed in this recreation of his room while Keisha paced back and forth, her thumb against her chin while deep in thought. This time, she went in alone without Bex who was off with Serenity elsewhere in the building. This was just between Keisha and Oscar. It was the way she wanted it and even more so the way Serenity said it had to be.

"I guess we do," Keisha responded.

"You have to ask me questions to see if I respond in the way I did before. It's a complex problem, I know, I wrote the examination procedures."

"So if you did, why didn't you come up with a better way to test this?"

Oscar raised his hand to his face. It was phasing in and out of visibility with each passing moment. The smoky nature of his form still astounded Keisha who didn't dare get close enough to see whether it was as flimsy as she perceived it.

"It's part of the reason why I asked for you to be here. You specifically. That law degree had to be good for something besides cheating people out of money that insurance companies owed them."

Keisha noted the insult. "That's something Oscar would definitely say."

"But it's not enough for proof."

"No, it isn't. I have no idea whether or not you shared these things with Serenity before you died. She may have programmed them into whatever illusion this is. I have no way of knowing."

"Then, how do we prove that this is really me?" Oscar asked, more of a leading question than one he actually wanted to know the answer to.

"I'm not sure. But, it's not going to be from you throwing those insults at me the way Oscar did when he was alive. He never did like the fact that I was a lawyer."

"It wasn't that you were a lawyer that I didn't like. It's who you represented."

"That's right," Keisha said, now remembering numerous arguments they had in the past. "But again, Serenity would have known that."

Oscar stood from the bed and started towards Keisha. She stopped pacing and backed away. Seeing her unease, the apparition stopped advancing and instead stood in the dim light of the nearby table. The light was playing tricks here. Whatever fogginess was in the room was shifting his form into particles, as if he was made up of static from a television.

"Maybe you could tell me how this is done. Perhaps that would help me believe it a little more," Keisha was beginning her cross examination.

"It's complicated."

"That's what Serenity said last night. Try something less cryptic."

Oscar turned a sly smile to her, the same smile she had known him to use in life when someone caught him off guard intellectually. For her, that was often. She always suspected that was a main part of his attraction to her.

"Sure. Well, this room is filled with a certain mixture of gases and other particles, most of them so microscopic you'd never know they were there. Polonium, radon decay, elevated levels of rock particles, some ionized materials, a cocktail of its own that's coming through those vents."

He pointed up to the slits in the ceiling above Keisha's head. They were all over the room and for the first time she noticed the subtle hiss of the ventilation system gently pushing this cocktail, as he called it, into the space.

"Isn't that dangerous?"

"None of it will harm you. It's not much different than what the Hessdalen lights are made up of."

"The what?"

"Hessdalen lights. It's an unexplained light phenomenon in Norway people have been seeing for decades. Some think it's ghosts, others think it's UFOs, we know it's something different," Oscar explained, almost dismissive of the issue as if the specifics weren't relevant. "That was just a small part of our research. It's not what's happening here, but part of how those lights are formed is how this lab can allow me to manifest here."

"Isn't that dangerous?"

Oscar wagged his finger at her insinuation. "You're referring to the research that shows most people who think they see ghosts are suffering from some level of carbon monoxide poisoning. No, there's no carbon monoxide in the cocktail. That would more likely put you over here with me."

"And where is over there?" Keisha asked. She had started her pacing again, keeping an eye on Oscar as she did and watching the shift in his form as she circled around him like a witness on the stand. "Can you describe it to me? What do you see?"

"It's the same but different. Everything is really quiet here. Still. Except when I come to this room, then it's all brought into sharp focus, like having bad eyesight and then being given the right prescription of eyeglasses."

"Who else is there?"

"That's ... complicated."

"You're favorite word," she noted. "Are you afraid to tell me certain things because she will hear?"

Keisha nodded to the cameras in the room. Oscar waved them off.

"Serenity really can't see or hear anything. Well, not really. All she's really seeing is you standing in this room, pacing back and forth, talking to some static and hearing a few fragments of what I say. It's like those EVP's: whatever I'm saying sounds like broken words hidden behind layers of white noise."

"She can't decode it?"

"She can, that's part of what the Hitchcock Algorithm does, but it takes a long time and she can't do it live. Besides, that's not what this is about anyway."

"Right."

The conversation had stalled. Neither of them really knew where to go now. Keisha had a whole list of questions in her head but none of them were going to get them anywhere. This ghost, or perhaps this AI fueled illusion, was too good at mimicking Oscar's personality, right down to his tendency to bite his lower lip when he was trying to come up with something to say.

"I know," he broke the silence. "Ask me something about how we broke up."

"What?"

"Go ahead. Ask me something I would know about how we broke up that I wouldn't have told anyone else. If anything could prove it, it would be that."

"I don't want to talk about that."

"Why not?"

"Because, I just don't."

"That's why you're here."

"No, I'm here because I thought you had left something behind in a will for me. I certainly did not come for this!"

"Keisha, you're not listening. I want to talk about how we broke up."

There was something strange about how he phrased this, as if there was something more to what he was asking that she didn't get right away. Keisha stopped pacing and stared directly at the ghost, locking her eyes on his. Oscar just stood there, waiting for her to ask a question with a slight tilt of his head forward as if to tell encourage her to do so.

"Okay, where did it happen?"

"That's not the right question," Oscar replied.

"What? How is that not the right question?"

"Ask me something else."

"Who initiated it? Did I break up with you or did you break up with me? Everyone seems to think the wrong thing about it."

"It's still not the right question."

He was becoming irritated with her as much as she was

becoming annoyed at him playing this game of mystery with her. It struck her then that this thing she was talking to had really gotten Oscar's personality quirks down. This was classic Oscar: making things more difficult than they needed to be with his cryptic words and displeasure when someone didn't get whatever he was hinting at.

"I don't get what you mean. I don't know what else you want me to ask about. We split up. It was a heated fight and you just walked out."

"What was it we were arguing about?"

Keisha took a minute to think back on it. "You had taken some job somewhere that was going to keep you out of the country for six months. I was pissed because you took it without even asking me what I felt about it."

"And do you remember what I said?" Oscar's question lingered for a few minutes while Keisha tried to remember.

"No. I don't. But, I don't know, what is it that you want me to figure out here?"

"Nevermind," Oscar said, as if he was already bored with the conversation.

"That's it?"

"That's it."

How fucking irritating this was. Keisha scoffed in frustration and turned on her heels to leave the room. She'd give this creation one thing, whatever it was had mastered the talent Oscar had for making her completely frustrated.

Before leaving the room she turned back one last time to look at him. The apparition was watching her as stoic as a statue, his grin tight and his eyes narrowed on her. Keisha knew this look too. Nodding to him, she left the lab and closed the heavy metal doors behind her.

Bex and Serenity were watching the encounter between

Keisha and Oscar on a set of flat screen monitors in a room down the hall from the lab. As Oscar had told Keisha, they couldn't see or hear much of him but got a crystal clear view of Keisha, her reactions, her words, her frustration, all in vivid color.

Only a few fragments hinted at any other presence in the room besides the lawyer. A flicker here, a mote of energy there, a few disembodied words hidden deep behind the humming of the ventilation system. To an outside eye, it would appear that Keisha was talking to herself and might have even had a mental disorder from the way she carried on near the end of the recording.

"So, explain this to me again," Bex asked Serenity while intently watching the monitors. "How is it that we can see and hear him in that room but your cameras can't pick him up?"

Serenity was leisurely leaning back in a chair on the other side of the brightly lit room behind a clear table made of glass. With her feet propped up on the desk, crossed at the ankles, and her head tilted back towards the ceiling, she showed about as much interest in the meeting between Keisha and Oscar as possible.

"Audio and video recording devices work on spectrums of sound and light that we can perceive. It can't perceive what Oscar is as anything more than a few anomalies. He's there, she's talking to him, he's responding, but you can't really pick him up on the cameras unless you cycle the footage and audio through a sequencer I designed. That'd take about six hours to fully get everything and by that time it'll be night. So, none of this really matters to me right now."

"But you wanted me to see it." Serenity had no come back for this and Bex took note of that. "This is what all those ghost shows do, isn't it? They set up cameras and see little orbs or whatever floating by. They capture voices on audio."

"Yes. Um, no. Well ... yes," Serenity's answer was confusing

Bex. "What those shows do is mostly fake. Theatrics, you see. They took the rumors and whispers of what had actually been captured decades ago and turned it into a fucking horror movie. So, there is some merit to what they do but it's not the same. Without knowing what to filter in and what to filter out of the video and audio you can't hear or see anything. A bunch of jackasses running around abandoned buildings aren't going to know what to do with what they capture."

"That still doesn't help me understand."

Serenity let out a long sigh. She was already bored with the process of waiting for the sequencer to start its business and Bex's incessant questioning wasn't helping time go by any faster. Her impatience was getting the best of her and in a huff she stood up from the chair and marched over towards Bex.

"You know what a radio is, right?"

"I'm not stupid."

"I'm not asking because I think you're dumb. I'm trying to establish a base from which to start this explanation. You know what a radio is right? Just say yes or no."

Bex's forehead furrowed as she begrudgingly answered the bitch's question, "Yes."

"So, look at it like this. A radio has different frequencies—different stations you can tune into. Say we're all on station 99.1. Oscar is on another frequency altogether, 100.5, right? Now, if you're riding in the car you'd never be able to hear anything from 100.5 while your dial is on 99.1. We'd have to turn the dial to the other station. The problem is we can't turn the dial. We can't change our reality into another reality.

"But, much like your radio, we can occasionally get another signal from another channel. Say you go into the mountains like you did coming up here. The radio might pick up another signal that'll bleed into the station you're listening to. You'll hear fragments of what's on that other station pop in and out. Well, that's a lot like what ghosts do. The few times people have heard or seen ghosts is when for some reason—mostly environmental factors, chemical factors, and so forth—the signals get crossed up. That's what we were able to do in a nutshell. Tune the environment in that room to such a state where we can hear that other station that Oscar is on."

The theory intrigued Bex. She had never thought of it in those terms but it was a concept she could grasp. It did, of course, beg other questions.

"How do you tune the environment?" she asked.

"Many ways," Serenity answer

red, her mood lifted by going into teacher-mode now. "Some of it is on a subatomic level so I won't get into detail about that. Then, there's the familiar items in the room which is why the lab looks like his bedroom. Parts of him are imprinted there so it's easier for him to attach himself than say a white room with four walls."

"I must admit, I can't even begin to understand how you two were able to do any of this."

"It wasn't easy, that I can tell you."

Serenity looked at the monitor again and watched as Keisha paced back and forth in the lab. She pressed a few buttons on the keyboard and turned a few knobs on a nearby control panel.

"This all means though that Oscar volunteered for this. He wanted to be turned into ... a ghost." Bex asked.

Serenity continued fiddling with the controls while she answered, "He knew he wasn't going to live long so he wanted to exist past this mortal coil. You see, what people often think about ghosts is that they're some manifestation of a spirit or some echo of residual energy. What they're missing is that the human mind is what controls the soul, not anything supernatural or spiritual. And the human mind is far more capable than we even give it credit for. It's all impulse, response, electrical, things that can be measured, amplified, and transferred. Once you know how it works, it's just like writing a computer program. His mind, or his program, was set to go elsewhere but he decided to stay because his time was cut short. Wouldn't you want to do the same if you were him?"

Bex watched the monitors while Serenity gave her answer. Half of her mind was focused on the screens while the other half heard the words, as if they were narrating the experience Keisha was having in the lab. Impulse. Response. It was all there, being displayed on the screen for her to witness, and at the same time, being completely misunderstood by anyone else who would witness the same scene.

♦

That afternoon Keisha and Bex had briefly discussed the morning's session with Oscar. The dynamic between the two women had changed greatly since they arrived as evidenced by Keisha's unwillingness to go into any detail about what she and Oscar had discussed.

What small bit of information she received from Bex had confirmed something she worried about. The conversation she had with Oscar was only one-sided and it would take hours for it to be decoded, which meant hours for her to understand what it was Oscar was trying to tell her before Serenity could hear his side of the conversation.

Armed with this information, Keisha spent most of the rest of the day in her room in secret while Bex worked up the courage to speak to Oscar herself.

It wasn't until the next morning however that Bex decided to enter the lab. Serenity said she would be watching just in case but Bex already knew the redhead's attention would be elsewhere, especially since she reeked of marijuana smoke just before letting Bex into the lab.

◆

"Do you remember the only painting I ever did?" Oscar asked midway through a rather apprehensive conversation.

"That's unexpected," Bex responded, the question catching her off guard. "I remember you not liking to paint. I remember me encouraging you to do some art."

"'*Art is what keeps the soul clean*'," he said, quoting something from their distant past.

Bex recognized the phrase—her phrase—was something it would be very hard for anyone else to know, further proof to her that this might indeed be the spirit of her former lover.

"Right. I remember the painting though. It was ... unique," she smiled.

"It was terrible."

"No, it wasn't terrible. It was your first try. It shows a progression though which is why I loved it."

Oscar cocked his head sideways, "A progression? How do you mean?"

"You can see parts of it where you were just starting, just learning, and still overthinking the whole thing. Then, there are other parts of it where you can see that you were just let your mind wander wherever it wanted. Those strokes were less rigid, less calculated, and more you."

"I see," Oscar stood from the bed he was sitting on and moved to a corner of the room.

Bex followed him with her eyes, still not comfortable with getting close to this manifestation. The doubtful parts of her mind were still in charge to some degree and kept her at a safe distance.

Oscar was going through the drawers of a closet in the corner of the room, searching for something. Bex knew what it was before he even showed it to her, the painting he had done all those years ago. He walked carefully towards her, still knowing she was fretful of him getting too close, and extended his arms forward to show her the painting. He stopped just as she started to recoil from his close proximity, backed up a few paces, and then presented the painting again.

"Yes, that's it. That's your painting," Bex said, trying her best to force a smile to cover her awkwardness.

"So, you think this says a lot about me?"

"In a way. You were always of two minds: one creative, the other analytical."

"But they really can't be separate now can they?" Oscar put the painting down on the nightstand next to the bed, the soft light of the weird bird lamp keeping the painting illuminated in the darkened room. "It's really just different parts of the same mind working together. I don't think I ever worked on a project that didn't require a bit of creative thinking. It wasn't always just by-the-numbers with me, Bex."

She didn't know about that. Their relationship in the past had always been about her trying to tap into his creative side and Oscar constantly denouncing that he even had one. This was the first chink in the armor, so to speak, of her being convinced this was actually Oscar.

"You don't agree," he said, noticing how unconvinced she looked.

"It's just that you—the old you—always protested. It's a bit inconsistent."

"Oh, I can see that. Yeah, it's been some time since we last talked, even before my death. Serenity kind of changed that with me."

The pot smoker got him to be creative?

"How so?" asked Bex.

Oscar sat on the bed, his form shifting quite a bit once he made contact with the sheets. He turned casually to look over his left shoulder at the painting on the nightstand.

"She has this theory that science and the spirit aren't separated, that they're all part of the same thing. They're not even two sides of the same coin. It's more like they're different parts that make up the coin. Chaos and order aren't opposites, nor is the scientific converse to the spiritual. Both need the other to exist in many ways. That was the breakthrough to write The Hitchcock Algorithm: merging the properties of both to tap into what is actually real."

Bex's eyes wandered over to the painting as Oscar continued to explain his change in attitude towards the right side of the brain. Her eyes traced every brush stroke, every scratch, every glob of paint that had been worked into the canvas, and then repeated that journey over and over again. The rigid triangles, precision lines, and other geometric forms all spoke to logic and structure; functional art. Each shape was married to a splash of paint, some thinned to be almost watery while others so thick they gave the work a third dimension, verging on impasto. Some of the shapes resembled something human, from an eyeball to the profile of a nose, while others looked like the etchings of a computer program trained to systematically trace lines in the exact same way, over and over again, onto a flat surface with little thought or emotion to them at all.

"Well, there's kind of the problem with this whole thing, isn't it? I can't verify what I don't know, and I don't know what happened between you and Serenity during your relationship."

"True," Oscar said, now turning his attention fully to Bex. "But, there are things that were between us that no one else would know. Important things."

She knew where he was going and didn't like it.

"Private things," he continued.

"I don't think I want to be reminded of that."

"He would have been beautiful."

"Stop."

"Your compassion and my mind."

"Oscar, please ..."

"I won't ever forget that night."

"Shut up! Shut up!"

Bex rushed to the door of the room, her memories of the one and only night they had attempted to sleep together, and how miserably it failed. She was to blame more than him. Her timidness and irrational fear of such an intimate encounter, despite the longevity of their relationship, fueling the ruin of that evening.

Reaching the door she fumbled with the latch to open it. Unable to get her mind around how to work a simple lock she started pounding on the door, yelling for Serenity (who she hoped was paying attention) to let her out.

Warmth came over her shoulder, something that pricked at her flesh like static but at the same time proved soothing. It was Oscar. He crossed her borders and had gotten close to her, touching her, the very thing she feared the most from this whole encounter.

"Even if I was still alive, you'd be scared of this," he whispered into her ear.

She couldn't see him but felt him pressing against her. His hand now rubbing at her shoulder, his torso just behind hers, his groin pushing against her backside. It was stimulating and a part of her wanted to just stand here and delight in the sensation. Just for a moment, she thought, just enough to get a piece of him back, a piece she had pushed aside so many years ago.

"You know we weren't ready for that," Bex said between quivering lips. "To have a child, to even be with one another. We weren't ready."

"I was," he whispered, now switching to her other ear. "I wanted you and I wanted our child. I wanted our family. It's all I ever wanted."

Bex closed her eyes and a tear found its way between her lashes, sliding morosely down her face to her quivering lips. This was too much, way too much.

"I know you did," she admitted.

"Then why did you leave? Why did you turn me away?"

"I don't know, Oscar. I didn't then, and I don't now. Please let me go."

Oscar slid both of his hands now down to her hips, pressing himself against her backside again so suggestively that Bex shuddered, letting out a gasp of pleasure that she immediately wished she could have hidden.

"Why?"

"Oscar. Let me go, please. I don't want to do this anymore."

On request, he let go. His presence was no longer on her and her heart skipped a beat, aching for the sensation the second it left her. This was insane. She was stirred by a facsimile of an old lover—*the* old lover—who she had let go into the arms of other women, lamenting her choice for years. And now, even if this was all a game, when she was given a chance again her old fears motivated her back to her old actions and she push him away, even in the afterlife.

"I think you do ..." his disembodied voice echoed throughout the room.

Bex turned back to look for him, perhaps to counter his assumptive, and accurate, appraisal of her emotions. But he was nowhere to be seen. His form had gone once again, disappearing into the darkness. She looked for the flickers of his body, some hint, but perhaps he had been struck just as hard as she was and retreated into a place of hiding.

Taking a deep breath, she opened the door and left the room. Whatever it was she could gain from this so-called experiment didn't matter anymore, she would not spend another day in this place.

◆

As it turned out, Serenity had left the control room some time ago and sought out Keisha who she hadn't spoken to the entire day. She had managed to piece together the audio from the lawyer's session with Oscar the day before and had a few questions she wanted to ask, mostly for the purposes of the study but also some for her own personal satisfaction.

It was easy to track anyone in the house with the extensive security system. Cameras and microphones were everywhere in the renovated hotel-turned-museum-turned-research facility. However, when Serenity finally reached Keisha's room she found it empty with only an open suitcase (half-filled) and a few notes scattered on the bed.

She searched the rest of the building but it was the lawn keeper who alerted her to where Keisha had gone. The two were outside having a conversation as one of the supply trucks was pulling up to the building. What could she possibly be talking to them about? Serenity didn't discount Keisha's skills as a lawyer so this was likely an attempt to get information about what was going on from people who worked there. Although it didn't worry Serenity too much, she didn't much like conversations she couldn't hear or control happening in her facility. Better to put a stop to it, who knows what small piece of thread Keisha might pull on to unravel the fabric of everything she had done here.

Before she could even get outside the lawn keeper had pointed Keisha in the direction of the waterfall. The woman was in great shape, much better shape than Serenity had been in from gorging on food and sitting in a lab all day for years, so trying to follow her was a daunting task. She cursed the lawn keeper for telling her where to go, she cursed Keisha for taking this trek through the overgrowth and up into the hillside, and she cursed herself for not spending more time on the elliptical.

What in the world could be up here? What was she looking

for? There was nothing at the waterfall that would tell her anything about the experiment, Oscar, or the facility itself. Serenity's body began to tire halfway up the hill, her legs aching from being used more in the last hour than they had for an entire season. Not to mention it was humid today and she started to perspire heavily, soaking shirt and shorts. Damn this woman. Damn her and her athletic genes!

"I figured you'd follow me up here. I'm surprised you actually made it," Keisha greeted Serenity who was literally clawing her way up the last few feet to the top of the hill.

"You ... are in ... good ... shape," Serenity huffed as she finally stood upright, stretched her limbs, and then knelt over with hands on knees, gasping for air.

Keisha gave the scientist a few moments to compose herself while looking out at the scenery. From here, the building looked like an outcropping someone had stuck into the side of a cliff. Isolated and lonely, the Cascada de Tequendama sat as a man-made structure in the midst of nature's beauty, yet at the same time felt as if it belonged here.

So close to the waterfall, the rushing water created a roar as it spilled over the side and down into the valley below. Serenity had to start their conversation several times, almost shouting in order for them to hear one another.

"Why are you up here?" she asked.

Keisha smirked as she plucked a piece of grass, "Just taking pictures. I want to remember this place after this is all over."

"I don't think you'll forget what's happening here. You're part of one of the biggest scientific and spiritual breakthroughs of human history. A picture isn't going to outweigh that," Serenity said, now showing her usual confidence and command.

"It's personal," Keisha responded.

"Yeah, I saw how personal it got. You and Oscar have a rich history, much different than the one I had with him. And from what I've seen, entirely foreign to what he and Rebecca had."

"You expected something else?"

"No, I'm just noting how someone can be so different depending on who they are with." She started to laugh, "I'm sorry, I know it must be strange for you to know someone is listening in to your private conversations."

"Unnerving would be the word I'd use."

"But it's necessary. I have to validate this as being authentic. It must be documented and studied."

"I get it, Serenity. But I have to ask, why have you been lying to us?"

"Come again?"

Keisha sucked her teeth at the fake innocence, "Oh, stop it! We're all smart women here. You knew we'd catch on that you weren't telling us everything. It makes no sense for you to have both of us here. You could have accomplished this with just one of us. Oscar wanted something, and I suspect you want something from the two of us. What is it? And if you say it's just research I'll throw you off the side of this waterfall, I swear."

It took a second for Serenity to register that Keisha was only joking about throwing her over the waterfall. "I don't know why Oscar wanted you two. Well, correction: I didn't know, I get it now. You both represent different sides of him. The two most important sides to him. That's something I could never do. He and I were linked by intellectual pursuits, not really love or passion. You and Bex ... what you guys had with him was real. It was chaotic and messy yet at the same time it made sense."

Serenity sat down in the grass, crossed her legs, and stared back at the museum. As she continued to explain her motives she picked pieces of grass and tossed them aside one by one, something she hadn't done since she was a child. One very long piece she wrapped around her finger, taking great care in this makeshift ring.

"I'm still not convinced he's Oscar. There's something off with this. Whether or not this whole thing is some elaborate computer program or artificial intelligence or some shit like that I don't know."

"Say what you will. It may or may not matter. I only really need one of you, like you said, to make this experiment a success."

"And the other one can't talk about it," Keisha nodded, realizing the endgame for Serenity. "So, no matter what, as long as one of us does what you want, you win."

"I wouldn't call it winning. I'd call it evolving. Think about it, we're shifting the entire definition of what reality is. And I sense your distrust and hostility towards me, it's been there long before you stepped foot into Cascada de Tequendama. You can be angry with me all you want, try to talk to the workers to find some evil little master plan, whatever the hell you need to do to convince yourself what you've experienced isn't what you experienced. But years from now, you'll look back and know that you had a chance to know him completely, not just for sex, and you threw it away because of ego."

She was a clever bitch, that much Keisha would give Serenity. There was no denying that she loved Oscar, as much as she hid it, and this was a competition between them all. It soured her to be involved in such a thing; three women pining over one man. No matter how much she told herself she was better than that, she couldn't escape the truth that Serenity had so deceptively laid out here.

"Can you be upset with me for wanting to merge all those pieces together:, the chaos, the order, the logic, the creative, the natural and the unnatural, to get the full picture of who he was down to his soul?" Serenity stood up and pointed to the landscape before them from the hotel to the cliffs to the waterfall and the pool down below. "No, you can't, because it's the very same thing you want."

◆

Once they returned to the museum Serenity was exhausted, high as a kite, and sweating profusely. She quickly removed her top as she entered the building and staggered towards the kitchen for a glass of water. Keisha followed behind her, not nearly as exhausted by the trek to the waterfall and back, and watched her host gulp two glasses before taking a breath.

"You look tired," Keisha exclaimed.

"I don't know how you're not," Serenity said, filling her glass for a third time. "It's hot up there. And my legs are killing me."

"Maybe you should just take a nap. We'll catch up later. You've given me a lot to think about anyway."

Serenity stretched her arms and sighed heavily. It wasn't a bad idea to rest now. There was nothing needing her immediate attention and it would be some time before the cypher would decode the conversation between Oscar and Bex. She nodded to Keisha, pulled out another joint, lit it, and then proceeded to her room where she would pass out. She stumbled at the bottom of the stairs though, dropping her joint on the floor.

"Fuck!" she yelled as she tried, unsuccessfully, to pick up her joint.

"Hold on, let me help you," Keisha said.

Being in better shape after the trip, Keisha picked up the joint, took a puff for herself, and then handed it back to an eager Serenity. The scientist was in no shape to make it up the steps and immediately began cursing the layout of the building for having such a tall stairwell. Keisha helped her up to her room where Serenity took a moment to pass the joint back to her before collapsing on the bed.

"No matter what I say, you are a fine woman, Keisha. Oscar never told me but I knew he missed you," Serenity confessed as she lay on her back with her hand cupped over her brow. "He missed both of you. He was a jerk. Well, I guess not so much a jerk because it's not like he waived it in my face but you know ... you know what I mean! I'm so tired. I'm just going to sleep here now, okay?"

Keisha took a moment to scan the room. It was filthy and disorganized with clothes strewn everywhere, wrappers crumpled on the floor, used cups stained to the brim from coffee that was at least a day old, and piles of papers stacked next to her bed in no discernable order. How such a woman could manage a project as detailed as the one Serenity was a mystery to Keisha but this disorganization did offer an opportunity, one that this whole excursion had been designed to reveal.

On the nightstand next to the bed was a set of key cards, the same set Keisha had seen Serenity use to open many of the doors in the lab and the other lower levels of the building. She waited as the redhead continued to ramble about her jealousy over Oscar's devotion to Keisha and Bex, and just as the woman turned over on her side to fall asleep Keisha seized her opportunity. She quietly swiped the key cards from the nightstand, extinguished the joint in the ashtray (where other roaches had been extinguished before), and left the room.

One of the benefits of the museum being set up the way it was without staff was that Keisha could walk the halls without worrying about much other than the cameras. Electronic eyes were just as good as human ones but that would be something she could hopefully remedy later on. For now, getting access to the room was enough.

The keys worked and the instant the lock released the door Keisha felt a rush. Her skin tingled at the experience: breaking into somewhere she wasn't allowed, finding out secrets she shouldn't be privy to. Serenity held all the cards during this entire experiment but it was time to turn the tables.

It only took five minutes for Keisha to gain access to Serenity's workstation, which was not locked or required a password to use which just further showed her confidence in controlling the situation—a false confidence. How much time Keisha would have was unknown but she worked fast, absorbing as much information as she could in her brain while making a copy of specific files on an external drive she carried on her keychain. Oscar had taught her enough about computer science that she was competent around the machines, not a programmer by any means but still above average for the everyday user.

"So, that's what's really going on?" she whispered to herself as her download of files completed. "You think you're so slick, Serenity. Don't you? But I'm better."

Keisha removed the external drive from the console and slipped it into her pocket for safekeeping. She also found the surveillance video files and wiped them clean. If she had more time and was more skilled perhaps she could erase herself from the footage but that was for more practiced hands. The best she could hope was that Serenity was so arrogant that she wouldn't even think to check the videos. No time to worry about that now. Armed with information, her greatest weapon both in the courtroom and outside of it, Keisha returned to her room and waited for night to fall. Closing arguments, if done well, require a skillful mind and a silver tongue. Keisha had both, and before the day was over, she'd end this fiasco in grand fashion.

♦

Waking up from her haze, Serenity forced her weary body to roll out of bed but neglected to put her feet down so she just fell onto the floor. Groaning now not only from her weary legs but the sudden impact of hitting the hard marble of her bedroom, she let loose a sarcastic "ouch" before clawing her way up to her feet using the bed for balance. It took a moment for her to regain her wits and then she immediately realized that she had been out for some time. The sun was starting to set outside the floor-to-ceiling windows of her abode and she desperately started searching for her keys. Where could they be? She reached into her pockets, looked under the bed, pushed aside all the trash and debris that littered her messy bedroom, until she finally saw them sitting on the nightstand.

Pocketing the card keys, she left her room knowing that she might be late for the next part of the experiment. Time was of the essence today, and she needed to complete her tasks if this whole endeavor was going to be worth it. A momentary slip, she thought, it wouldn't ruin anything. She'd just have to adjust.

On her way down to the main floor she ran into a despondent Bex who was starting out at the waterfall, her eyes red and her arms crossed defiantly. She had been crying clearly and whatever was said between her and Oscar had upset her.

"Are you okay?" Serenity asked as she staggered towards Bex, her equilibrium still not fully returned to her.

Noticing this, Bex answered in kind, "Are you?"

"Just had a bit much. Keisha led me on some walk through the woods out there. Right there, in fact, to the top of that waterfall."

"It's a magnificent view," Bex said stoically.

"Seriously, Bex. Do you want to talk? Did something happen while I was gone?"

"Nothing you won't find out about once you review the

video. I was just thinking, that's all. I've already gone through this in my head a thousand times since this morning. I want to leave, but right now I just want to get some rest."

Serenity's eyes widened, "Yes, rest would be good. You should take some time and just sleep. I just had a nap myself. This whole thing must be exhausting for you."

Bex didn't respond her thoughts clearly elsewhere and her eyes focused on the scenery outside. Seeing that this conversation was going nowhere, Serenity left her guest to her thoughts and continued towards the control room where she had pressing work.

"You haven't seen Keisha have you?" asked Bex before Serenity left.

"Not since we got back. I'm sure she's around. Where is she going to go?"

"True. I just wanted to ... I don't know, I think I need to talk to her. No offense. It's just she and I are close and ..."

"You don't have to explain," Serenity saved Bex from having to go into her drawn out reasons for not wanting to share. "You two are tight. I get that. It's why he wanted you both here. Go get some rest. If you want to talk later I'll be here, okay?"

A smile finally crossed Bex's face, reserved as it was. She nodded to Serenity and then went back to watching the waterfall.

Night came quickly and with a new moon the sky outside was pitch black. If not for the lights inside the building there would be nothing to see. The effect was rather strange in Bex's bedroom, making the huge windows look like nothing more than sheets of black decorating the room. It turned into a blessing though as she wanted to sleep the rest of the evening away. She turned the lights off in the room forcing it into darkness, all except for the subtle green glow of an electrical strip near the television across from her bed.

As she drifted, her ears also picked up a sound she hadn't noticed before, a hissing sound from somewhere in the dark. She didn't know where it was coming from but she knew it was there. No matter, she needed to rest. She needed to sleep. She needed to forget her conversation with Oscar, at least for tonight.

Thirty minutes later her eyes flashed open, her mind telling her to wake up. Given the blackness of the night, she wasn't quite sure her eyes had opened until she blinked a few times. Turning from her side to her back, she could see the dim green of the power strip panel on the opposite wall. But something was different. It was distorted, twisted by something between the bed and the wall. Was she really awake or was this just a dream? *Go back to sleep, it's in your head*, she thought. Then, the distortion moved.

She knew what this was.

"Oscar?" she whimpered, half hoping it was him and half hoping it wasn't.

The bottom of the bed depressed, the weight of her visitor pulling the mattress down. What an underhanded move, to come in such darkness, to use the night to enter her room.

The shapeless form didn't answer, but she could feel it now pressing against her legs, then up her thighs. What felt like fingertips fluttered against her stomach and then out to her arms. Bex lay prone on the bed, as if paralyzed by the experience, but fully capable of moving. She didn't want to move. This was just a dream after all, and what harm could come from this fantasy?

She cursed Oscar out loud. Damn him for getting in her head this way, for making her feel sensations she tried to bury, to relieve regret she had stashed away in the attic of her mind to be forgotten over time.

"I can't," she whispered, now feeling the sensation of flesh on her cheek. A pair of lips perhaps, pressing gently from her neck to her chin to the back of her ear, her special place, the place Oscar knew so well. She gasped as her prone body began to relax, her knee bending upwards and outwards, allowing a path for this shapeless form to press on her more sacred places if it chose to. It responded in kind, a hand she presumed, going to her thigh and raising the leg off the bed entirely, holding it there while increasing the pressure of its form between her legs.

The notion of this being dirty, being taboo, came and went between each rush of gooseflesh and tremor of pleasure. She shouldn't be doing this. It was wrong. What did it say about her to have this dream, this fantasy that she had obviously been storing in the back of her mind since the minute she found out about this bizarre experiment?

Damn him.

"I want to be inside you," she heard his voice in her ear.

God, she could feel his breath. Was that even possible? No, this must stop. Gently she pushed against the form, but in the darkness she didn't know if it was a shoulder or his head, it didn't matter. She pushed this dream back and it complied.

"I want to be inside you," it repeated, this time softer.

Now that it was off of her she felt more at ease. Her eyes strained now to see him. The darkness was both seducer and oppressor, creating this tantalizing scenario that she wanted so salaciously yet also denying her the one thing she wanted to go along with it: to see Oscar.

"Relax and you will see," he said. "Relax."

Something about the way he said the word made her shudder. Her muscles loosened, her breaths slowed, and her eyes softened to the darkness. There it was. A shoulder she thought. Some flickering of color that outlined his neck, his bicep, his torso. He had come to her nude, ready to press his skin against hers. As the glimmers of color continued to outline him, they found his wrist and hands, just for a brief moment before his fingers went to the top of her jeans. He slid a finger between the fabric and her stomach, another trademark of Oscar's she had known so well. Where his flesh met hers was like fire, warming and exciting.

"Relax."

Bex reached down to meet his hand. She wanted to press him further but in the darkness her judgment was off and she missed his arm completely and found his prick, her hand clasping it for a few moments before she realized what it was. Initially, she wanted to recoil when she realized her error. Her hand wouldn't move. Instead, she tightened her grip around his cock, thick and hot in her palm, the texture of it addicting as she slowly glided her fingers from his shaft to the head as it ticked just a few inches from her groin.

"I shouldn't," she said, but it was a weak protest.

Reaching back now to his hand she guided him to unbutton her jeans. The shapeless form did so in response, sliding her jeans off with one fluid motion. She ached at the momentary departure of his flesh from hers and reached out into the blackness to receive him again. Her lover returned quickly much to her satisfaction, his full weight now upon her. Every inch of him that touched her was a ripple of pleasure, as if her body itself was statically charged, crests of energy gliding just underneath her skin from head to toe. His lips found the special spot behind her ear again and again the same response. Her legs opened as if on cue, but this time she was exposed and wet. The danger of it was exhilarating. No more barriers. She trembled with anticipation, so much that the sheets beneath her were soaked.

"I shouldn't," she repeated one last time, this one the least convincing of all. "Please Oscar ..."

She felt the shapeless form sliding off of her once again

mid-sentence. The absence felt cold, as if death had replaced his touch with its own cold chill. The subtext of this did not escape her. It was cruel. It was unbearable. It wasn't right.

"Please Oscar, fuck me," she sighed.

The tingles returned, first on her wrists, then between her thighs, and then pressing against her flower. He slid inside her with a practiced confidence, slow and filling, as if he knew just how to build the sensation, drawing the experience out as he inched more and more of his cock inside. As luxurious as his touch was on her skin, it was tripled here. She gripped the shapeless figure, dug her nails into the darkness while raising her head off the pillow and her hips to meet his decadently methodical thrust. Her mouth was open in a gasp as she held her breath, the penetration almost too much as he slid deeper and deeper. In the dark she had no frame of reference for his physique, and at a certain point she felt as if he was never going to stop entering. But her lover knew just when to stop, retract, and re-enter.

Bex exhaled finally. She wanted this years ago. She wanted this earlier in the day. She wanted this now. No one else would know, it wasn't any of their business what private fantasies she had. This was too good, too long overdue to cast aside. What harm was a dream after all? Tonight, and only tonight, she'd have Oscar. She'd have what she had talked herself out of, thinking it was for the best, and ultimately regretted doing so. And sure, there would be no family scenario, no marriage, and when she woke the only evidence would likely be her bedsheets and a ghostly tingle throughout her body, but so what?

Keisha may have wanted resolution while Serenity craved some insight into Oscar, but this was what Bex wanted. Something the two of them had with him that she didn't, and for the next hour, she would feel no shame in that truth.

♦

The audio files for Bex's last interaction with the spirit in the lab had finished processing by the time Serenity returned to the control room. She started going over the files as she lit herself another joint and kicked her feet up on the panel. It wasn't but a few moments later that someone was knocking on the door. It was Keisha who looked none too pleased as she entered the room.

"Where have you been?" Serenity asked casually as she muted the audio track she was listening to. "I haven't seen you since our little hike."

"Cut the crap, Serenity. I'm here to speak my mind before Bex and I leave this little show you've concocted here."

"I don't know what you mean."

Keisha pushed past Serenity and headed to the video displays on the far wall. There were several but the one she wanted to draw attention to was in the center of them all. It was a video feed of the lab.

"I know what you've been up to," she said to Serenity in an accusatory tone.

At first, Serenity met Keisha's anger with shock, then resignation, and finally laughter. The lawyer was none too pleased about the response. Pressing the issue a bit more would perhaps change Serenity's tone.

"I figured something was off which is why I had quite a few conversations with your staff. That led me to researching the companies they worked for, which led me to discover how this place was renovated into your little private lab here."

Serenity's laughed stopped.

"You've been wondering where I've been? I had to get away from this place to get a signal so I could connect to the internet. I talked to a few people back home. One of the benefits of being a lawyer is I have a lot of contacts, Serenity. A couple of them know some secret people too."

Keisha started walking towards Serenity as she continued to reveal her findings. Each step enhanced by another bomb dropped.

"Carbon monoxide caches. Infrasound embedded in the lab area. Research in subliminal messages and high frequency white noise. All of which are used often to disorientate people. All of which are also known to be the cause of hallucinations, including giving those exposed to it the feeling that they're seeing ghosts.

"Then, there's Oscar. Yes, he was trying to give me a clue earlier. We broke up because he took a job with a company that I had defended in a carbon monoxide poisoning scandal. I called him a hypocrite because he gave me such a hard time for defending it. The conversation got heated and that's when we broke up. He tried to tell me without you knowing he was.

"I have to admit, it's a pretty elaborate set up you've got going on. I just have one question though. Why go through all of this? Just to play games with me and Bex? What's the point?"

Serenity sighed and patted Keisha on the shoulder in a condescending manner. Keisha pushed her hand away, her face still twisted into a scowl. She wanted answers, not more games. She was a few moments away from slapping the pot smoking bitch in the face if she kept this up.

"You have been so, so fucked with, Keisha," Serenity replied. "I have to say, I'm a bit sorry for doing it. It was worth it in the end."

"You think this is funny?"

"Well, first let me explain. You're not totally right and you're not totally wrong. And I know you feel manipulated but you really shouldn't be upset. I didn't anticipate that you'd find out this early but at this point it doesn't really matter."

Keisha took a seat now and relaxed. As angry as she was,

and as much as she had figured out on her own, it seems that this whole deception went deeper. She'd entertain Serenity's storytelling for a few more minutes.

"So, you fill in the blanks then. What was I right about and what am I missing?"

Seeing that Keisha was not going to attack her now, Serenity sat down at her workstation and began bringing up several charts and graphs. There was a myriad of data here all color coded, tagged, organized, and accented with numbers and calculations that Keisha couldn't begin to decipher. Serenity continued her explanation as she typed away on her keyboard.

"It's true, there are gases and particles and soundwaves used in that room that are known to manipulate the human mind. I told this to Bex before but tricking you wasn't the intention of the experiment. You see, so many of these anomalies over history have all of those things in common: infrasound, ultrasound, chemicals, light manipulation, suggestion, and so on and so on. Many scientists simply dismissed it as the cause of people seeing ghosts or experiencing paranormal events. But what if they weren't the cause of the experience but a *conduit* to the experience?"

Keisha could see Serenity's excitement to finally be able to reveal this. The woman was in her element, so enthused by the theory and the process that the morality of what she had done didn't seem to matter.

"Remember what I said before about radio signals? In order to break into another signal you had to use all of these elements to understand what the pattern was. I could do it on my own but my results were limited. Oscar and I didn't have enough of an emotional history to conclusively say whether or not what I was seeing and experiencing was actually him or just a result of the stimuli that was in the room. In fact, it was Oscar who knew that part of the equation was necessary to validate our findings. When he knew he was going to die of cancer he said that you two would be the ones he wanted to prove his theory. Now, the big question is: are you two seeing something real or is it all a hallucination? Hard to prove right?"

"You're insane," Keisha said flatly, completely unimpressed with Serenity's diatribe.

"Yeah, he said you were short-sighted about these things. No matter. You and Bex have proven it though. Well, more Bex than you. The pipes run throughout the building, so I can create the environment anywhere. The final part was to flood Bex's bedroom with the same algorithm of stimuli and see whether or not the manifestation was real."

"You did what?"

"I moved the environment outside of the lab and into a place where she wasn't expecting it. And she responded. Boy, did she respond. Look there," Serenity said as she pointed to one of the video screens on the wall.

There, Keisha watched a recorded video of Bex in bed having intercourse with an unseen figure. Even with the video tuned to night vision, her suitor was invisible except for the shifting form beneath the bedsheets, its body given shape by the flow of fabric around its incorporeal shell.

"Jesus Christ," Keisha said. "What in the hell is that?"

"That is Oscar," Serenity explained, her voyeurism taking over as she watched the coital liaison. "She wanted that so badly. I have to be honest; I thought it'd be you. Oscar thought it'd be you. They never slept together, did you know that?"

Keisha punched Serenity so hard that she was unconscious before hitting the floor. Keisha then smashed the keyboard, swiped the keys from Serenity's pocket, and locked the door behind her as she left. The mad scientist wouldn't be an issue for a few minutes, more than enough time to leave this building and the memory of it behind. Her hand stung from the punch, but the satisfaction of knocking out the sociopath far outweighed the pain. All that was left was to pull Bex out of her ill-conceived coupling and leave this place.

♦

Bex awoke from her dream and slowly put back on her clothes. Lightheaded, she stumbled out into the bright hallway and down the stairs in search of food. She had such a craving now for something sweet. Chocolate, she thought, that would satisfy her sweet tooth.

Once she entered the dining area her legs started to feel week. What was this? It was only a few more steps to the kitchen so she shook it off. One benefit of this whole ordeal was that the kitchen was fully stocked so she had every manner of chocolate she could want from cookies to cake. She opted for a giant slice of double chocolate cake with extra icing. God bless whoever had made this.

No need to use a fork, there wasn't anyone else here watching, except the cameras. She scooped up a heaping chunk of icing with her finger and sucked it clean. Delicious. This was the distraction she needed after such a vivid dream. It had been too realistic though, too on the nose, too much of her subconscious taking her to a place she wouldn't dare go in real life. Bex allowed herself a few moments to luxuriate in the memory, every touch of her dream lover coming back in waves to the point she got goosebumps.

"Rebecca," said a disembodied voice near her ear.

The surprise of hearing her name jolted her erect. Cake spilled onto the floor and she soon followed, both of her legs completely giving out beneath her. A stabbing pain was tearing at her insides and she had no idea why. Tears formed as she tried to breathe slowly, hoping that doing so would ease the discomfort. It didn't. Another series of stabs doubled her over on the floor.

"Bex!" came another voice, this one was attached to a living person.

Keisha found her friend in a heap on the floor. No time to wonder what happened, they needed to leave. She knelt down and rubbed Bex's back gently.

"What happened? Are you okay?" Keisha asked.

"I ... I don't know," Bex replied. "My stomach hurts. Just give me a minute."

"We need to go, Bex. There's a lot you don't know. They set us up. Both of them."

"What are you talking about?"

"I'll explain on the way home. We just need to go now!"

The lights went out in the entire building as if on cue. Keisha and Bex clung to one another in the darkness, fearful and disoriented. The sound of gas being released could be heard coming from all around them. Keisha knew what this meant. Although she had locked Serenity in the control room she had not castrated her of any power. Her fears were confirmed as the woman's voice boomed over the speaker system.

"I hate to do this," said Serenity's voice in the dark. "But as I said, I only need one of you. Oscar's isn't the only spirit here. That waterfall has such a history to it. Suicides, rituals, worship, all part of local lore. Scream if you must, cry if you need to, but the experiment is over."

Keisha knew they had to move fast. Even though she was just as terrified as Bex she had to be strong. With every ounce of energy she could muster Keisha lifted Bex off the floor and dragged her through the pitch black dining area.

They bumped into a few tables as they scampered sightless through the rest of the building, using the walls and their vague memories of the layout to escape. Bex's strength was slowly returning and as they made it into what they assumed (and hoped) was the large foyer of the museum they could finally see some illumination.

The recessed panels of the walls were now a sickly bright green, slivers of luminance in the long void between them and the exit. A strange smell filled this corridor, a mixture of rot and citrus, clogging their senses and watering their eyes. The air was ice cold and their breaths burst from their lips in grey wisps as Keisha continued to pull Bex towards the entrance.

"We're almost there. We're almost there," Keisha kept repeating, more for herself than Bex.

That's when the voices came. The language was foreign to both of them but they were certain whatever was being said wasn't pleasant. All were men, all whispering ghastly words, some from afar and others as if they were standing right next to them. Next was the touching. At first there were just fingers poking at them, then a set of fingers brushing through their hair as they continued to the door. Keisha tried to hold it together but when one of these invisible souls tugged at her hair she started to scream.

Bex howled she was wrenched away from Keisha's grip and hoisted into the air. Keisha could barely see her even with the dim lighting but she could tell that her friend was being lifted off of her feet and carried as if ten men were hoisting her up above their heads. Without thinking, Keisha took hold of one of Bex's arms and tugged. There was no way she was leaving her friend to whatever horrors these spirits had in mind for her. It took a few tries but she was able to drag Bex from her captors, both women crashing to the floor in a heap.

The voices became increasingly angry. Threats, screams, howls, all manner of viciousness came from this cacophony of twisted voices that surrounded the women as the stench of rot and citrus increased. They were running out of time.

Bex pushed herself back up to her feet and despite the agonizing pain she felt in her legs and abdomen started a mad dash towards the door. Keisha wasn't far behind but the spirits were still pulling and tugging at her clothes. For whatever reason, their attempts were getting weaker the faster they ran, but their rantings continued to echo along the walls, increasing with frequency and venom, to the point where Bex and Keisha felt their eardrums were about to burst.

The doors was getting closer and just as Bex neared them she felt a cluster of hands grab hold of her body, from head to toe, preventing her from taking another step. Keisha felt the same, her head snapping backwards as the spirits stretched their bodies. They wanted to tear them limb from limb, their arms and legs being pulled to their limits.

There was no escaping this building. Indeed, the experiment was over.

Through a stream of tears and screams Bex forced her eyes open one last time. The door was just a few feet from her but something had changed. She could see a figure there, the outline just barely formed in the green light of the hallway. She knew this body that was manifesting. She had felt it before. It was Oscar.

She wanted to call out to him but she felt a hand around her throat, tightening its grip as she struggled to free herself. His face disappeared as he started walking towards her but she could still make out a hint of his form in the dark, as she had in her bedroom before. He gently touched her cheek and as he did the other hands that were bound to her released their grip. She coughed as she looked for him in the darkness. His form had moved beside her and stroked at her midsection with the delicacy of a feather.

Keisha continued crying out for help. Bex turned to watch as Oscar's flickering form approached her friend. Words were exchanged between the two but something was different. Why wasn't she being released? What were they saying? After a few moments, Bex could see his outline moving towards her again, his face being revealed now in clouds of emerald and disappearing just as quickly. He took her hand and placed the car keys in her palm, then touched her midsection with the delicacy of a feather. She knew this touch, her flesh tingling with the same sensations from before.

"Live for us," he spoke, his form dissolving back into the blackness of the night as the words lingered on the air.

"Bex!" Keisha screamed.

The grip on her arms and legs were tightening. The tugging on her hair was beginning to rip her scalp.

Conflicted, Bex looked at the keys in her hand and back to Keisha. What could she do? What should she do?

"Bex!" again she cried.

Keisha's ribs were cracking now, splinters of bone puncturing her organs. Livers, lungs, intestines, all were being squeezed free of their contents.

Live for us, Bex heard echoing in her head now, over and over again as she stared at the keys. Keisha was reaching out for her. The look of terror on her face was enough to draw a tear. Bex began to take a step forward but then stopped mid step. She could feel the air of the hallway pushing back on her even with this movement, the smell increasing, the voices of the dead threatening her again.

Live for us.

"Bex! Bex!" Keisha cried out hysterically, blood now streaming from the corners of her mouth and eye sockets.

With resignation Bex closed her hand around the keys, turned towards the door, and exited the museum leaving Keisha behind. Astonished and panicked that she had been abandoned, Keisha screamed Bex's name repeatedly. Her cries were so loud that Bex heard them outside the building as she slowly stumbled to the car, her face devoid of any emotion. As she settled into the driver's seat and closed the door, the screams abruptly stopped. Taking a moment to collect herself,

Bex started the vehicle and quietly drove away.

She was still scared of driving on this winding road especially in the pitch black of this moonless night. It still made it difficult for her to navigate the vehicle. She couldn't do it, terrified that she'd drive over the side of the road and down into the cliff to that dramatic death she so feared.

Bex stopped the car and turned off the engine. What the hell had just happened? What had she done? She left her friend to die in a house of horrors. She left a psychopathic narcissist in a lab where she had control over the dead spirit of her lover. And her lover! Oscar, she had slept with his spirit and tried to convince herself it was a dream. And now she was left here in the dark to try to find a way out. No, it was too much.

At this moment the speakers of the car started blaring music. Something had turned on the radio and it wasn't any question to Bex who had done so.

"Live for us," Bex said quietly to herself, and in a true sense, also to Oscar.

A calm came over her. She quickly scanned the radio stations and decided on one devoid of music or talk. Instead, she chose a station whose signal was mixed between two competing broadcasts, each struggling through a haze of static to dominate the speakers.

Casually, Bex started the car up once again and confidently drove through the winding road of the cliffs above the Bogota River on her way back to the airport. She took one look back at the museum in the rear-view mirror, rubbing at her midsection as she watched it disappear in the darkness behind her.

Postmortem V

With only one soul to claim, the outcome was a bit hard to determine as to who actually won that hand. The demon scratched at his chin for some time before lighting another cigar and puffing away, his confusion growing with every puff of smoke he blew out from his cracked lips. As for the angel, she sat quietly as she reorganized her cards, also seemingly perplexed about who would claim the soul of Keisha.

While she had been ripped apart by a host of angry souls, that didn't necessarily put her in the camp of either. Her life as a lawyer who defended shady companies and the powerful that trampled over the weak didn't exactly help her value to the angel, and at the same time, the demon couldn't lay a claim over her because of her genuine good nature in trying to save her friend, ultimately leading to her own demise.

A tough call on this hand.

"You take it," the demon finally grunted. "A soul like that will just lament. There's no taste to her."

"I have a hard time claiming someone who spent their life making money off of the misfortune of others as a worthy prize. It doesn't matter how much she sacrificed for her friend, she would be worth nothing back home. You take it."

Omar watched the two go back and forth trying to pawn off this woman's soul on one another. After five hands, this one had caused the most confusion and he could see why. In fact, he could identify with Keisha far more than any of the other poor spirits who had lost their lives during this entire game.

After another minute or two of debating, both angel and demon decided the hand was a wash and discarded the lawyer's soul into a pile of its own, the same as they had done with Garrett before her.

This can't be how it worked. Omar was so sickened by the cavalier attitude with which these two entities played with human lives through manipulation, coercion, misdirection, divine intervention and demonic possession, that he had half a mind to get up from the table and leave them to their sick entertainment. If this was what higher beings did, then he didn't find them any more evolved or awe-worthy than the common thug on the street in his old neighborhood.

"How many more hands?" he dared to ask.

"Do you have somewhere to go? Are we holding you up?" the demon answered in a powerfully menacing tone.

Omar needed to be careful again. He didn't want to test this monster's temper any more than he already had today. "No. I was just wondering how you would know who wins the game."

"Settle down now," the angel said. "We've played hundreds of hands before you even showed up. I'd be a bit more reserved if I were you. You're still between heaven and hell here and there's no guarantee that you're meant for one or the other just like that woman. Let us complete our business. You'll know soon enough where you'll land."

That was true. Omar didn't have a choice here. He was at their mercy whether he liked it or not. Whatever he felt about the game didn't matter. It was either sit here and watch or be the demon's meal, there weren't any other options.

"I think he's getting mad," the demon chuckled.

"Shall we play the next hand then?" the angel asked, her hands sliding over causally to a deck of cards that until now Omar hadn't noticed. They had been by her side the whole time at the opposite end of the table. The artwork was slightly different than that of the cards they had been using so far. What made this so special?

"Oh, he'll like that. Yes, let's play that hand."

What were they up to?

"Okay, here we go. Remember, this counts as double for whoever wins the hand. We can use enchantments," the angel said.

"As if I'd need any. You're very quick to play a hand you know you'll lose," the demon added haughtily.

"Ah, don't be so quick to pound your chest just yet. Nothing is for certain until the hand is dealt," said the angel as she quickly dealt the demon his cards. "So, let's begin."

She turned over a card in the middle of the table. Omar leaned forward to look at the image on the card's face, and with a sudden wave of realization, his mouth opened in surprise.

"I know him," he said.

The demon and angel didn't respond, they simply grinned as they organized their cards in their hands. Omar stood from his seat and continued to stare at the card, now pointing at it, his finger trembling.

"That's the little bastard who brought me here in the first place!

Revelations of the Broken Martyr

I t was midafternoon at the Econo Trip Motel, a rather seedy place that sat just outside of the city near the airport. Known mostly as a place where prostitutes would take their johns or, in some cases, use as their temporary homes due to the cheap nightly fee, the collection of rundown bungalows was nestled just far enough off the main highway that it didn't draw too much attention from the authorities. It wasn't as if the police didn't know what the place was used for, but since it was off the radar enough from the average citizen who would be offended by such places, they left the patrons and owners of the motel to their business.

Such places saw many things that those with a taste for the

underbelly of society craved as a distraction from their normal lives as productive citizens. Here, you could be anyone you wanted. No credit cards were accepted by the management, only cash and whatever valid (or in most cases invalid) form of identification you had on you. Married men, sex addicts, college students looking for a cheap date when they couldn't convince a coed to sleep with them, all knew of the Econo Trip Motel and had spent their $42.50 for a few hours in the rather disgusting rooms. Each unit decorated with cheap furniture, stained carpets from decades of use, walls that had been painted over in excess, barely working bathroom facilities, and the residual smell of thousands of cigarettes smoked and extinguished.

Sitting by the one and only window of the motel room farthest from the main entrance was a small man with thinning hair and a bright pastel yellow suit. He crossed his legs while tapping a spoon against the side of a teacup, casual in his demeanor but clearly impatient. The other occupant of the room was in the bathroom moving objects around, fiddling with the shower curtain, and various other activities that the yellow-suited man could only guess at. But this was nothing new. He had played out this scenario time and time again, the process so boring at this point in his long existence that the changing shapes of clouds outside proved more entertaining.

"Can I expect you to come out soon or will I have to come get you?" he addressed to the bathroom occupant.

The commotion in the bathroom paused, then came a whimper, then it started again with more vigor. His warning was heard but not heeded. Thirty seconds he'd give it, and if by that time the bathroom dweller didn't emerge, he'd have to go get them. It wasn't as if he had anything against doing so and he certainly didn't fear getting his hands dirty, but as with the rest of this task, it bored him.

"I'm coming out! I'm coming out now!" a shrill female voice

shouted from behind the bathroom door.

Marissa stumbled out into the main room with her clothes barely covering her and her hands shaking uncontrollably. Her dirty blonde hair hadn't seen shampoo in days and her arms were covered in sores and blemishes, all telltale signs of her favorite recreational activity. A professional, in the loosest sense of the term, who had just finished enjoying the fruits of her labor but still retained a sense of embarrassment about her habit that she felt the need to hide it behind closed doors.

"You certainly took a long time," the yellow suit commented as he turned to watch the woman struggle to straighten her top.

"I need it. You stress me out, Kutner."

The man recoiled from hearing her speak his name. Very few dared to. He let it pass this time. Marissa couldn't handle any sort of assault verbal or physical right now and he needed her to finish the job he had paid her for.

"When will you be ready?" he asked.

"Just give me a few minutes dammit! I need to come down a bit. That hit was more than I thought it was. Good shit though. I'll always give that to you, if nothing else, you always bring me good shit."

"Clearly," he said with a dishonest smile, his contempt for this woman ever present.

Marissa took her time to put on her shoes fearing what Kutner had in mind for her now. Sure, he had given her what she wanted and the high she felt was something extraordinary, but as with all her johns now was the part where they wanted their cut. The things she had done over the years for a few twenty dollar bills or a baggie of heroin sickened her to think of, so she simply didn't think about it. Men were disgusting. Men sought out disgusting things. It was the price of her addiction.

This john was different though. Kutner had never sought

anything perverse with her in a sexual manner; his requests were more psychological. There were times he would simply stare at her or want to watch her attract other clients from the comfort of the back seat of his car. A strange little man he was. She almost preferred if he had some sort of fetish involving feet or whips or tickling, anything besides just being a creeper who watched her and asked invasive questions.

Of course, Kutner knew she was stalling for time. He turned towards her, his legs still crossed and lifted his cup of tea to his lips. With a sip he swirled the drink in his mouth, rolling his tongue over to push it between lips and gums, and then swallowed hard, letting the warmth of his drink slowly crawl down his throat. Marissa watched him as he did this, shook her head, and then went back to putting on her boots.

"You are a really strange man," she muttered. "So, are you going to tell me what you want or am I supposed to guess, honey?"

Kutner grinned and then turned his attention back to the window. Marissa followed his gaze and understood what had held his attention all this time. Another working woman was on the other side of the dirt parking lot arguing with what clearly was her employer. She knew that conversation. It was one she had many times when she was younger and had done everything in her power to avoid having again. Pimps around this area were often aggressive, and from the looks of things, the argument was about to reach that level.

"It's a curious lifestyle, isn't it?" Kutner said as he continued watching the pair in the parking lot. "The women trade their virtues for money, drugs, liquor, day after day until they forget the reasons they were doing it. Oh, sure the claims originally were for their children or to get extra cash for school or whatever other noble cause they might actually have had in the beginning. But then it deteriorates into that."

He pointed with the spoon to the conflict outside, jabbing at the two as if he could actually touch them from here with the utensil.

"It's harder than you think to get away from them," Marissa reflected.

"I'm not saying it isn't. The pimps aren't without their own misery too. Yes, they pump their chests and walk around like peacocks, but beneath it all is this sense of failure. They can't make anything. They can't create anything. They can't even have the pleasure of sex with their whores. Always wondering whether or not the orgasm she's having is performance or pleasure. No matter how much money they make, they are stuck in this filth, in this grime, in this gutter of society."

"You're quite opinionated today, hon," said Marissa, now fully dressed and taking a seat at the table next to Kutner.

"Just observations."

"And what about our clients? You see what's so wrong with us, what about them? What about you?"

"I dare say I'm a bit different than a client, as you put it, wouldn't you agree? I have never, nor would I ever, contact you for intercourse. But you aren't completely wrong. Your clients are culpable as well. Without them, there is no industry for you and your peers to be stuck in this life. There is no interest in pimps to have women under their thumb like what we're seeing now. But again, they're not all to blame. The perverts, yes. Men who cheat on their wives, girlfriends, husbands, boyfriends, looking for a thrill that they can't get in their normal lives and using other people, knowing full well that they're enabling drug addicts and abusers.

"The lonely man I'm not as disgusted by. Much the same way I don't really find you disgusting, in case you were wondering. They have been abused emotionally by a world that finds very little use to show them love. All they really want is communication, a human connection, something that others have denied them. I can't fault them any more than I fault you for being harshly pushed towards addiction."

Marissa tried to follow Kutner's logic, and to some extent, she could see where he was coming from. But she wasn't the brightest of people, so most of his words went over her head. He was just babbling high-brow nonsense in her mind. Still, he made it a point not to insult her, and in fact, made her out to be a victim. She liked that. It's how she saw herself and knowing that he respected her struggle made his company more palatable.

"It looks like they're done," Marissa said, moving the focus back to the arguing pair outside.

"Not yet," Kutner replied.

Marissa didn't understand what he meant. The argument had seemingly stopped. Without warning, the pimp punched his employee in the stomach. She doubled over in pain as he kicked her twice to drive home his point. Both Kutner and Marissa watched as he snatched up the woman's purse and took a wad of cash for himself. He barked profanities at her before leaving the scene, and the woman left in a sobbing heap in the dirt and broken asphalt of the parking lot.

"It all seems so petty," Kutner said as he stood from his seat and closed the blinds. The show was over and he cared very little to watch this woman squirm on the ground. "They have no idea what's out there. No idea at all."

"And what's out there, Kutner? A better life? Do you know how many men have tried to tell me that? I thought you'd be smarter," Marissa replied.

"Nothing like that, love. There's so much beyond this little life here. I'm not talking about angels coming from the sky, the voice of God booming, insects taking over the Earth, nothing like that. But here in places like this; the backdoors of society, there are strange events that sting at nature's sensibilities, mock the Holy Ghost's creations, dampen the flower of innocence. This is where they happen. All just inches from them, not in some grand movement of the heavens. Yes, it's true. Behind the stained doors, dripping faucets, and stained bedsheets of the forgotten and discarded are malevolent miracles, each and every day, only seen by those wise enough to look or unfortunate enough to be victims."

He was clearly insane. Marissa had no idea what he was talking about and a few of the words he used were beyond her vocabulary to understand. It was, again, just the rambling of someone who read too many books and thought himself more important than he really was.

"Whatever," is all she could respond with.

She needed to find her purse and leave if he wasn't going to be asking for anything else. Where was it? This was a bad habit of hers, constantly misplacing her purse when she was high. One of these days she was going to regret it.

While she searched around and under the bed, Kutner put his index and middle finger to the side of his head, the fleshy part just under the ear and just above his jawbone. Up and down he massaged the area as if coaxing something from inside. He then winced just slightly as he reached up to his ear and took hold of a squirming insect that emerged.

"Well, if you want me to stay any longer then you're going to have to pay for another hour. I've got things to do," Marissa informed Kutner, completely unaware of what he was doing.

Not finding her purse under the bed, she got back up on her knees and turned to find Kutner's hand going to her throat. She tried to fight him off immediately, screaming for help, but the man's strength was unnatural. There was no give to his grip on her windpipe. With a grunt he tightened his hold on her, forcing her mouth open as she gasped for air.

"Yes, the truest miracles are just behind doors like these," he whispered to her.

Marissa watched in fear as he placed the squirming insect into her open mouth. Completely incapable of stopping him or closing her jaw, she sobbed as the creature worked its way through the soft palate at the back of her mouth, up through her sinuses and nestled itself somewhere near her brainstem.

"Shh, hush now my dear. Don't fight it. You're about to touch something on that other side, the side you cower from in your worst nightmares and fondest of dreams. Just be quiet now and let my friend do his work. We have much more to do today."

His words echoed through her head while everything else became numb. Her sight blurred, her mouth lost all sense of taste, her skin went cold and dry. Whatever it was he had put in her was rapidly at work on her system. Before she completely blacked out, she was Kutner open her purse, not to take money, but to add another stack of bills to it. Whatever for? It didn't matter. It was unlikely she'd ever know the answer to that question.

♥

It was a half hour commute from the rundown motel to Kutner's next destination in the city. Traffic never had bothered him as he enjoyed spending the time listening music, in particular, jazz. Music was a human invention that he had grown quite fond of. As diverse as the species, music had something to offer all the time among its different genres and forms. Esperanza Spaulding had caught his attention as of late, and he had listened to her latest album so many times, he had nearly every word and note committed to memory.

This was also the downside of this current task. As much as he would like to share the brilliance of this artist with his passenger, she was in no condition to understand. He wasn't sure Marissa would be of sound mind to do so in her natural state anyway. The woman had never shown much of an appetite for anything beyond the realm of Walmart or McDonald's. She sat now with her seatbelt on staring blankly out the window as the city slowly crept by.

One more exit to go and they would be at their destination. His work would be completed, and he could go back to other endeavors he cared for. This was wet work for him. It was getting his hands dirty. It was milling with the scum of humanity, a task which he found to be beneath a creature of his stature. Regardless, it had to be done.

"Here we are, love," he said to his mindless passenger.

They had reached the exit. A few more turns and he'd find Hanover Street, where the real work would begin.

"Wait a minute," Omar interrupted the game, his face ashen with realization. "Is this how he found me?"

"Calm down, Omar," the angel warned him.

"No! I want to know what the fuck this is. What is going on here?"

"I think the lady asked you to sit," the demon admonished.

"Enough of this. I want to know what's going on. Who is this woman?"

Both entities ignored him as they continued the game. Omar's protests continued, but it was pointless to continue. He had no power here and whatever revelation he was about to get—and he knew it wouldn't be anything good for him—would be something he'd just have to suffer through.

Kutner stopped two blocks up from his destination. Parking was atrocious in this part of the city. Everyone had twice as many vehicles as the street would allow. Time was wasting, and he needed to wrap this up soon.

He helped Marissa from the car, holding her hand gently as she stumbled over her high heels.

"Keep it together. It's just a few blocks that way," he said to her.

"Where are we going?" Marissa asked.

Even though she had no control over her body, there was a hint of her personality still there. Kutner's insect had been bred for this specific task. They were known as broodsac in darker circles, but this particular kind had been engineered not only to gain full control of its human victims but to also leave enough of the host's brain intact, so they were aware of what was happening.

He housed many within his own body, but fortunately for Kutner, they had no effect on his species. His physiology was so foreign from that of humans that the broodsac had nothing to latch on to, much less control.

"Here we are," Kutner smiled as they passed by the neighborhood children playing along the sidewalk.

A few of them took note of the obvious hooker and the strange man in a bright yellow suit. How could they not? Even the couple across the street couldn't help but spy from their windows, both men gawking at the odd people who were visiting their neighbor.

♥

"Stop it!" Omar howled again.

The spirits continued to ignore him. They really believed he'd just stand here and let this play out? he thought. No, this was not going to go on any longer. This was his neighborhood, his neighbors, his house they were going into. *Why were they there?*

"I'd pay particular attention to this next play I'm going to make," the demon snickered as it lay another card down on the table.

♥

Marissa unlocked the front door with her keys. This was her home. Kutner pushed her in gently while closing the door behind him. Up the stairs they went to the top floor of the duplex. The lower half belonged to another family, but the top floor was where she lived. Once there, a hint of her recognized the doormat and its dirt-covered message of "Welcome Home." She bought it years ago when she moved into this place.

"Go ahead. Open it," Kutner whispered to her.

On command, Marissa inserted the key and turned the lock. Inside was sparsely decorated with most of the furniture cheap and falling apart.

"Quaint," Kutner said as he surveyed the space. "I believe she's in the back room, love. This is where I leave you. You know what to do."

Marissa turned to him with a blank stare. He watched her gaze for a moment. What few fragments of consciousness that were aware inside Marissa's body struggled to fight. Two tears rolled from her eyes as her face trembled. It was no use. Even with this small breakthrough, the broodsac was still in control.

Kutner lifted her hand to his lips and gently kissed it before taking his leave of the apartment. He left her there, this sad woman, trembling and terrified as her body pushed itself towards the bedroom.

"Marissa isn't her name," Omar said. "This isn't happening now. This is from earlier. This is from the day I died."

The demon applauded him sarcastically. "Give the man a prize," he mocked. "Time here is not what you think it is. We couldn't even begin to explain to you as I doubt you'd be able to comprehend it."

"Oh, I get it," Omar said, his tone rising up now to pure fury.

"What surprises me," the angel said, "is that you never knew your wife's work name. *Marissa* ... it sounds so original for someone in her line of work."

"Fuck you," Omar spat. "We did what we needed to get by."

"Fuck me?" the angel scoffed with her hand to her chest as if insulted by the remark. "I think you are the one who is fucked here, Omar. Unless ..."

"Unless what?"

The angel was not giving him an answer. Instead, she let the thought linger with him. Omar wasn't having any of it.

"Unless what? Stop playing games with me. You're talking about my family here!"

"Why don't you tell us what happened, Omar?" the demon suggested. "I want to hear."

"Yes, how about you explain what she did. What you saw. How you got here."

Omar bit his lip. The circumstances of his death had come and gone so quickly that he hadn't had time to process them. This man (if you could even call him that) Kutner had immediately jumped on his death as a way to lead him here. That much was clear now. What wasn't clear was that this had all been orchestrated for him to be at the mercy of these two entities and their sick card game.

"I want answers after this," Omar said calmly as he took his seat.

The demon and angel put down their playing cards and

gave Omar their undivided attention. While they already knew what happened, it was clear they wanted something else from him. An admission of guilt perhaps? Omar didn't have any to give, but he could recount what had led him to tumble down the stairs in the first place.

"I came home that day and found them there," he started flatly.

"Found who?" asked the angel.

"You know. Marissa ... or *Monica*, which is her real name ... and my princess Bella."

"You found them where?" the demon pressed Omar.

"In the bedroom ..."

Monica opened the door of the bedroom and there kneeling at the side of her bed was her daughter Bella. The girl was eight-years-old and had a face of pure innocence. Round cheeks, reddish-brown curly hair from her mixed heritage, and the brightest round blue eyes. She was praying out loud, so Monica could hear every word, every wish, every hope of this child.

Even though she was young, Bella was quite aware of the realities of her life, which included the harsh truth of her parents. Omar was a drug dealer, peddling his poison on the streets. Even though he had taken a steady job and paid his taxes, the bulk of their income came from hustling. Her mother was a prostitute. The kids at school and various television shows allowed Bella to draw the connection between the clothes she found her mother wearing when she came home late at night and her profession.

Omar never intended for his wife to become a junkie. She had found his stash and sampled the product behind his back.

It led to an addiction that she had hidden but soon became obvious to him. Unfortunately, by the time he discovered his wife's extracurricular activities she was already pregnant with Bella.

The chemicals took their toll on the child. Despite being an adorable looking little girl, Bella had suffered slight brain damage. While she was keenly aware of many things and able to excel in school, her motor functions never developed past that of a three-year-old. She could walk but would often stumble, her perception of distance was underdeveloped, her motor skills in general were so poor that she'd often need her parents to feed her if she suffered a serious fit. At eight, she had already suffered through three strokes that had caused her right hand to twitch uncontrollably from time to time.

They had destroyed their child.

Monica confided all of this to Kutner in their previous meetings. As she crept closer to her unsuspecting daughter, her memories of those conversations started flooding back to her. She had told him too much. Kutner knew where they lived, who her husband and daughter were, much of their history, and worst of all she had confessed in a drug-induced state that she wished her daughter would die. It was an embarrassing admission but the toll of taking care of her day after day was wearing her thin. The money for treatments was what had driven her deeper into the life of prostitution and her husband back into the world of the drug trade.

What in the hell had she done? Truly, she didn't want her daughter to die. Her selfish side, her narcissistic desire to have her old life back had driven this. She wanted to be free. Bella would never recover.

"... and God bless daddy. I know he's working hard God to take care of me ..." the child continued on, unaware of her mother's presence.

Bless her heart. No, she can't do this. Fuck whatever Kutner had put into her system. Fuck her deplorable ramblings about wishing she never had a daughter. Fuck Omar for leading her down this road.

But what could she do? Her body was not hers to control. She was five steps now from Bella, her hands outstretched and aimed towards the child's neck. It wouldn't take long, and Bella was in no condition to fight her off even if she wasn't ill. No, there must be a way.

"... and God please do something nice for mommy. She needs a nice day. She is so tired all the time. I just want her to have a nice day ..."

Monica's eyes welled with tears. Her body wouldn't stop. She screamed inside, mentally clawing at the walls of her mind to prevent this. God, stop this. Stop this.

♥

"When I came in, she already had a hold of her," Omar continued the story. "I didn't know what to do. I couldn't begin to understand what I was seeing. She was killing her. She was killing our baby."

"What did you do?" the angel asked.

"I ... I ..." he could barely bring the words to his lips. "I just froze. I watched her do it. I couldn't move."

"You let her kill your daughter?" the angel asked, her cold eyes narrowing on Omar.

"Such delicious evil," the demon mused. "Go on with the story!"

If he weren't so afraid, Omar would have beaten the demon to a pulp right there and then. "I just backed away. I had to get out of there. I had to leave. I couldn't ... I just couldn't stand it anymore."

"And that's when you fell down the stairwell, hit your head, and stumbled out into the street. That's when you were hit by the truck, right?" the angel said.

"Yes," Omar quietly admitted, his head turned down to the floor, his eyes red, and his whole body quivering.

"A coward," the demon grunted. "You wanted her dead too, didn't you? You didn't want to take care of your child anymore because she was ill. A child you made ill in the first place."

"Fuck. You." Omar said, his eyes rolling up to meet the demon's gaze.

The monster laughed at him as it puffed away on a new cigar. It was freshly lit. The glowing end burned brightly in the dark warehouse. It was an opportunity, a foolish one, but he knew where this was going. His soul was damned on so many levels that there was no hope of redemption here. If these would be his last moments before becoming a meal for this spawn of Hell, he'd make the demon fight for it.

"How delicious your sins will taste on my tongue," the demon laughed as it licked the end of the cigar, its forked tongue twirling over it like a worm latching onto a branch.

This was the moment.

Omar grabbed the cigar and yanked as hard as he could. The demon screamed in pain, his tongue nearly ripped from his mouth. He relaxed his muscles and let the cigar go, but Omar was quick, faster than the demon could have imagined. With a flick of the wrist, Omar twirled the lit end of the cigar around and jammed it into the demon's eye.

It feels pain! Omar thought. A rush of euphoria swelled through Omar's spirit, the first real sensation he had experienced in some time. They had lied to him. These entities weren't as all-powerful as they had presented themselves. If the demon could feel pain, then it could likely be killed, and after what had seemed like days of being bullied, ridiculed, tortured, and mocked by this fucking demon, the bastard would go back to Hell remembering Omar Snellings.

"You can change it," the angel said calmly as she watched her opponent thrash about in anguish. "Omar! Did you hear me? You can change it."

Omar dropped the cigar and turned towards the angel. She had backed away from the chaos with her hands pressed together and her wings fanned out. Even though she wasn't as omnipotent as he had thought, this knowledge didn't take away from the pure beauty of this creature. In the darkness, she still shimmered with a radiance that was truly divine.

"I can change this?" Omar asked.

"If I let you play my hand, you have a chance to change this. I don't do this for you; I do this for the child. Your soul was damned long before this. I cannot change that nor would I, but you have convinced me that the girl, Bella, is a light that should not go out now."

Part of him was disappointed in the fact that this would not fix his fate. As she said, he was damned long before this ever happened. He held out some small hope that doing something to change this would redeem him, but there was no hope in it.

"Such spirit in you, Omar," the demon cackled as it stood from the table. "Why bother? You know you are coming with me."

"If you can take me."

"Child, do you think that little display hurt me? No, I am beyond pain as you would know it. No matter what you do to me, you have no power over me. I savor the pain; it only increases my appetite. And trust me, I will suck the meat from your bones and drink blood from your skull. This angel is trying to trick you; you can't change your daughter's fate."

"Sit at the table, Omar. I allow you to play this hand for me."

The demon protested angrily, "You cannot do that! They are all mine!"

"I can and I will," the angel spat back. "You know the rules.

Divine intervention is allowed in the game. So is human choice. It's up to Omar to decide though."

"Of course I'll save my daughter," he said.

"If you do, she'll live a rough life without her parents. She'll be-alone for many years. She'll be mocked and cast aside. Know that before you decide."

Omar turned to the table and looked at the playing cards. Was saving his daughter really saving her if she'd lead a pained life? Perhaps letting her die would save her from all that misery.

Something the demon said had struck him though. *They are all mine.* If he didn't save his daughter, he would be condemning her to far greater pain than any she would have in life. Even at that, as this game had shown him, Bella's fate was not set in stone and surviving the game would free her from ever being in it again. Her life would have possibilities.

With his mind made up, Omar took the angel's seat at the table. The demon watched with furious disdain as Omar played the final card of this round, the one of sacrifice.

The moment the card was turned over on the table, he was shot back into the bedroom. His wife had her hands around Bella's neck already. This time, he didn't freeze. He broke Monica's grip on the child and forced her back against the wall.

"Stop it, Monica! Don't make me hurt you," Omar pleaded.

The broodsac was too strong. Whatever was left of Monica in there wasn't responding. She lunged at Bella again, but Omar wrapped his arms around his wife and pulled her to the ground. Bella cried as she watched her parents struggle on the floor of the bedroom, unable to understand what was going on.

"Get out of here, Bella!" Omar shouted at his daughter. "Go now!"

"But daddy! What's wrong with mommy?"

"Bella, just go! Baby, I love you, but you have to leave now!"

Bella stumbled across the bedroom and grabbed at the door. Her handicap slowed her progress, but she managed to work her way down the hallway and out of the apartment.

Omar held on to Monica as the woman screeched and clawed towards the door of the apartment. If he didn't know better, Omar would have assumed she was having a mental breakdown but he knew what had caused this. It wasn't the broodsac either, it was him.

He turned Monica's face towards his as she continued to thrash about in his arms, trying to break free to go after their child. Her eyes were white, her pupils pinpricks, her veins pulsing like blue stains under the skin.

"I'm sorry, Monica. I'm so sorry," he whispered to her.

The words appeared to calm her. For a moment, Monica became lucid and seemed to acknowledge her husband's presence. It was only for a moment. The insanity returned and without warning, she bit into his throat. Her teeth clenched tightly around his windpipe and she pulled viciously. Omar tried to fight, but it was useless. A stream of blood poured from the wound as she broke flesh free between her teeth. He pushed her away, clutching at the wound and gasping as his life spilled out onto the floor.

Monica hovered over him like a rabid animal, trails of crimson dripping from her lips as her body heaved with every breath. She just watched Omar as he gurgled and coughed his last breath. Gently, his hand fell from his throat and his body relaxed. Twice now he would face death. He knew where he was going and accepted the eternity of torture he was heading to. But this he did for his daughter whose life he had condemned from birth, now given new life through his own demise.

Within moments of Omar's passing Monica began to cough. She was slowly regaining control of her body as she thrashed about on the floor, spitting up blood and mucus next to the dead body of her husband. With one final push, she forced a painful obstruction from her throat. It didn't go willingly, raking tiny hooks against her esophagus as it came out.

There on the floor was the broodsac, its size eight times that of when Kutner had placed it in her body. Even though she was still in a haze, Monica had enough wits about her to grab the nearest weapon, a lamp next to her daughter's bed, and began smashing the insect with as much force as she could muster. Her shrieks pierced the walls of the home, alerting every neighbor on the block of the nightmare that was happening.

After nearly a minute, she had no energy left to strike the creature and dropped the weapon on the floor. Her eyes adjusted to the light and she wanted to see her handiwork. At least the damn thing was dead.

To her horror, there was nothing there. No carcass of the broodsac, no stain of its body left behind, just the smashed pieces of a lamp next to the growing pool of blood coming from her husband's body.

Had she lost her mind? She must have! What had she done? Her husband's body lay here and her daughter ran for fear of her life.

My God, I tried to kill my baby!

The neighborhood had gathered in front of the Snellings' house as the police and fire department arrived on the scene. Some of the elderly neighbors had surrounded Bella trying too protect her from the horror of what was happening. Even though they didn't know the specifics, they knew enough that this child had escaped some nightmare and needed to be kept away from the flashing lights and commotion. Above all else, she absolutely needed to be shielded from the sight of her parents: her father a bloody corpse carried out on a gurney and her mother a deranged madwoman in handcuffs being arrested.

Bella sat in the back of the ambulance while the paramedics examined her for any injuries. Ms. Page from down the street explained to them that the child had disabilities but didn't seem to be harmed beyond that.

"It's going to be alright, dear. It's going to be alright," Ms. Page kept saying, trying to reassure Bella.

The child clearly couldn't understand what was happening and just sat there with a blank stare. Ms. Page and a few other neighbors tried to offer her food and drink, some asked if she needed to talk, but Bella was not hearing a word of what they said.

There was one thing that did break her from her trance. Beyond the bodies and vehicles and emergency lights was a man in a bright yellow suit. He stood at the end of the street watching, his suit so obnoxiously bright that it was hard to miss him. Bella stared as he surveyed the scene and then suddenly locked his eyes on hers.

The child didn't flinch, but she knew there was something peculiar about this man. In kind, the man nodded towards Bella with a disturbingly polite grin and then continued to walk away from the crime scene.

"I hope we are even now," Kutner whispered to parties unseen. "I have other games to attend to."

DID YOU ENJOY THIS STORY?

For independent authors, reviews are the lifeblood of a book. Outlets like Amazon, Barnes & Nobles, Kobo, iTunes etc. use reviews to determine what books they will promote and where they rank.

If you found this book enjoyable we'd love to hear what you thought about it. From detailed reviews to a short sentence just saying that you liked it, any feedback is much appreciated.

Use the link below to post your thoughts:

Amazon US: https://www.amazon.us/dp/B076VCF6N2
Amazon UK: https://www.amazon.co.uk/dp/B076VCF6N2
Amazon CA: https://www.amazon.ca/dp/B076VCF6N2
Amazon AU: https://www.amazon.au/dp/B076VCF6N2
Amazon IN: https://www.amazon.in/dp/B076VCF6N2

ABOUT THE AUTHOR

Clive Reznor is a new horror author with a background in the Deep Web where he created short horror stories on various websites under another alias.

While he keeps his life private, his pen name tells much about what influences him as a creator. An avid fan of horror legends like Clive Barker and the industrial music and lyrics of Nine Inch Nails front man Trent Reznor, the stories and situations that Clive Reznor tells mix the metaphysical with the mundane, the supernatural with the superficial, in a post-New Weird form of storytelling.

Based in the State of Maryland in the United States, Clive Reznor continues his work on various websites and promotes much of his public creative writing through his Twitter account.

Website: www.aoestudios.com
Twitter: www.twitter.com/clivereznor

Made in the USA
San Bernardino, CA
26 August 2018